The
Seaside Café

Also by best-selling author Rochelle Alers

The Innkeepers series
The Inheritance
Breakfast in Bed
Room Service
The Bridal Suite

The Book Club series
The Seaside Café
Coming in December 2020:
The Beach House

The Perfect Present
Christmas Anthology 2017:
A Christmas Layover

ROCHELLE ALERS

The Seaside Café

KENSINGTON BOOKS
www.kensingtonbooks.com

DAFINA BOOKS are published by

Kensington Publishing Corp.
119 West 40th Street
New York, NY 10018

All Kensington titles, imprints, and distributed lines are available at special quantity discounts for bulk purchases for sales promotion, premiums, fund-raising, and educational or institutional use.

Special book excerpts or customized printings can also be created to fit specific needs. For details, write or phone the office of the Kensington Sales Manager: Kensington Publishing Corp., 119 West 40th Street, New York, NY 10018. Attn. Sales Department. Phone: 1-800-221-2647.

Dafina and the Dafina logo Reg. U.S. Pat. & TM Off.

ISBN-13: 978-1-4967-2186-0
ISBN-10: 1-4967-2186-1
First Kensington Trade Paperback Printing: June 2020

ISBN-13: 978-1-4967-2187-7 (ebook)
ISBN-10: 1-4967-2187-X (ebook)
First Kensington Electronic Edition: June 2020

10 9 8 7 6 5 4 3 2 1

Printed in the United States of America

She riseth also while it is yet night, and giveth meat to her household and a portion to her maidens.
—Proverbs 31:15

Chapter 1

Kayana Johnson groaned when she heard her cellphone's alarm go off at 4:00 a.m. It was the beginning of the tourist season, and she'd slept restlessly throughout the night. Once again, she had been plagued with the dream where she'd grabbed a large kitchen knife and stabbed her husband until he lay with lifeless, unseeing eyes staring up at the ceiling. It was only when she realized he was no longer breathing that she'd calmly walked over to the sink and washed the blood off her hands before calling the police. Afterward, she had sat down at the table and waited for them to come and arrest her.

Kayana quickly sat up, as if jerked by a wire attached to the top of her head. It wasn't a dream but a nightmare, one she'd had over and over since her divorce. As a counselor, she knew she had to let go of the demons that had plagued her relentlessly; however, forgiveness was slow, much too slow in coming for her emotional healing.

Sweeping back the sheet and lightweight blanket, Kayana swung her legs over the side of the bed and walked to the minuscule bathroom in the two-bedroom apartment above the restaurant that had been in her family for more than three decades. The Seaside Café had become her sanctuary, a place where she now felt most at home. As a young girl, after classes were over, on weekends, and during the summer months, she'd watched her mother and grandmother concoct the dishes that had made the restaurant a popular dining spot with locals and vacationers alike.

Located on Coates Island, North Carolina, several miles south of Wrightsville Beach, the Café, as the locals called it, offered panoramic views of the dunes, the beach, and the Atlantic Ocean whether one was seated inside or on the screened-in patio. The island boasted a population of a little more than four hundred permanent residents, but that number swelled to more than a thousand during the spring and summer, when bungalows, boardinghouses, and several bed-and-breakfasts were filled with singles, couples, and families who returned year after year. A decade ago, a developer had purchased several tracts to build twenty one-bedroom condos. After ongoing protests from residents, he was approved to construct ten two-bedroom units. Vacationers were given bumper stickers to park personal vehicles in designated lots, because from late May to Labor Day, their cars were not permitted on any road on the two-mile island. Tourists were able to get around by walking or on bicycles or local jitneys, unlike locals, whose bumpers were stamped with a large red R and their license plate number. Local deliveries were exempt from the vehicular restrictions.

Her Grandma Cassie was gone, and her mother had relocated to Florida, to help take care of her grandchildren. Kayana's brother-in-law had had an epiphany after ten years of marriage and suddenly decided he'd wanted to be single again. Kayana didn't know what it was about the Johnson sisters, but their marriages had imploded within three months of the other, and she wondered if the brothers-in-law had been engaged in a conspiracy to rid themselves of their wives.

Since moving back to Coates Island to help her widower

brother run the Café, Kayana wanted to thank her husband for his duplicity because it was the first time in a very long time that she could be Kayana Johnson and not the wife of the revered Dr. Hudson. She no longer had to be the consummate hostess for his colleagues who came to admire the opulent five-thousand-square-foot showplace in Atlanta, Georgia, that was much too large for two people. And she didn't have to skin and grin for his bougie family, who'd believed James Hudson had married down rather than up. Now, in hindsight, she was able to say good riddance to him and his plastic family and friends. The folks who came into the Café were a constant reminder that down-to-earth people still existed.

Taking off her nightgown, she left it on the hook behind the bathroom door. Kayana had made it a habit not to close the door because it made the space feel even smaller than it actually was. It was furnished with a shower stall with barely enough room for one, a commode, and a vanity. What she missed most was a bathtub. She'd made it a practice several times a week to soak in the garden tub, with pulsating jets of warm water massaging her body. However, the shower stall had become a welcome trade-off if it meant that, at the age of forty-six, she had total control of her life and destiny.

She brushed her teeth, followed by gargling with a peppermint mouthwash, and then covered her chemically straightened hair with a shower cap and stepped into the stall. She completed her morning ablutions in record time, and it was exactly 4:45 when she descended the staircase and turned on the lights in the restaurant's kitchen. Kayana had arranged with her brother that she would oversee the preparation of breakfast and make the sides for lunch and dinner, while Derrick was committed to preparing dinner, which had allowed him more time to spend with his daughter, Deandra.

The girl had taken her mother's death hard, and even after four years, the teenager still deeply missed her. Kayana had finally convinced her brother to let Deandra spend her summer recess in Florida with her grandmother, aunt, and cousins before returning home to begin her senior year at the mainland's high school.

During the off-season, the Café only offered a buffet brunch from 10:00 a.m. to 2:00 p.m. Monday through Saturday. But from the Memorial Day weekend to the Labor Day weekend, diners were served a buffet breakfast from 7:00 to 10:00, lunch from noon to 2:00, and a sit-down dinner between the hours of 5:00 and 8:00 p.m. Sundays were the exception, with brunch from 10:00 a.m. to 1:00 p.m.

Kayana preferred preparing a buffet breakfast because she didn't have to wait on customers who wanted individual orders. She'd fill warming trays and replenish them when necessary, while varying the menu with sliced seasonal fruit, in addition to the ubiquitous scrambled eggs, grits, bacon, ham, sausage, pancakes, waffles, home fries, and French toast; milk, coffee, herbal teas, and bottled water were also available with the fixed price. She made oatmeal on request for those looking for a hot-cereal breakfast. Her brother had contracted with vendors on the mainland for their baked goods, meat, and fresh fish.

The dinner menu hadn't changed much over the years except for the addition of a few Asian-inspired recipes. During a trip to New York City, Kayana had visited several Korean restaurants and found herself instantly addicted to several of their dishes. Once back in Atlanta, she'd experimented with Korean barbecue and after a few attempts was able to duplicate some of her favorites.

She opened the walk-in refrigerator-freezer and removed a crate with dozens of eggs to bring them to room temperature; in a half dozen large plastic containers, cut-up chicken marinating in buttermilk lined two shelves. Minutes later, she set a box of apple-cured slab bacon, another with locally made pork sausage, and a half dozen ham steaks on the prep table. Working quickly, Kayana mixed up pancake and waffle batter, and set a large pot of grits on the commercial stove.

The chiming of the bell echoed throughout the restaurant, and she glanced at the closed-circuit monitor. It was minutes before six; the college student her brother had hired the year before as a dishwasher and busser had arrived. Wiping her hands on the towel tucked under the ties of her bibbed apron, she disarmed the security system and walked out of the kitchen to the front.

She opened the door, smiling. The lingering aroma of burnt wood mingling with the distinctive smell of saltwater wafted to her nostrils. Her brother, Derrick, had built an addition at the rear of the building where he smoked brisket, pork shoulder, ribs, pork belly, and chicken. Steaks were aged and then grilled to order in a wood-burning oven.

"Good morning, Corey, and welcome back."

The tall, raw-boned young man with shaggy, sun-streaked light-brown hair and large brilliant blue-green eyes flashed a shy smile. "It's good to be back. I like going to school in Michigan, but I sure miss seeing the ocean."

Kayana opened the door wider, waited for Corey Mason to enter before she locked it after him. "I felt the same way when I lived in Atlanta." The young man, who lived on the mainland with his single mother, had earned a partial academic scholarship to attend the University of Michigan and had worked a few odd jobs throughout high school to save enough money to supplement his student loans. He was one of several part-time employees working at the Café during the summer season.

Corey followed her to the kitchen, where he washed his hands in one of the three sinks and then slipped on an apron. "It looks as if you're going to have a lot of business. I saw many more cars with vacation stickers this year than we had last summer."

Kayana smiled. "We can never have too much business."

She wanted to remind Corey that she and her brother depended upon new and returning customers to keep the restaurant viable during the off-season. Derrick had made it a practice to raise prices between eight and ten percent every other year to offset the higher costs for food and utilities. Earlier in the year, they'd added wine and beer to the menu, and Kayana knew it would substantially increase their revenue.

Aware that there was only an hour before they would open the doors to the public, she placed strips of bacon and sausage links on baking pans and put them in the oven. Ham steaks sprinkled with cinnamon and brown sugar were grilled on the heated flattop, flipped, and then cut into bite-size pieces. Forty minutes later, Corey carried platters of meat into the dining area and placed them on warming trays. Stacks of pancakes and waffles followed, and then hot, creamy grits. It had been two years since her return to Coates Island, and Kayana was still in awe that she felt more comfortable working in the kitchen than she had counseling patients as a hospital social worker.

Corey had just set out pitchers of chilled orange, grapefruit, and cranberry juice, along with the bowl of fruit, when the clock in the kitchen chimed the hour. Reaching for the remote device, Kayana raised the shades and unlocked the front door. She also switched on several televisions set up around the restaurant, muting them and activating the closed caption feature. She tuned them to all-news, weather, and sports channels, while contemporary tunes spanning several decades flowed from hidden speakers as a steady stream of customers walked in.

She knew every permanent island resident, and recognized the names and faces of those who'd summered on the island the year before, greeting them with a smile and thanking them for returning. Many of the vacationers were educators who took advantage of their summer recess to bring their children to the seaside community to swim, fish, and relax. Kayana saw a woman walk in and knew instinctually she was a first-timer. The slender redhead, cradling a book, stood at the entrance, glancing around for an empty table. Smiling, Kayana approached her.

"Good morning, and welcome to the Café. I'm Kayana, one of the owners."

The woman returned her smile. "Thank you. How long do you think it will be before I can get a table?"

Kayana's eyes were drawn to the book title, *Les Misérables*, which happened to be one of her favorites. Only this edition was printed in its original French. "We have a policy here that you can sit at any table with an available chair. It's a way for folks to get to know one another."

Bright-blue eyes sparkled like polished topaz in a lightly freckled pale face. "I like that policy."

Kayana nodded. "It works for us."

"By the way, I'm Leah, and I noticed you staring at my book. Have you read it?"

"I have—several times, but not in French," Kayana admitted. "It happens to be one of my favorite novels."

Leah's smile grew wider. "Mine, too. Maybe we'll get a chance to discuss it."

"I'd like that." Since returning to the island, Kayana rarely got involved with vacationers who frequented the restaurant. Most came in to eat before going into town to browse the shops lining the main thoroughfare. Mothers congregated on the beach, while their children competed making sandcastles or frolicking in the surf under their watchful eyes. Teens tended to congregate on the sand, listening to music until sunset or sometimes later. However, no one was permitted on the beach after midnight, and the regulation was strictly enforced by local law enforcement.

Leah Kent smiled at the cook, silently admiring her flawless, nut-brown complexion with orange undertones. Her near-black, chin-length hair covered with a white bandana emphasized the roundness of her small face. Leah hadn't come to Coates Island to make friends, but to unwind and figure out what she wanted to do with the next phase of her life. However, there was something about the other woman's warm smile and laughing eyes that silently communicated she had found a kindred spirit when it came to books. And it wasn't just any book but her favorite: a classic.

It had taken months for her to research vacation properties once her husband informed her that he'd planned to take their twins sons to Europe with him as a gift for them passing the bar exam. What had originally been scheduled as a month-long stay was extended to two months when Alan added a two-week African safari to their itinerary. Once she realized she would have at least six to eight weeks to herself, Leah decided to rent a bungalow at the seaside resort and indulge in everything she'd been denied back in Richmond, Virginia.

"I'm free twenty-four-seven, so you'll have to let me know when you're available," she told Kayana.

"Are you staying on the island?" Kayana asked.

"Yes. I'm renting one of the bungalows."

"I'm always free on Sunday evenings, so you can come by at six, and we'll hang out on the patio."

Leah smiled again. "You've got yourself a book club buddy."

"That's a bet. It's been nice talking with you, Leah, but I have to get back to the kitchen."

Leah went to find a table and again felt her decision to vacation on the island was certain to change her outlook as to her future.

When she'd parked her brand-new Audi in the designated lot for vacationers, she'd felt as if she'd been liberated. She'd driven the sedan out of the showroom two days ago on the very day she'd celebrated her forty-eighth birthday. Purchasing the car and driving from Richmond to summer on Coates Island was an act of rebellion. It had been the first time she hadn't conferred with her husband about a big-ticket purchase, and it was to be the first time in their twenty-eight years of marriage that she and Alan would take separate vacations. Now she knew how people who were incarcerated felt when told they would be released from prison. Although still married, Leah had mentally divorced her husband years ago. In that instant, she made herself a promise not to think of or dwell on the man with whom she'd had some good as well as too many bad times.

Leah found a table for two with an empty chair. "Is anyone sitting here?" she asked the young woman with close-cropped hair who appeared totally absorbed in the magazine spread out on the table in front of her.

"It's yours if you want it," she said, without glancing up.

Setting her book on the table, Leah adjusted the strap of her colorful woven tote and walked over to the buffet table. Reaching for a plate, she filled it with two strips of crispy bacon, a serving spoon of scrambled eggs, and home fries. She passed up the mini corn muffins, because she knew she wouldn't be able to stop until she'd eaten at least three or maybe even four. Baked goods were her Achilles heel whenever she tended to overeat. There was enough room on her plate for sliced melon, and she decided to set it down and go back for coffee.

"I hope you're not on a diet because you're skinny as hell," the young woman at the table said when she returned.

Leah stared at her plate as she struggled not to lose her temper. Then her eyes met a pair of large brown eyes with gold flecks that reminded her of a pair of tortoiseshell eyeglass frames she wore whenever her eyes tired from prolonged reading. A hint of a smile lifted the corners of the full, sensual mouth of the woman with whom she was sharing the table. She looked very young, but as the mother of sons in their twenties, Leah had become quite adept in judging ages, and she knew she was close to if not at least thirty.

"No, and that should not be any of your concern."

The woman's smile vanished quickly. "You're right about

that. It is none of my business. Sit down and enjoy your break-fast, because I'm leaving." She closed the magazine, picked up her plate and walked away.

"What a snot," Leah said under her breath. It was her fa-vorite word for the students in her school who'd believed they were so privileged that they could say and do anything they wanted without regard to the consequences.

She would make certain to avoid the rude woman during her stay, even if it meant standing up until someone at an-other table vacated a chair.

Cherie Thompson walked out of the restaurant and headed for the beach and folded her body down on the near-white sand. She knew she should return and apologize to the woman who'd asked to share the table, but an overwhelming wave of helplessness rendered her impotent. Today was the anniver-sary of one of the darkest days in her life, a day when she'd lost a part of herself.

The baby she'd carried to term and delivered was one she would never see, hold, or claim as her own because of an agreement she'd made with a man she'd at one time loved more than she'd loved herself. Although she'd been well compensated, it still did not diminish the pain of having to give up her son, which was the only and last connection be-tween her and the man she could never have.

Two days after giving birth, she returned to her condo and sank into an abyss of depression that swallowed her whole. She'd only left her bed to relieve herself, brush her teeth, and down copious amounts of coffee, something she'd given up during her confinement. After several days of not taking a bath or shower, she discovered she found it hard to cope with her own body odor. She'd filled the tub with bath salts and hot water, waiting until the water was cool enough not to give her a first-degree burn, sat there, and cried until spent.

It took a week for her to shake off the self-pity. Cherie finally washed her hair, ate enough to regain some of her energy, and called her favorite stylist to ask him for an appointment.

The profusion of black curls that had contributed to her signature look lay on the salon floor, and when she stared at her reflection in the mirror, she did not recognize the image staring back at her. That's when the person she'd known all her life was gone and would never return.

Cherie lost track of time, reliving all she had experienced over the past three years until the sound of unrestrained children's laughter captured her attention. A father, pretending to be a monster, lumbered along the sand, dragging one leg as his young son and daughter ran to escape him. She smiled at their antics, her dark mood suddenly lifting. She had never been able to resist the sound of a child laughing. It had been the reason she'd accepted a position to work at a childcare center. But that was before she'd discovered she was pregnant. She'd continued working until her last month, then took off to prepare herself for the inevitable. At that time, Cherie had believed she was ready to give up her child, but in the end, she discovered that if she could've changed her mind, she would have.

Pushing to her feet, she made the ten-minute walk to return to the restaurant and stared at the back of the woman she'd insulted. Walking over to the table, Cherie took the chair she'd vacated. She knew she'd shocked the redhead when she looked at her as if she'd grown a third eye.

"I'm sorry I insulted you. Will you please accept my apology? I'm . . . I was having a bad day."

A network of fine lines fanned out around a pair of bright blue eyes when the other woman smiled. "As for bad days, I've had enough of those to last me a lifetime. So, of course, I forgive you."

Cherie extended her hand. "Let's begin again. I'm Cherie Thompson, and it's nice meeting you."

Leah took her hand. "I'm Leah Kent, and it's a pleasure to make your acquaintance."

Cherie's eyebrows lifted. "Are you always this proper?"

Leah lowered her eyes. "Proper decorum is something we attempt to instill in the young girls at my school, but unfortunately we are losing the battle."

"You're a teacher." The query was a statement.

"Yes. But right now I'm headmistress at a private school for girls whose parents pay through the nose for us to turn their unmanageable, rude, and spoiled little girls into ladies so they can make proper wives for so-called upper-class wealthy men."

Cherie smothered a laugh. She knew exactly what Leah was talking about. "Why did you call them 'so-called upper-class'?"

"Just because you have a lot of money doesn't mean you are upper-class. Would you call a drug trafficker upper-class because he's amassed a fortune selling death? No," Leah said, answering her own question. "It's home training that produces class."

"Don't you mean breeding?" Cherie asked.

Leah nodded. "Yes. Up north, you call it breeding, and down here we say home training."

"Do you also speak French?" Cherie had deftly changed the topic of conversation away from private schools for the elite because it would open a chapter in her life she'd closed and did not want to revisit.

"Yes, but not as well as I read it. Have you read *Les Misérables*?"

"It was required reading in one of my high school's literature classes."

"Did you enjoy it?"

Cherie stared over Leah's shoulder. "I never really completed any required reading."

"Did you pass the class?"

"Yes."

"How could you when you hadn't read any of the books?"

"I read the Cliff Notes." Grinning, Cherie pointed at Leah when her jaw dropped. "Gotcha!"

Slumping back in the chair, Leah narrowed her eyes. "That wasn't very nice."

"I couldn't resist teasing you, because you should've seen your expression when I said I hadn't read any of the books. My literature teacher warned the class at the beginning of the school year that he would assign a quiz every Friday, and we had to read the required pages because what was going to be on the tests couldn't be found in Cliff Notes."

A slow smile flitted over Leah's features. "It looks as if he was one step ahead of his students."

"He claimed he knew every cheating trick in the book and that he'd forgotten what we were attempting to concoct. But I must admit he was an incredible teacher who kept everyone totally engaged in the classics. By the way, I got an A in all of his classes." Pushing back the chair, Cherie stood. "I've intruded on you enough, so I'll leave you to read your book."

She felt a lot better walking out of the restaurant the second time now that she'd apologized. It had taken more than twenty years for a poor girl who'd grown up in public housing to reinvent herself; she'd learned that having good manners was her entrée into a social milieu that she would've been denied without them.

Cherie Renee Thompson no longer lived in public housing, and she had graduated college. However, it was marrying well that had eluded her; it was something she'd wanted all her life, because she didn't want to repeat the cycle of poverty and hopelessness that had plagued most of the women in her family.

She'd requested and was granted a two-month leave without pay from her position as the parent coordinator for the childcare center, and she prayed that, once she returned to Connecticut, she would know for certain which path her life would take.

Chapter 2

The rear door to the kitchen opened, and Kayana was shocked when she saw her brother walk in. It was only after eight. He usually didn't start his day until ten. "Why are you here so early?"

He set the keys to his pickup on a shelf with a metal toolbox. "Deandra called me early this morning, waking me out of my good sleep to complain that she's never having children because *your* sister's kids have completely turned her off motherhood."

Kayana gave her brother an incredulous look. He was the total package: brainy, tall, dark, and extremely handsome. Derrick Johnson, a masculine version of their beautiful mother, had been awarded full athletic and academic scholarships to several top colleges, and he'd eventually selected the University of Alabama. He'd become a standout as a running back for the Alabama Crimson Tide football program, and there were rumors he would eventually be drafted into the NFL. However, after tearing his ACL during his senior year, Derrick's dream of turning pro vanished. With a double major in accounting and finance, he was able to secure a position with a Wall Street investment firm, where he met, fell in love with, and married a money manager. When his wife announced he was going to be a father, Derrick and Andrea talked about buying property in a suburb close to New York City, but no one was more surprised than Kayana when they decided to move to Coates Island, where they purchased a newly built beachfront home; both had admitted that, despite earning a lot of money, they were overworked and stressed out from the Wall Street grind and wanted a more relaxing lifestyle.

Derrick assisted his mother and grandmother working at the Café, while Andrea divided her time taking care of their baby daughter and managing the restaurant's finances. Their fairy-tale marriage came to a crashing stop years later, when Andrea complained about extreme fatigue and excruciating back pain. It was only after Derrick convinced his wife to go to the doctor that she was diagnosed with stage-four pancreatic cancer. Andrea refused to undergo chemotherapy, and her husband made certain she was comfortable; two months following the initial diagnosis, she passed away at home with her loved ones looking on.

"Why is Jocelyn *my* sister, and not yours?" Kayana asked.

"Because you two have always been thick as thieves."

"Maybe it's because we're only eleven months apart. And my niece claiming she doesn't want children should put your mind at ease that she won't become a teenage mother."

Derrick stared at her with large near-black eyes. "I'm definitely not ready to become a grandfather."

Kayana wanted to tell him that he'd waited until thirty to become a father when many of his peers with whom he'd gone to high school were fathering children in their teens and early twenties. "A lot of men are grandfathers at forty-eight."

Derrick slipped on an apron and then put his favorite painter's cap on his cropped graying hair. Like their mother, he'd begun graying prematurely in his early twenties. The lighter strands contrasted dramatically with his unlined mahogany complexion.

"Thanks, but no thanks. I'm happy just being a dad at this time in my life."

Kayana returned her attention to chopping sweet pickles. The Café's pasta salads—mac and cheese, deviled egg macaroni, and Southwestern chicken and macaroni—were customer favorites that sold out night after night. Her personal favorite was her Grandma Cassie's mac and cheese, which she was able to duplicate down to the last ingredient.

"What was Deandra complaining about?"

"She says Jocelyn's kids won't listen when she tells them something."

"That's because Jocelyn doesn't believe in disciplining her children."

Derrick washed his hands, dried them on a bar towel, and then tucked it under the ties of his apron. "I had a long talk with Errol after he split from Jocelyn, and he told me they couldn't agree on child rearing. She accused him of being too strict, while he claimed she let their kids run amuck to do whatever they wanted."

Kayana's hands stilled. This was the first time she'd heard why her brother-in-law had left her sister. When she'd asked Jocelyn why she and Errol broke up, she gave her an inane excuse—that he hadn't wanted to be married any longer.

"What about Mom? Are they running her ragged?"

"No, because they're Grandmama's babies, and she claims she's earned the right to spoil them rotten."

"I want no part of that," she said under her breath. Although Kayana loved her sister and always enjoyed interacting with her niece and nephews, it was apparent they knew who they could get over on. She'd never had any children, but if she had, then she would've wanted them to at least be well-behaved.

She couldn't reveal to her brother what his daughter had confided in her. Kayana had taken family leave to be with her family during Andrea's last days, and Deandra told her in confidence that she never wanted to have children because she didn't want to die and leave them alone. Kayana realized Deandra's losing her mother at thirteen was doubly traumatic because of their very close relationship. Deandra said there wasn't anything she couldn't talk to Andrea about because she trusted her implicitly not to repeat it—not even to her husband.

As a young adult, she should've been hanging out with her girlfriends, talking about the boys they liked or what they'd wanted to be once they grew up, but Deandra had retreated into her own world, where she went to school, came home, and sat at a table in the restaurant to do homework as her father and aunts had done years before.

Kayana had urged Derrick to get counseling for his daughter, and once they were enrolled in family therapy, the teenager began to emerge from her cocoon. She'd become involved with several clubs at the high school, while joining some of her friends for slumber parties. Derrick had closed the restaurant to host a surprise birthday party for Deandra's seventeenth birthday, and when she walked in to find many of the school's eleventh graders in attendance, she'd nearly fainted in shock. The celebration had become the most talked about event at the school that year.

"Miss Johnson?"

Her head popped up, and she saw Corey poking his head through the kitchen's door. "Yes."

"We're running low on eggs."

"I'll make up another tray." Breaking eggs in a large metal bowl, she added light cream, whisked them until they were frothy, and then poured the liquid on the heated flattop coated with clarified butter. They cooked up quickly, and she ladled the fluffy eggs onto a tray and carried it into the dining area. A knowing smile touched her mouth when she recognized someone from the prior summers who'd come to the Café for breakfast and dinner.

The high school mathematics and economics teacher had recently purchased a two-bedroom bungalow from an elderly widow who'd left the island to live in Texas with her adult children. News of the sale spread like wildfire when folks whispered to one another about people from the North coming down to displace them. Kayana wanted to tell them that if they didn't move or put their properties up for sale, then there was no need to concern themselves about being displaced. While most locals welcomed vacationers because it meant extra money to supplement their income, there were still a few who resented the influx of folks who crowded their narrow streets, talking too loudly, and feared the disruption of their bucolic way of life.

"Welcome back, Mr. Ogden."

Graeme Ogden stared at Kayana Johnson like a dumb-struck adolescent coming face-to-face with a girl he'd had a crush on. And, if the truth was known, he did have a crush on her. The first year he'd come to spend the summer on Coates Island and walked into the Seaside Café, he felt like Michael Corleone in *The Godfather* when he first saw Apollonia Vitelli. It was as if he, like the fictional character, had been struck by a thunderbolt. He didn't know what it was about the pretty African American cook with a bright smile and stunning features that had him fantasizing about her. Although she'd greeted him by name, he was more than aware that she was able to recall the names of many of the people who frequented the eating establishment during the summer season. He also knew she was single once he overhead several locals talk about Kayana returning to the island after her divorce from a prominent Atlanta-based doctor. Rather than sit and eavesdrop on their conversation, he got up and moved to another table. Just knowing she wasn't married was enough to fuel his curiosity to find out more about her on his own.

"Thank you, and I'd really like for you to call me Graeme. I think after a couple of years of knowing each other, we could be a little less formal." He noticed an expression of indecision settle into her delicate features before it was replaced with a warm smile.

Kayana handed the tray of eggs to Corey. "Then Graeme it is."

"Does this mean I can call you Kayana rather than Miss Johnson?" Graeme felt as if he'd been poleaxed when she lowered her eyes. The expression was so demure that it reminded him of another woman who'd bewitched him within minutes of his meeting her for the first time. Although there was no physical resemblance between Kayana Johnson and the woman who had become his wife, Graeme still could not figure out why he'd become so fixated on the restaurant cook.

Kayana smiled and then gave him a direct stare. "I'm either Kay or Kayana to everyone on Coates Island, and yet you insist on calling me Miss Johnson."

"That's because when I'd asked one of your waitstaff when I came here two years ago your name, he said Miss Johnson."

"Corey has always called me Miss Johnson, but you may call me Kayana."

Graeme inclined his head as if she were royalty. "Thank you. Is it possible for me to order a Western omelet made with egg whites?"

"Of course."

He watched as Kayana turned and walked through the swinging doors leading to the kitchen. Graeme felt as if he'd somehow broken through the formality that had existed between him and the cook. When observing her, he'd discovered Kayana to be friendly and easygoing with the customers frequenting the restaurant. There were a few occasions when someone complained about their order, and she calmly reassured them that she would prepare something else more to their liking. Not once had he witnessed a change in her expression when interacting with a dissatisfied customer or detected an inflection of annoyance in her voice. That's when he'd wanted to intervene and tell the difficult diner that there was nothing wrong with their order. Every dish prepared in the Seaside Café's kitchen was exceptional; he knew because he'd sampled most items on the menu.

Searching for an empty seat, Graeme found a table with an elderly couple. "Good morning. Do you mind if I share your table?"

The white-haired, bespectacled man wearing a Boston Red Sox T-shirt gestured to the chair opposite him. "Please sit."

"Did I hear a New England accent?" the man's wife asked.

Smiling, Graeme sat. "Guilty as charged."

"We're Claude and Edna Ferguson, and we live in Worcester. This is our fifth time coming here for vacation."

A beat passed, and Graeme realized the couple expected him to introduce himself. "Graeme Ogden from Newburyport." Although he'd spent most of his childhood in Boston, he now called the historic seaport city home.

What, he mused, were the odds of meeting a couple from Massachusetts when during the prior two years the few he had opted to interact with were from Michigan or Ohio. Graeme had made a practice not to become involved with those on the island because he'd come to Coates Island to work and not socialize. He didn't hang out on the beach or in the town square to watch movies or listen to prerecorded music.

"That's a really pretty little city," Claude said.

Edna leaned over the table. "How long will you be here?" she whispered, as if it was a secret.

"Probably a couple of weeks." Graeme had no intention of revealing his plans to a couple of strangers.

"Did you come down with your wife?" Claude asked.

Well, I'll be damned, Graeme thought. Had he chosen to sit with a pair of retired interrogators? As soon as Kayana finished with his omelet, he was going to sit out on the patio to avoid what was certain to become an inquisition.

As if on cue, Kayana approached the table. "Here's your omelet. Enjoy."

Coming to his feet, Graeme took the plate. "Thank you." He turned to the Fergusons. "Thank you for allowing me to sit with you while I waited, but I'm going to eat on the patio."

Kayana walked with him over to the buffet table. "Did the Fergusons put you through the third degree?"

He gave her a sidelong glance, noticing for the first time that she wasn't as tall as he'd thought. The top of her head came to his shoulder. "How did you know?"

"I usually don't engage in gossip about my customers, but most folks know never to share the Fergusons' table because you'll end up being asked about your entire life, beginning with your birth weight."

Graeme smothered a laugh as he picked up a serving spoon of home fries and placed it on the plate next to the fluffy omelet. "I just witnessed that. Thanks for the heads-up." For the second time in a matter of minutes, he watched Kayana walk. He had never seen her wear anything other than a chef's tunic, black checkered pants, and a bibbed apron. Her telling him about the Fergusons had him feeling as if they were co-conspirators.

Kayana walked back into the kitchen to resume making the pasta salads. "Graeme Ogden unknowingly fell prey to the Fergusons' interrogating him."

Derrick gently mixed a large bowl of lump crab with Old Bay and other spices before forming them into crab cakes. "He's been here enough times to know to stay away from them."

"He usually keeps to himself."

"That's because he prefers to sit and stare at my sister."

Kayana went completely still. "What are you talking about?"

Derrick smiled. "Are you so turned off on men that you don't know when a man is interested in you?"

She went back to grating cheese. "You're talking out the side of your neck."

"No, I'm not, little sister. There were a few times when I caught the man gawking at you with his tongue hanging out, and I wanted to tell him not to be so obvious."

Kayana made a sucking sound with her tongue and teeth. "The next time you see him look my way, you should tell him your sister isn't interested. And even with his gawking, he could have a wife hidden away somewhere."

"You've been reading too many Gothic novels where men hide their wives away in a dungeon or locked room in order to seduce the heroine."

"Don't knock my books, Derrick," she said defensively.

"I happen to know that Graeme Ogden isn't married. Covering dinner allows me to talk to our customers when I ask them if they're enjoying their meal or just chatting about other things. He's a teacher and enjoys coming down here to get away from it all."

"Single or not, at this time in my life I want nothing to do with a man."

"Not all men are like James."

"I'm aware of that, but giving him almost twenty years of my life, only to be traded in for a newer model, still galls me."

"You're only forty-six, Kay, and—"

"Please let it go, Derrick," Kayana said, cutting him off.

She knew her brother wanted to see her with someone, but that wasn't going to happen—at least not yet. Two years, when compared to two decades, wasn't long enough to get over her ex's deception. If he had only told her he wanted out of their marriage, instead of her seeing him and his mistress coming out of a downtown hotel when he'd told her he was going out of town for a conference. She would've become his genie and granted his wish, because she didn't believe in staying in or continuing a toxic relationship or marriage.

"Is it because Graeme isn't black?"

Kayana cut her eyes at Derrick. "His race has nothing to do with it. I just don't want to get involved with anyone, and please let's leave it at that."

"Yeah, yeah, yeah," Derrick intoned.

"You've been single longer than I have, so hush your mouth."

"The difference between you and me is I have a child and you don't."

"What does that have to do with anything?" she asked. "Deandra has one more year of high school before she goes off to college. Are you going to wait to become a grandfather to begin dating again?"

Filling the sink with enough water to cover racks of ribs, he added a cup of vinegar. "You're pushing it, Kay, with your grandfather yakety-yak."

"Consider yourself fortunate if you're able to attain that honor because that's something I can never claim. Luckily, I have nieces and nephews I can spoil rotten."

Kayana had been married less than a year when she discovered she was pregnant. She had been within weeks of completing her first trimester when she began hemorrhaging, and the doctors were unable to stop the bleeding. Kayana was not given the option of becoming pregnant again after undergoing an emergency hysterectomy. Subsequently, she and James had discussed adoption, but whenever she brought up the subject, he said they were still a family even if they didn't have a child or children. After a while, they simply dropped the topic.

"Can you answer one question for me, Derrick?"

"What's that?"

"You went to see Errol about breaking up with Jocelyn. Did you do the same when I told you I was divorcing James?"

Removing a pair of disposable gloves, he met Kayana's eyes. "No, because I knew you could hold your own with him. Being the youngest, Jocelyn has always had us to fight her battles, and I doubted whether she would've been able to stand up to Errol. Now, if James had gotten funky with you, then I would've driven down to Atlanta and kicked his bougie ass."

She laughed. "I managed to beat him without lifting a finger, and because we didn't have a prenup, he had to give me what I asked for or I was ready to drag out the divorce for infinity and beyond."

"Damn, Kay, you've watched too many *Toy Story* movies."

"Those are Jocelyn's kids' favorite movies."

Kayana was relieved that she and her brother could talk about things other than the lack of a man in her life. She knew she would not be able to engage in a meaningful relationship unless she forgave her ex. Otherwise, the next man would bear the brunt of her simmering rage, and that would be unfair to him.

Derrick had asked whether dating out of her race was a deal breaker, and for Kayana it wasn't. While in college, she'd gone out with two men who weren't black and found them no different from the African Americans she'd dated. Although she never lacked for dates, it had taken her a while before she'd had a serious relationship, and she knew it had to do with her parents' divorce.

She also thought about her brother's reference to Graeme Ogden's interest in her, and she wanted to tell him he was delusional. The tall, middle-aged man with large gray eyes, which reminded her of dark clouds rolling across the sky before an impending thunderstorm, did not appeal to her. Whenever he visited the restaurant, she rarely gave him a passing glance, as she did most of the patrons. She greeted everyone politely, and her sole concern was making certain they enjoyed what she and Derrick had prepared for them to eat.

Graeme Ogden planned to summer on the island and then return home at the end of the season, while she would have her hands full cooking and serving at the restaurant. What little time she had to spare she tended to spend reading, because there was no room in her busy schedule for romance.

Chapter 3

Kayana always looked forward to Sundays. Once the restaurant closed at 1:00, following brunch, she had the rest of the day for herself. After showering and changing into a pair of cropped slacks, a T-shirt, tennis shoes, and a straw hat to protect her head and face from the brilliant late-spring sun, she set off on foot to go into town to browse the variety shop; she wanted to purchase something for Derrick and Jocelyn's children. Deandra liked cloth-covered journals, Jocelyn's sons were into Legos, and her daughter had amassed a collection of stuffed bears. Reaching into her tote, she removed a pair of sunglasses and placed them on the bridge of her nose.

She waved to people she'd known all her life as they drove slowly along the paved road. Although there was no posted speed limit, most residents did not exceed more than twenty miles an hour. It felt good to walk. It had become her only form of exercise since moving back to Coates Island. One of the rooms in the Atlanta house was outfitted as a home gym where she worked out regularly. The backyard was as opulent as the interior, with an outdoor kitchen, inground pool, jacuzzi, and swim-up tiki bar.

It was a source of pride for James whenever he'd entertained. And they'd done a lot of entertaining, so much that Kayana told James it had to stop, because she felt as if they were running a catering hall. It stopped for several weeks before starting up again. It wasn't until she saw her husband and the woman coming out of the hotel together that she'd realized why he had invited his colleagues to their home so often. Having a crowd had provided the perfect cover for him and his mistress to openly socialize together. Kayana did not want to believe the shy, soft-spoken, butter-wouldn't-melt-in-her-mouth intern had smiled in her face while she was sleeping with her husband. She didn't blame the woman as much as she did James. After all, he was the married one.

Kayana knew she had to let go of the past or she wouldn't be able to move on. She wasn't looking forward to getting married again, because she'd been there, done that. Then she remembered the plaque she'd hung on the wall in her office at the hospital. It was the Serenity Prayer, and she would recite it whenever she felt stressed out. Now she didn't feel stressed, yet she knew she had to accept the things she couldn't change. Her husband had left her for another woman because she was able to give him what Kayana couldn't: a child. And now she was relieved that they hadn't had children, because as a child of divorced parents she hadn't wanted the same for her children. She repeated the prayer over and over to herself, and miraculously she felt free, freer than she had in a very long time.

A wide smile parted her lips as she quickened her step. She hadn't intended to stop in the bookstore, but now that she recalled her conversation with Leah, Kayana decided to pick up a few titles as possible choices for their upcoming book club discussion. Particles of sand grated under her feet as she moved onto the grassy surface of the road when she heard an approaching vehicle. A jitney filled with vacationers drove by. The fee vacationers paid to park their cars for the season afforded them free jitney rides around the island from 6:00 in the morning to 10:00 at night. However, the owner of the jitneys did charge those wishing to go over the bridge to the mainland a nominal fee.

Graeme Ogden walked into the bookstore on Main Street and knew he'd made the right decision to purchase property on Coates Island because it reminded him of Newburyport with its historic quaintness. Small, independent bookstores were now as scarce as hen's teeth, and whenever he found one, he usually lingered there for a while; although not electronically challenged, Graeme still preferred reading a physical book. And much to his delight, Turn the Page Bookstore was stocked with current best-sellers and older titles in most popular genres. Wooden benches with enough room for two were positioned in the aisles so customers could sit and read before making their purchase.

The first year he'd summered on the island, he'd felt right at home. The furnished bungalow was no larger than the detached carriage house, converted into an apartment for the caretaker, on the three-quarter-acre property where he'd vacationed with his parents during the summer months, but it suited his needs. The bungalow was far enough away from the other small houses to allow him a modicum of privacy. However, there had been a few drawbacks. The plumbing and the electricity needed updating, along with the kitchen and bathroom. It was only after he'd rented the house the following year that he'd decided to buy it.

Graeme had just turned down the fiction aisle when he saw her. Kayana sat on a bench, a tote, shopping bag, and straw hat next to her. He smiled. It was the first time he'd seen her in street clothes. His gaze lingered on her bare arms. She was so engrossed in what she was reading that she wasn't aware of his approach.

"Are you enjoying it?"

Kayana's head popped up, and it took several seconds before she recognized him. "Yes, I am. I see you discovered our bookstore."

Graeme stared at her straightened hair, parted off center and ending at the jawline. Her hair would've been raven black if not for several strands of gray. "It's one of the reasons I decided to buy property here."

"You mean it wasn't the delicious food at the Café that had you coming back?" she teased, smiling.

His smile matched hers. "That, too. May I sit down?"

Kayana shifted the tote bag and hat to her right side. "Of course."

Graeme made certain not to sit too close and invade her personal space. Not only did Kayana look good, but she smelled delicious. Her perfume was a sensual, woodsy-floral blend of sandalwood, vanilla, and another flower he couldn't identify.

He gave her a sidelong glance. "How often do you come here?"

Extending her legs, Kayana crossed her feet at the ankles. "Not as much as I'd like."

She hadn't seen Graeme in the restaurant since the morning he'd asked for the omelet. Either he'd stayed away or had come in when she was working in the kitchen. She'd unconsciously dismissed Derrick's allegation that Graeme was interested in her, and when she'd looked up and seen him standing there, she saw curiosity, not lust, in his eyes.

"Do you ever get a day off?"

Kayana stared at Graeme's crisp khakis and matching deck shoes. "I don't get days, but hours off during the summer season."

"Are you saying you work seven days a week?"

Seeing him this close made her aware that his eyes weren't as dark as she'd originally thought. They were light gray, with dark centers that reminded her of the mist that occasionally shrouded the island. His sandy-brown hair, with glints of gold and silver, was cut military-style. His features were well-balanced for his lean face, and Kayana didn't think of him as handsome or attractive, but interesting. It was his eyes and voice she'd found worthy of note. The instant he opened his mouth, she'd known he'd grown up and/or was educated in the Boston area.

"Yes."

Graeme sandwiched his hands between his knees. "That must get exhausting."

"I try not to think about it because there are advantages to working for yourself. I don't have to put up with a boss breathing down my neck, and my brother and I set our own schedules."

"Did you always want to be a chef?"

Kayana knew she was right about Graeme. He *was* curious about her. "I'm not a chef, but a cook. Derrick and I learned everything we know watching my mother and grandmother."

"You must have been an excellent student, because the dishes you and your brother serve are exceptional."

She smiled. "We just try to keep the family tradition going. By the way, how do you like living on the island?" Kayana asked.

"You know about that?" he questioned.

"You mean about you buying property here?"

"Yes."

"If you live here long enough, you'll learn that there are no secrets on Coates Island. When the widow Hutchins left to live with her daughter in Texas, everyone knew it was a matter of time before she would stop renting the house and put it on the market." Elderly residents who hadn't passed away tended to move in with family members and rent out their bungalows rather than sell, because there was a wait list for vacationers willing to pay exorbitant fees for the summer season.

"They were selling it for more than I was willing to pay because it needed a lot of work," Graeme admitted. "After a lot of back-and-forth negotiating, we were able to agree on a price, and the first thing I did was contact an architect and have him draw up plans to open up the interior."

Shifting on the bench, Kayana turned to give him a direct stare. "Do you plan to live here permanently?"

"Probably not until I retire."

She knew that would not be for a while, because Graeme didn't appear old enough to retire. Kayana estimated him to be in his late forties or early fifties. She'd also noticed he appeared to be in good physical shape and didn't have the paunch that occasionally afflicted middle-aged men who'd let themselves go.

"You will certainly become an anomaly. The only folks who retire on Coates Island live here year-round."

"Why do you make that sound like a bad thing?" Graeme asked.

"Quite the contrary. I grew up here and had an incredible childhood. Everyone knew one another, and parents looked out for each other's children. The kids who lived on the mainland were jealous of us because we had the beach as our playground and the ocean was our swimming pool. The only thing they had that we didn't was a movie theater. But during the summer months, everyone was treated to Friday night movies in the town square, and the tradition continues to this day."

"Do you still go to the Friday night movies?"

Kayana shook her head. She'd seen most of the family-oriented movies, and if she'd wanted to see other than a PG or PG-13, then she would drive to the theater on the mainland. "Not any longer."

"What do you do during your downtime?"

"Read." She was hard-pressed not to laugh in Graeme's face when his jaw dropped.

"Are you saying you spend time reading when you're not working?"

A shiver of annoyance washed over her, and Kayana struggled not to unload on him. He was no different than James, who'd taunted her relentlessly whenever she settled down to read. When he wasn't at the hospital or on call, he couldn't just relax and enjoy their time together. And if he did stay home, he had to have hordes of people around.

"Would you have been less shocked if I told you I spend my free time smoking weed?" Kayana knew she'd struck a nerve with Graeme when a rush of color suffused his pale face. Within seconds, she regretted lashing out at him, but it was too late to retract the acerbic retort. "I'm sorry. I should not have said that," she said, apologizing.

The seconds ticked by as Graeme stared at Kayana. Not only was he shocked by her comeback; he was also puzzled why she would even mention smoking marijuana. Was she being defensive because she'd had or someone close to her had had a drug problem? He'd believed his query was innocent enough for her not to come at him as if he'd openly insulted her. His first impulse was to get up and walk away, but he decided against it.

Graeme knew very little about Kayana Johnson other than she was part owner of the Seaside Café and that she was divorced. The latter he had uncovered when the chatty real estate agent handling the sale of the bungalow offered an overview of the permanent residents on the island. He'd been tempted to delve further into her background, then decided he preferred uncovering things about her on his own. After all, he had planned to live on the island and therefore would get to see her in his daily comings and goings. He'd told her that he'd intended to live on Coates Island once he retired, but in reality, he'd recently retired from teaching after twenty years to concentrate on his second career as a writer.

And at the age of fifty-two, he could realistically write for another twenty years before settling down to read every book in the extensive collection he'd amassed during his lifetime. First editions of classic and rare-edition books and music recordings were housed in his library in Newburyport, and Graeme knew if he were to transport even half the collection to North Carolina, it would take up every square foot of the bungalow and force him to sleep on a blow-up mattress in the corner of the bedroom. As a young boy, he'd thought of his parents as hoarders because of the number of books they'd bring home after scouring bookstores that sold out-of-print titles. Then there were the auctions and estate sales, where they'd paid what he'd believed were excessive amounts of money for musty-smelling autographed first editions and vinyl recordings. It wasn't until after they'd passed away and he went through their legal documents that he realized that the value of their book and record collection was appraised at more than seven figures.

"There's no need for you to apologize. I had no right to question you about what you do in your spare time." Lowering her eyes, Kayana flashed what passed for a demure smile. The gesture was so innocent, so charming that he found himself holding his breath.

"I'm addicted to books," she admitted.

Throwing back his head, Graeme laughed loudly. "You have a partner in crime, because I too am addicted to books."

"What do you read?"

He smiled. "Everything. However, I am partial to legal thrillers and books written by Clancy, Patterson, and Baldacci."

Her eyebrows lifted questioningly. "You only read male authors?"

"No. I occasionally will read a female author."

"Name one, Graeme."

"Octavia Butler."

A soft gasp escaped Kayana. "I love her writing. But it's been a while since I've read her."

Graeme saw excitement light up Kayana's eyes. It had

been years since he'd met a woman who liked books as much as he did. "I've read everything she's written. I wasn't much of a science fiction reader until I read *Kindred*, and then I was hooked."

"I haven't read all of her work, but *Clay's Ark* really affected me. I had recurring dreams about women who gave birth to mutant, sphinxlike children after they'd contracted a microorganism brought back to Earth by the one surviving astronaut of the spaceship *Clay's Ark*."

"She was truly a genius."

"I think I'm going to recommend reading one of her titles."

Graeme listened intently as Kayana told him about a meeting with a vacationer later that evening to talk about forming a book club. Watching her reminded him of images of young kids opening presents on Christmas morning. "I believe I saw a copy of *Kindred* when I was looking through the science fiction section."

Kayana stood. "I think I'm going to buy it."

Graeme rose with her. "Don't you want to check first to see if you can download it electronically?"

"No. I much prefer holding the physical copy to reading it on an electronic device."

He smiled. "I feel the same way."

"It looks as if we have a few things in common," Kayana said, as she gathered her belongings.

"When it comes to books, I'd say we have a lot in common. Maybe one of these days we can get together and discuss the books we've read."

A beat passed. "Would you like to join our book club discussion?" Kayana asked.

Although Graeme found the invitation very tempting, he knew reading books and having to discuss them would take away the time he needed to complete a manuscript and submit it the second week in September. As it was, he was behind schedule and needed to catch up in order to make the deadline. "Thank you for the invite. It's very tempting, but I'm going to have to pass. Maybe next summer."

"I'm going to hold you to that. Now, if you'll excuse me, I'm going to buy *Kindred* and begin reading it before I meet with my book club buddy later on tonight."

"How are you getting back?" Graeme asked.

Kayana smiled at him over her shoulder. "I'll either walk or take a jitney."

"Don't bother. I'll drive you back."

"You don't have to—"

"I insist, Kayana," he interrupted. "It's much too hot to walk or stand out waiting for a jitney." If driving her back to the restaurant meant spending more time with her, then Graeme was more than willing to do it. After dropping her off, he would return to the bookstore to look through the out-of-print titles.

She smiled. "Okay."

Kayana discovered the bookstore had several of Octavia Butler's titles, and she decided to purchase *Parable of the Sower*, *Parable of the Talents*, and *Kindred*. A shiver of excitement eddied through her when she anticipated a reading marathon. It had always been that way with her when she discovered a writer's work she really liked. She looked for everything they'd written and literally lost herself in the world they'd created, shutting out anyone and everything around her. She was aware that some people became avid readers for entertainment or escape, but for Kayana, it was both. She retreated into books whenever she sought to escape her parents' incessant arguing. The arguments finally stopped once they were divorced, but for her, the die had been cast. She'd become an avid reader.

Kayana set the books on the counter and then reached into her tote for her wallet. "I'm going to take these."

The owner of the bookstore smiled, exhibiting a mouth

filled with teeth stained by years of smoking cigars and chewing tobacco. The slightly eccentric man wore a ski cap year-round despite the temperature, and Kayana wondered if he had any hair. Lenny Davies and his retired librarian wife had bought the bookstore from the former owner more than twenty years ago; they had updated the interior, and she'd scanned all of the books electronically.

"I reckon you're starting your summer reading."

"Yes, I am, Mr. Davies." She noticed slight trembling in his right hand when he picked up the books to scan the bar codes and suspected he might have Parkinson's. Living with a doctor and working in a hospital had afforded her a front-row seat to the challenges faced by the many patients who came through the doors.

"You picked some good ones."

Kayana wanted to tell the man that she probably wouldn't have chosen Octavia Butler if Graeme hadn't recommended the science fiction writer, because she tended to favor the classics. It had been a while since she'd read Henry James, Dumas, Richard Ellison, Edith Wharton, Jane Austen, and James Baldwin. She'd kept up with the best-seller lists and read those that appealed to her. Although not partial to biographies, she did read and enjoy Michelle Obama's *Becoming*.

"I'm looking forward to enjoying them," she said, handing Mr. Davies her credit card.

"I didn't read much before the missus and I bought this place, but now I'm like that character in that *Twilight Zone* episode who was addicted to reading. He hid out in the bank vault to read and didn't know that an atomic bomb had exploded that left him last person alive on earth. He couldn't believe his good luck because there was nothing to stop him from indulging in his addiction."

Totally intrigued by the tale, Kayana asked, "What happened?"

"His glasses fell off, and he stepped on them and shattered the lenses."

"Are you saying he needed glasses to read?"

"Yes."

"Oh, how awful."

Mr. Davies shook his head. "It was the saddest episode I ever saw."

Kayana wanted to tell him that she rarely watched television because she didn't have the patience to become that involved in a program to commit to watching it week after week. But once she opened a book and found herself engaged in the first few pages, she became a part of the characters' lives.

"It had to be devastating for him." Kayana could not imagine anything that would keep her from reading. She signed the receipt and put the bag with her purchases into the tote. "I'll probably see you again before the end of the summer."

"If there's any book you want, just call me and I'll order it for you."

"Thank you." Kayana put on her hat and sunglasses, and walked out of the bookstore, nearly colliding with Graeme. His hands went to her shoulders to keep her from losing her balance. For an instant, she felt the strength in his fingers as he tightened his grip on her bare skin. "I'm sorry. I didn't see you standing there."

Graeme dropped his hands and reached for the tote and shopping bag. "I decided to wait outside because Mr. Davies tends to be a little long-winded. By the way, I'm parked around the corner."

Kayana smiled and nodded. "It appears as if you're getting to know a little something about the locals."

"They regard me as an outsider, and most are suspicious as to why I've chosen to move here."

Kayana walked with him to the parking lot, skirting people standing around in small groups as they waited for the next jitney. "It's going to be a while before they consider you an islander." Graeme stopped next to a silver Range Rover, opened the passenger-side door, and waited until she was seated before handing her the tote.

"I'll put your shopping bag in the back."

She smiled at him. "Thank you." She was grateful that Graeme had offered to drive her back because the heat had intensified and her tote was considerably heavier because of the books.

Graeme punched the car's START engine button. "Where do you live?"

Kayana turned to look at him. "You can drop me off at the restaurant."

"The restaurant?"

"Yes. I live in an apartment above the restaurant."

"I thought you grew up here."

"I did. But after I graduated college, I moved to Atlanta and lived there for twenty years. I moved back a couple of years ago."

Graeme shifted into REVERSE and backed out of the space. "I thought you'd always lived here."

"That's a very long story," she said.

"Too long for a short drive?"

"Yes."

It would take Graeme less than three minutes to drive from the business district to the Café. The ride ended quickly as he maneuvered into the lot behind the restaurant and parked without shutting off the engine.

Graeme placed a hand on her arm. "Don't move. I'll help you down."

Kayana unbuckled the seat belt and waited from him to get out and come around to assist her. He opened the door, and she placed her hands on his shoulders as his fingers tightened around her waist. She had to admit that the Range Rover was higher than her SUV. And the last thing she wanted was to step down awkwardly and sprain her ankle—an unfortunate incident she'd experienced in the past.

Graeme held her aloft for several seconds before slowly lowering her until her feet touched the ground. She looked at him through the lenses of her sunglasses. There was a hint of a smile touching the corners of his mouth.

"Thank you for the ride," she said when he opened the rear door and handed her the shopping bag.

He winked at her. "Anytime."

Kayana turned and walked to the back door leading into the restaurant, aware that Graeme hadn't moved to get into his vehicle. She unlocked the door and then disarmed the security system. It was only when she'd closed and locked the door behind her that she heard him driving away.

She mounted the staircase leading to the apartment, recalling the short time she'd spent with Graeme Ogden. She did enjoy talking with him about books and authors. But at no time had he appeared to come on to her, which had put her totally at ease with him. And Kayana liked listening to him because of the distinctive New England inflection in some of his words.

"He's nice," she whispered under her breath.

Kayana entered the living room and set her tote and shopping bag on a low table. The clock on the fireplace mantle chimed the hour. It was five, and she'd told Leah to meet her on the patio any time after six. An hour was enough time for her to change into something more comfortable and put up a load of laundry before her book club partner arrived.

Chapter 4

Kayana set platters of different types of cheese, seedless grapes, sliced strawberries, and stone-ground wheat crackers on the table on the enclosed patio, along with small plates and serving pieces. She'd also put together a caprese of sliced tomato and mozzarella drizzled with a balsamic vinegar glaze and topped with fresh basil, and a charcuterie plate with smoked ham, olives, cured sausage, and a pâté made with chicken liver.

Diners were able to take advantage of the screened-in patio regardless of the weather. During the colder months or in inclement weather, the pocket doors were closed to the elements; woven shades, when raised, provided diners with picturesque views of the beach and ocean, while, at the same time, they were afforded complete privacy from those outside looking in.

Kayana didn't know whether Leah had had dinner, but had prepared a light snack in the event she hadn't. She'd just returned to the dining room when the sound of the bell echoed throughout the restaurant.

Peering through the blinds, she saw Leah and opened the

door. A narrow dark-green headband holding her hair off her face matched a green floral midi-sundress. It was apparent the woman had spent time in the sun, as evidenced by the bright-red color on her nose and bared arms.

"Welcome."

Leah flashed a warm smile. "Thank you. I have a confession to make."

Kayana's expression changed at the same time she bit her lip. She didn't want to believe their book club had met its demise before it even began. "What is it?"

"I hope you don't mind that I invited someone else to join us. I ran into her again and told her I was meeting with you to talk about books, and she seemed very interested. She's younger than we are, but I feel she can offer another perspective to our discussions."

She was looking forward to talking about books with another person who shared her passion for the same genre. "Of course not. The more the merrier."

"I told her we were meeting here at six, so she should be coming soon."

The words were barely off Leah's tongue when a young black woman with cropped dark hair wearing white shorts, a matching T-shirt, and red leather flip-flops walked up the steps. Kayana remembered seeing her once or twice when she'd come in for breakfast during the past week. She'd also noticed that she preferred sitting alone, wondering how she and Leah had connected. As she came closer, Kayana realized the younger woman hadn't selected her clothes off a department-store rack, but from a boutique geared to those who selected garments without first checking the price tag. And she knew the crossbody designer bag had cost her at least five figures.

"Welcome. I'm Kayana Johnson."

"And I'm Cherie Thompson, and thank you for allowing me to join you."

"As I told Leah, the more the merrier when it comes to

talking about books. Please come in before someone walks by and thinks we're open for business." Kayana closed and locked the door behind Cherie. "I've set up a table for us on the patio where we can talk and share a light repast. I wanted to hold out serving beverages until I asked what you'd like to drink."

Leah and Cherie shared a look. "Do we have a choice between alcoholic and pop?" the redhead asked.

"Yes. I was thinking about making a pitcher of sour apple martinis—that is, unless you'd prefer something else. And I also have wine and beer on hand."

"I'm good with the martini," Cherie said.

"I'll also have the martini," Leah said in agreement.

"Y'all make yourselves comfortable on the patio while I whip up the cocktails."

Waiting until the two women retreated to the patio overlooking the rear of the restaurant, Kayana walked into the kitchen and reached for a bottle of vodka, sour apple liqueur, and butterscotch schnapps. Opening the refrigerator, she took out a bottle of cranberry juice and a chilled glass pitcher. She measured the liquid into a shaker, along with ice cubes, and shook it until condensation formed on the outside of the shaker, then strained it into the pitcher. She went back to the fridge to get three chilled martini glasses, which she then placed then on a wicker tray with the pitcher.

When Derrick had decided to add cocktails to the menu, Kayana had had to brush up on her knowledge of mixing drinks. When married, she'd become the consummate hostess for the many dinner parties she and James hosted, planning the menus and occasionally preparing the food. Most times, she assumed the role of mixologist because it meant not having to engage in inane chitchat with her phony in-laws.

Kayana carried the tray to patio and set it on the table with the cheese and fruit. "Don't be shy, ladies. Eat, drink, and be merry."

Leah reached for a plate and speared slices of caprese and several grapes. "Everything looks too pretty to eat."

Cherie picked up her plate. "It looks as if you went to a lot of work for us to just talk about books."

Kayana halted filling the glasses with the chilled cocktail. "I didn't know if Leah had eaten dinner, so I decided to offer her something to eat."

Cherie lowered her eyes, apparently acknowledging she had been summarily chastised. "Perhaps I spoke out of turn. It's not that I don't appreciate what you've prepared, but if we're going to meet again like this, then I'd like to bring something. I was raised to never go to someone's home empty-handed."

"I believe we all have been raised to do the same," Leah added. "However, I am more than appreciative of the offer, because I did not eat dinner."

"There you go," Kayana said smugly, as she continued to fill the martini glasses, handing one to Cherie and one to Leah. She sat and raised her glass. "I'd like to propose a toast to the inaugural meeting of our Seaside Café Book Club." She touched glasses with Leah and then Cherie before taking a sip.

Cherie pressed a hand to her chest. "Whoa! This is really strong."

Leah looked over the rim of her glass at Cherie. "Perhaps Kayana should've carded you before serving you that drink."

Cherie narrowed a pair of large, slanting, clear-brown eyes and glared at Leah. "Very funny."

Setting down her glass, Leah speared an olive and popped it into her mouth. "How old are you?"

"I just turned thirty-three."

Kayana stared at Cherie. "You look a lot younger than that."

"I may look young, but right about now I feel twice that age."

"Did you come to the island with someone?"

Cherie shook her head. "No."

"Bad breakup." Kayana's question was a statement.

"Something like that."

Knowing it was time to stop delving into Cherie's personal life, Kayana picked up a plate and filled it with fruit, crackers, and pâté. "I think we should get to know a little bit about one another before we begin talking about what types of books we want to read. Leah, do you want to go first?"

Leah took another sip of her drink before touching a napkin to the corners of her mouth. "I'm Leah Berkley Kent from Richmond, Virginia. I'm the mother of twenty-seven-year-old twin sons who both just passed the bar exam. Right now, they're traveling abroad for the summer with their father. I'm forty-eight, a teacher by profession, and I recently celebrated my twenty-eighth wedding anniversary."

Kayana noted that Leah had said her sons were traveling with their father rather than her husband. She'd counseled enough women to pick up on certain words and phrases whenever they referred to their significant other. And she didn't have to have the intelligence quotient of a nuclear physicist to glean that Leah wasn't an underpaid schoolteacher who lived from paycheck to paycheck, because most of the summer rentals on the island ranged from twelve hundred upward to eighteen hundred a week, and the eternity band of diamonds on her left hand totaled at least two or maybe even three carats.

Cherie stared at the red liquid in her glass. "You married very young."

Leah pressed her lips tightly together as if to stifle the first thing that came to her mind. "Yes, I did." She paused. "Cherie, you're next."

Cherie set down her glass, inhaled an audible breath before letting it out slowly. "I'm Cherie Thompson. You already know that I'm thirty-three. I've never been married and don't have any children. I have an undergraduate degree in early-childhood development, and I'm currently on leave from my position as a parent coordinator at a Connecticut childcare center. I plan to hang out here until just before the

Labor Day weekend. And, before you ask, I'm not involved with anyone."

Leah chewed and swallowed a plump ripe strawberry. "Are you opposed to marriage?"

The air shimmered with friction as Cherie glared at Leah. "Just because I'm not married doesn't mean I'm opposed to it."

Kayana didn't know what it was, but she detected somewhat of a power struggle between the other two women and wondered if it had something to do with Leah's attempt to be maternal. After all, her sons weren't much younger than Cherie. "I guess it's my turn," she announced, hoping to diffuse what was becoming a tense situation. "I'm forty-six, divorced, and I've never had any children. In my former life, I was a hospital psychiatric social worker, but I gave it up to assist my brother in running this venerable establishment that has been in our family for more than thirty years."

"Did you grow up here?" Leah questioned.

"Yes. My family is a direct descendant of the man for whom the island is named, and the Johnsons are one of the oldest families to inhabit Coates Island."

"Please tell us about him." Cherie's eyes were as bright as newly minted pennies. It was apparent she'd gotten over Leah questioning her about marriage.

"Yes, please do," Leah chimed in.

Kayana thought it odd they wanted to hear about her family's history rather than talk about books. "Half is true and the other half legend, but there is factual evidence that Draymond Coates was an eighteenth-century pirate who found safety in coves throughout the Caribbean to moor his smaller, faster ship, the *Black Dragon*, from British warships that sought to capture him and his crew and return their plunder to the Crown."

"Was he British or an American?" Cherie asked Kayana.

"He was a British subject. Draymond was only twenty when he was caught stealing a farmer's hog. He was jailed, and then exiled from England as an indentured servant to a family who owned a sugarcane plantation in Jamaica, where he'd worked alongside African slaves making sugar, molasses, and rum. He escaped after six years and joined up with a band of miscreants who preferred stealing to working. After a while, he and a small group of criminals commandeered a British merchant ship, cast out the captain and crew on a deserted island, and renamed it the *Black Dragon*."

"Did they ever capture him?" Leah asked.

"No, because he had Mother Nature on his side. His preying on British merchant ships finally ended when the *Black Dragon* went down during a hurricane and all onboard perished except Draymond Coates. Historical records claim the legendary brigand washed up on the beach and was taken in by a family of free people of color. He recovered, changed his name to Duncan Johnson, and married one of the young women; they had eight children together, with six surviving to adulthood. Even though it states they were married, the fact is black folks knew it wasn't legal, because marriage between whites and blacks was forbidden at that time, but she was so fair in coloring, she could pass for white."

A slight frown furrowed Cherie's smooth forehead. "Do you know for certain that you are a direct descendant of a pirate?"

"Yes, because my sister searched an ancestry website, and she was able to go as far back as Draymond Coates's grandparents, who were born in Hampshire, England. Remember, he married a free woman of color, so she and their children were recorded in the census."

"What makes you believe part of it is a legend?" Leah questioned.

"Historical records claim that when his ship sank, it was carrying a cargo of gold coin and jewelry estimated to be worth two million dollars in today's money. Salvagers spent years searching the area where the *Black Dragon* went down, and when they finally located it, there were no gold coin or jewels, leading them to believe the captain had buried his treasure somewhere in the Bahamas before the hurricane blew him off course after he'd attempted to sail back to Jamaica. And here again, it may be a legend, but there was talk that when Draymond washed up on shore, the people who rescued him said he'd sewn emeralds and other precious jewels into the waistband of his trousers."

"That should have made him quite a wealthy man," Leah commented.

"I'm not certain what he did with the stones, but he made his living as a blacksmith—a trade he'd learned from his father and grandfather before he was shipped to the West Indies. He had a thriving business that allowed him to build a modest home for his wife and children."

Picking up a knife, Cherie spread a small amount of pâté on a cracker. "What I don't understand is if North Carolina was part of the British Empire, couldn't they have arrested him here?"

Kayana shook her head. "No, because by that time the colonies had declared their independence from England, and Britain's focus was sending thousands of well-trained soldiers to America to quell the rebellion rather than find and hang a pirate."

Cherie applauded softly. "That's sounds like a plot for a historical romance novel."

Kayana suddenly had the opening she needed to broach the reason for their meeting. "Do you read romance novels, Cherie?"

The young woman lowered her eyes. "I occasionally do."

"I read them more than occasionally," Leah admitted.

Cherie shot Leah a questioning stare. "But . . . but why would you? You're married."

A rush of color suffused Leah's face, as the redness on her nose blended into the blush. "Just because I'm married, you think I shouldn't read romance novels?"

Again, Kayana sensed tension between the two women and knew that if it continued, their book discussions would be fraught with hostility. "I think we should settle something right now before we go any further. I'd hoped we would be able to read and discuss books with a modicum of respect for one another's opinions. I don't like judging folks, and I'd like the same from others when it comes to me. And as mature, educated women, there is no need to be at one another's throats because someone says something that rubs the other one the wrong way."

"Aren't you the social worker?" Cherie chided, sneering.

The fragile hold Kayana had on her temper snapped as she rounded on Cherie. "I don't know what your problem is, but I'll be damned if I'm going to allow you to insult me and anyone I've invited to my home. Either you get your personal shit together, or you can walk the hell out of here and never come back."

She and Cherie competed in what Kayana thought of as a stare-down. She had met a lot of young women like Cherie when she was a social work intern, and most times, their hostility and negative attitudes came from personal relationships with the men in their lives. Some of them were the third or even fourth baby mama and there was always baby mama drama, or they'd discovered he was married or had cheated on them. She'd wanted to tell them to just walk away and their lives would be less stressful, but that would not have solved their dilemmas.

Kayana felt her heart turn over when she saw tears fill Cherie's eyes. It was apparent her tough-girl stance was nothing more than a façade. And then she remembered her saying she had taken a leave from her employment, which probably meant she needed to take a break in order achieve a semblance of balance in her life.

"If you need some time for yourself before you decide if you want to become a part of our book club, then I suggest you do that, because Leah and I could always use a third opinion."

Reaching for a cocktail napkin, Cherie dabbed her eyes.

"Look, I'm sorry." She forced a smile. "It seems as if I'm doing a lot of apologizing lately."

"I'm a witness to that," Leah said under her breath.

Kayana wanted to tell Leah to let it go and not continue to antagonize Cherie. "Well, Cherie, what do you want to do? Are you in or out?"

She sniffled. "I'm in."

"Good. That calls for another toast. Cherie, do you want to make it?"

Smiling through unshed tears, she raised her glass. "Here's to a summer filled with delicious food, excellent cocktails, new friends, and lastly, but not the least, interesting books."

"Here, here!" Leah and Kayana chorused.

"Perhaps we need to eat and drink a bit more before we start talking about what we want to read this summer," Kayana suggested.

Leah drained her glass. "I like the sound of that."

Picking up the pitcher, Kayana refilled Leah's and then topped off Cherie's and her own. "It looks as if I need to mix up another batch of martinis."

"Do you mind if I watch you make them?" Leah asked.

"Of course not. Come with me."

Cherie popped another cracker topped with pâté into her mouth. "You'd better hurry because I intend to eat up everything on this table before you get back."

Kayana and Leah shared a smile as they left the patio and walked toward the kitchen. "I think I'll add a little more cranberry juice this time to make it less potent. I can't have you and Cherie getting arrested for public intoxication."

Leah sat on a stool near the prep table, watching Kayana as she measured the ingredients for the cocktail. "I can assure you that I'll need at least three or more drinks before I'm over the limit to be deemed legally drunk. Don't look at me like that, Kayana. I'm not an alcoholic, but it isn't often I get time to myself to let off some steam."

Kayana gave the schoolteacher a direct stare. "Do your sons still live at home?"

"No. They attended college and law school in New York City, and they still have an apartment there. When I asked, now that they've passed the bar, if they were coming back home to practice, both claimed it would be like culture shock after living in the Big Apple for ten years. My boys are rather closemouthed whenever I ask either of them if they're involved with a young woman."

"At their age, they have time before they consider marriage or even starting a family."

"You're right, but I find it odd that they've never talked to me about the women they've dated."

"Are you saying you believe your sons are gay?"

Leah shook her head. "No. They're straight."

"If they're straight, then why are you so concerned about who they're dating?"

"I don't know. I suppose it's just that I miss my boys."

Kayana noticed Leah had referred to them as boys. They weren't boys but twentysomething men. She knew she was thinking with her therapist head, but wondered if perhaps their mother had been the smothering type and that they just wanted to get far away from her and live their own lives. She wanted to ask Leah about her relationship with her husband, but decided against it; she did not want to delve into Cherie's or Leah's private lives because then they might expect the same from her.

And Kayana knew she had to stop relating to her book club companions as a therapist. After all, Cherie and Leah were adult women who didn't need her analyzing everything they did or said. The days when she provided counseling for patients and their families were behind her. She'd also shared a private practice with another social worker in downtown Atlanta, but only part-time. She would fill in whenever the other therapist exceeded the limit she'd determined for her caseload or whenever Mariah went on vacation. She had been filling in for Mariah when she witnessed James and his mistress coming out of the boutique hotel. It was apparent he'd forgotten she would be in the Buckhead neighborhood that evening seeing clients.

Kayana had to admit that she was a creature of habit. While living in Atlanta, she had risen at the same time every day, weekends notwithstanding, to work out in their home gym. On the days she had to go into the hospital, she left early enough to avoid the horrendous Atlanta traffic jams. She wasn't scheduled to begin working until 8:00 a.m., but she could always be found in her office between 6:30 and 7:00.

The days James was scheduled to work the night shift or was on call was her time to retreat to the space she'd called her sanctuary and indulge in her passion: reading. The cozy room was decorated with overstuffed chairs and love seats with bright floral fabric, table and floor lamps, floor pillows, scented candles, and live plants in hand-painted pots. An extensive playlist of her favorite songs and show tunes coming through a hidden speaker provided an atmosphere for total relaxation. Reading and working out were essential for her release of tension.

She vigorously shook the shaker and then poured a small amount into a glass, handing it to Leah. "Let me know if it's too strong."

Leah took a sip. "It's perfect. Do you always put your bar glasses in the refrigerator?" she asked when Kayana opened the fridge and took out three more martini glasses.

"Yes. Instead of using a lot of ice to dilute the drinks, my brother decided to chill the glasses instead."

"You would sell a lot more alcohol if you served weaker drinks."

Kayana gave Leah an incredulous stare. "That's not what we're about, Leah. This place has built a reputation over the years by offering folks good food and drinks and good service. Of course, we're in business to make a profit, but not at the expense of shortchanging those who come here. And after the vacationers leave, we still have to treat the local residents well, or we'll have to shut down."

"You're right about good food and service," Leah admitted. "You're right up there with the best."

Kayana knew Leah was echoing what so many patrons had said over the years. As a child, she'd accompanied her grandmother to farm stands and chicken farms, where Cassie meticulously examined the leaves of greens, the skin on white potatoes, and the color of chickens before making her selection. If the foodstuffs didn't pass her muster, she refused to purchase them. Her motto was "Nothing but the best for the Seaside Café." And the tradition had continued to the present day, when Derrick had vendors bring their products to the restaurant for his perusal. He had become even more nit-picking than Grandma Cassie when it came to selecting meat and fish, and he was no-nonsense when supervising the wait-staff. Not only would he not tolerate lateness; his disapproval extended to being rude or indifferent to customers.

She filled another pitcher with the cocktail, handing it to Leah. "Please carry this. I'll bring the glasses." The two women returned to the deck, and Cherie stood and took two of the glasses from Kayana.

"I never liked liver, but this pâté is off the chain. How did you make it?" Cherie asked. "Or is it a family secret recipe?"

Kayana smiled. "It's a knockoff of a New Orleans recipe for chicken livers with bacon and pepper jelly. I rinse and cook chicken and duck liver in boiling water for about two minutes, drain the pieces on paper towels, and then sauté the liver in finely minced onion and bacon cooked in duck fat. I add sea salt and ground peppercorns, and put it all into a food processor until smooth. I store it in an airtight container in the fridge for about an hour for everything to marry before serving."

"Kayana, I don't remember it listed on the menu," Leah remarked, as she spread a small amount of liver on a cracker.

"That's because it isn't. I only make it when entertaining."
The pâté was always a hit with her guests whenever she and
James hosted cookouts and dinner parties.

Cherie leaned forward on her chair. "We're so busy eating
and drinking that we haven't talked about the books we
want to discuss."

"Which genres do you like?" Kayana asked her.

"Romance, women's fiction, and African American literature."

"I'm partial to the classics, and British writers in particular," Leah said. "What about you, Kayana?"

"I also like the classics. However, I'm not opposed to considering other genres."

"Like what?" Cherie and Leah said in unison.

"Science fiction. I was talking to someone earlier today
about writers, and when the name Octavia Butler came up in
conversation, I remembered I'd read one of her novels and
how much I'd enjoyed it."

Leah clasped her hands together. "I love her novels. In
fact, she is my favorite science fiction author."

Cherie gave Leah a questioning look. "Didn't you say
you're partial to the classics?"

"That's only because I taught English lit for years. But
when it comes to reading for pleasure, I'll cross genres."

"Is that what we want to do?" Kayana questioned. "Are
we going to choose books from different genres?" She stared
at Leah, and then Cherie. Personally, she was open to reading
works by authors she'd never read before.

Cherie massaged the back of her neck as she rolled her
head from side to side. "I wouldn't mind reading other genres. I've heard of Octavia Butler, but never read her."

"And I wouldn't mind rereading her," Leah volunteered.
"I read *Kindred* a long time ago."

Kayana's smile reached her eyes. "I've never read *Kindred*,
so would you mind if we begin with it?"

Reaching into her crossbody, Cherie took out her cell-phone and tapped several keys. Seconds became minutes as she read the prologue. "Yes. I'd like to make this our first title." She glanced up. "How many books and how often are we going to meet?"

"How about every Sunday?" Leah questioned. "It shouldn't take more than a week to read a book."

"You forget Kayana has a business to run," Cherie reminded Leah. "And if we do meet once a week, then she shouldn't have to put out a spread like this. I'm willing to bring wine and soda."

"And I'll bring the ingredients for a charcuterie," Leah volunteered. She paused. "Kayana, are you all right with us meeting here every Sunday?"

Kayana nodded. "I'm good." She and Derrick had worked out a schedule by which both would have time for themselves. Late May through early September were their busiest months, and for the subsequent nine months, they'd committed to serving only one meal from Monday through Saturday. She pressed her palms together. "I guess that does it. We'll meet here next Sunday at six, and we all should be ready to discuss Ms. Butler's *Kindred*."

"Boom!" Cherie said under her breath. "I just downloaded the book."

Leah smiled across the table at Cherie. "I'll download my copy when I get back to the bungalow, because if I do it now, I'll start reading and won't be able to stop. Are we going to decide now what we're going to read next?"

"I made the first choice," Kayana said, "so why don't you go next, and then it can be Cherie's turn."

"I'd rather go after Cherie, because I still want to think about it."

Resting her head against the back of the chair, Cherie closed her eyes. "I've decided to compromise." She opened her eyes. "Because Leah likes the classics and I am partial to romance, I'm going to select Jane Austen's *Pride and Prejudice*."

Leah let out a little shriek before putting her hand over her mouth. "Bless you, my child," she crooned. "*Pride and Prejudice* is my favorite Austen novel."

It was also one of Kayana's favorite works written by the author, but if she'd had to pick one book to read over and over, it would be *Mansfield Park* because Austen was willing to focus on the subject of infidelity and slavery in the Americas. "I suppose we have our reading assignments for the next two weeks."

She didn't have to purchase the book because it was part of her reading library. When she'd moved from Atlanta to North Carolina, she'd left everything behind with the exception of her clothes, jewelry, and books. The smaller bedroom in the apartment had been set up as a reading studio, with a convertible love seat, comfortable armchairs with footstools, and bookcases packed tightly with her treasured books. Kayana had also purchased framed prints of James Baldwin, William Shakespeare, Toni Morrison, John Steinbeck, and Zora Neale Hurston to hang up on the bare walls. The space wasn't as large as the one in Georgia, but after she'd put her own special stamp on the room, it was an equally inviting place for her to read and while away the hours.

Kayana also couldn't wait to begin reading *Kindred*, and if or when she ran into Graeme again, she would thank him for recommending the book and author. "Leah, how long do you plan to stay on the island?"

"I'll be here through the second week in August."

She estimated they could realistically read and discuss five books before disbanding the Seaside Café Book Club. With the approach of dusk, the sun was a large orange ball in the darkening sky. An invisible bond began to form between the three women that had nothing to do with books when they talked about what was trending in the news. It didn't take Kayana long to realize that Cherie, despite her sharp tongue and being quite opinionated, was very intelligent. There was no doubt she would bring another approach to their upcoming book discussion.

Other than Mariah Hinton, Kayana hadn't been able to get close enough to any other woman in Atlanta to regard her as a friend. Her colleagues at the hospital were just that—colleagues, and nothing more. She'd occasionally join them after work for dinner or drinks for someone's birthday, but she never entertained them in her home. It was James who'd invited his friends, family members, and some of the doctors over to celebrate a particular holiday or to host someone's promotion and/or retirement.

Kayana was beginning to feel a special kinship with Leah and Cherie because they all had something in common. They were readers.

Chapter 5

Graeme rose early, let Barley, the two-year-old toy poodle mix out to do his business in the fenced-in yard, cleaned it up, and then walked down to the beach as the sun was rising. He wanted to finish a run before it got too hot. He'd discovered he was more creative in the early-morning hours, but since coming to the island and taking up permanent residence in the renovated bungalow, it appeared as if his creative juices had suddenly dried up; he knew he had to do something to kickstart himself into gear because he had three months in which to submit his latest manuscript.

He had managed to write the first chapter before driving down from Massachusetts, and although he'd been on Coates Island for almost two weeks, he hadn't typed more than five pages. Graeme knew it wasn't as much writer's block as it was malaise. He'd believed he would have come to grips with losing his wife eight years ago; since that time, he'd dated several women, but guilt would not permit him to commit to any of them, which left him feeling unfulfilled. And it wasn't about sex. That he could get from any woman willing to go to bed with him. It was about companionship.

om he could talk ; home to his wife. ld have been her good day instead sations that could the number of hours lors, who'd all told him esponsible or to blame for

He wante once se dn't argued with her, she would to drive to Boston to stay with her stantly harangued her daughter to di- would have stayed at the house in New- hen he walked through the door later that ld have been there to greet him. And when he ning himself, it was his mother-in-law who became the focus of his anger because she hadn't forgiven Graeme for wooing her precious daughter away from her.

Jillian's death had shattered his and her mother's lives. He had requested and was granted bereavement leave for a month before he was able to return to teaching. His wife's passing had so dramatically affected Susan Ellison that she finally had to be institutionalized after several suicide attempts, the last one of which resulted in her being declared brain-dead.

Susan languished for nearly a year, hooked up to a ventilator, until her brother requested that she be taken off life support. She was buried in the family plot next to her husband, son, and two daughters. Graeme believed his mother-in-law had gone to her grave holding him responsible for depriving her of her last surviving child.

Graeme felt the heat from the rising sun on his back as he jogged along the beach. The pedometer strapped to his upper arm beeped once he reached the one-mile mark. He was breathing heavily as he turned to retrace his steps. Running on the sand proved a lot more challenging than when he used a treadmill. The smell of saltwater, the soft sand under the soles of his running shoes, and the sound of waves washing up on the beach with the incoming tide transported Graeme to a place where he was able to clear his head of the real world. He could hear the character he'd created for his ongoing fictional series—about a retired covert operative who becomes the champion for the falsely accused and disenfranchised—telling him it was time for him to have a love interest. In prior books, the character, like himself, had become a recluse after losing his wife when she was killed in a hit-and-run. However, it wasn't a vehicular accident that had claimed Jillian's life. She had unknowingly walked in on a robbery in progress at a convenience store, giving the store clerk the opportunity to reach for a firearm from behind the counter; in the ensuing shootout, she was struck in the head by a bullet and died instantly.

Writing had become a catharsis for Graeme. It had taken him more than a year to research and plot his first novel, and then another year to revise it until he felt satisfied that he had an anti-hero willing to go above the law for the underdog. He'd completed two manuscripts before working up the nerve to submit one to a publisher.

Six months later, he was offered a two-book contract. However, Graeme wanted the publisher to adhere to certain conditions, and he knew that it wouldn't be possible to negotiate for himself unless he secured an agent. He found one willing to represent him, and she wasn't timid when she communicated his demands: He would publish under a pseudonym, would not submit a photograph of himself, and would never commit to a book signing. It took some legal maneuvering before the publisher agreed, and Graeme and his agent celebrated privately when the first book made the best-seller list within three weeks of its release.

No one at the high school knew that Mr. Ogden was the creator of the literary world's newest popular fictional protagonist. Zachary Maxwell was described as a cross between

Bruce Wayne and Bryan Mills from the *Batman* and *Taken* movie franchises. His character's life mirrored his creator's, though no one suspected Graeme was moonlighting as a writer.

He returned to the house and went into the bathroom to shower and shampoo his hair. The spray of lukewarm water sluicing down his body revived him. Normally, Graeme would've gone to the Seaside Café for breakfast, but not this morning. His breakfast would consist of coffee, toast with peanut butter, and yogurt topped with granola. Although his cooking skills were limited, he wasn't completely inept in the kitchen. He could boil eggs, put together a salad, grill steaks and corn, and bake potatoes.

Dressed in a pair of shorts, a T-shirt, and well-worn leather sandals he should have discarded years ago but hadn't because they were that comfortable, he made his way into the kitchen that looked out onto the open floor plan. An interior decorator had chosen furnishings in keeping with the humid subtropical setting, with seat cushions and pillows in colors of blue, green, and soft yellows. The colors were repeated in the second-story bedrooms, with verandas that had views of the ocean. It was a sight Graeme never tired of waking up to. He had chosen the smaller of the two bedrooms as his study, and whenever his mind wandered, he found himself staring out the windows for inspiration. The contractor had installed a white PVC fence that enclosed the backyard and provided a modicum of privacy from his nearest neighbors, while a landscaping crew had worked their magic as they laid sod, planted trees and brushes, and strategically placed large planters overflowing with ferns and flowering cacti. There was something about the refurbished bungalow that felt more like home than the one in Massachusetts, and Graeme attributed that to its size; it was much smaller than the property he'd inherited from his parents. He knew eventually he would have to sell the historic house with eight bedrooms and servants' quarters.

He finished breakfast, cleaned up the kitchen, then retreated to his study to call his agent, glancing over at Barley
curled up in his bed in a corner of the room. The tiny, sand-
colored animal had become his constant companion since
he'd adopted him from a shelter after the dog had spent the
first four months of his life in a puppy mill overrun with seventy other dogs. Graeme had always had pets when growing
up and had gone through separation anxiety when he had to
leave them with the household staff when he and his parents
summered abroad. Jillian was allergic to cats and did not like
dogs, and without the sound of children's laughter, the large
house was as silent as a tomb.

Graeme knew he could telephone Alma McCall at any
hour because she'd admitted to being an insomniac. He dialed her number and then activated the speaker feature.

"To what do I owe the pleasure of hearing your melliflu-
ous voice this morning?"

Graeme smiled. "What happened to 'Good morning,
Graeme'?"

Alma's deep throaty chuckle came through the speaker.
Years of smoking had lowered her voice several octaves, and
there were occasions when people mistook her for a man.
"Good morning, love."

He ignored the endearment because Alma had recently
married a woman whom she'd dated for years. "I need your
feedback about introducing a recurring female character that
could possibly become a love interest for Zack."

Alma laughed again. "So, your hero is tired of jerking himself off."

A frown settled into Graeme's features. "There's no need
to be vulgar."

"And there's no need for you to be so puritanical, Graeme.
You're an incredible writer, but whenever I ask you about
your social life, you tell me nothing's happening. I'm older
than you are, and even if I wasn't married, I'd still get more
action than you."

Graeme struggled not to let loose with a litany of profanity he was certain would shock the woman, only because he'd made a concerted effort to monitor whatever came out of his mouth after the unbridled argument with Jillian. It hadn't mattered that his wife had goaded him relentlessly for weeks until he finally exploded with an expletive-laced tirade that ended with her storming out of the house and his life.

"I'm only going to say this once, Alma. This will be the last time you will ask me about my personal life." A beat passed. "Now, what do you think of my idea of introducing another character?" In Alma's former life, she'd been an editor for several best-selling writers until she tired of reading and editing manuscripts, and having to put up with petulant, egotistical authors who'd treated her as if she were their personal slave or valet. When her company offered her an incentive package to retire, she took it and transitioned from editor to agent.

"I think it's a wonderful idea. Do you know who she is?"

Graeme smiled. "Yes. She's a journalist for the *Washington Post*. She's also separated from her wealthy husband, who has just initiated divorce proceedings, and when I introduce her to Zack, there's definitely an attraction."

"Where do they meet for the first time?"

"It will be at his favorite Starbucks. She orders a chai tea, and then sits at the table next to his to read the newspaper."

"Does she soften him, Graeme? Because readers love him, even though Zachary is one hardnose, scary-ass dude."

"She doesn't soften him that much. But their interaction will allow readers to see another side of Zack's personality, one he has kept hidden from them."

"It sounds good. After you introduce her, send me the chapter so I can give you my feedback."

"Thanks, Alma. Take care."

"You, too."

Graeme rang off and set the phone on a corner of the desk. Even though he'd gotten Alma to warm to his idea, he still had to work up a complete character dossier for his female protagonist. He had to decide on her name, then go forward from there.

It took several hours for him to create a personality for what would become a recurring character in the next two books in the series. He took a break to heat up two crab cakes he'd brought home from the Café. The crab cakes, potato salad, and cole slaw would sustain him until it was time for the evening meal. Whenever he went to the Seaside Café for dinner, he always ordered enough food to take home to last him for several days. Once he started writing, he'd spend long, uninterrupted periods of time at the computer, stopping at intervals to eat to keep up his energy, then going back and writing until exhausted. He'd learned that once he left the house, his creativity deflated like someone letting the air out of a balloon.

Graeme completed the dossier and wrote the scene in which his new character appears on the page for the first time. He rarely included female characters in his books unless they were victims and only if they moved the plot forward. Zachary Maxwell's widowed mother and divorced sisters were the only women he interacted with. And setting his home base in a small Maryland suburb close to DC, where he'd grown up, added authenticity to his character's familiarity with the area.

He wrote and rewrote the scene until he felt comfortable enough to send it to Alma. Graeme knew his agonizing over every word and phase slowed his progress, yet he never felt comfortable moving on to the next scene or chapter until he was satisfied with what he'd written. His agent had accused him of being a perfectionist, and when he looked back, he realized he'd always been that way. His late mother had accused him of being too hard on himself, and it was only when he was older that Graeme understood that it had come from being abandoned at birth by a woman who'd given him away to a childless couple.

He was eight when his mother and father disclosed that they'd adopted him, and even at that age, he was so grateful for their love and protection that he'd become the good son who'd excelled in school and did everything to make them proud of him. His parents were gone, but his need to be the best hadn't waned. It was what made Graeme Norris Ogden an excellent math teacher and a best-selling fiction author.

He reread the chapter for the third time, and then clicked the mouse and sent it as an attachment to Alma. Standing, Graeme rolled his head from side to side to relieve the tightness in his neck. Sitting for hours put a strain on his shoulders and back, and he made a mental note to call a sports club on the mainland to schedule a massage.

Graeme knew that if he didn't leave the house, he would embark on a writing marathon and not stop until fatigue overtook him. He walked out of the study and into the bathroom to shave and shower before driving to the Café for dinner.

Kayana wended her way through the tables in the restaurant and out to the patio. It was the dinner hour, and she rarely shared a meal with the patrons, preferring instead to eat in the restaurant's kitchen or her apartment. She found an empty table for two in a corner and sat down to wait. Unfortunately, she hadn't turned on the air conditioning in the second story, and the buildup of heat was stifling, forcing her to sit outside until it dissipated.

"May I join you?"

She knew it was Graeme even before glancing up. She hadn't seen him since Sunday. The week had been unusually busy, affording her little or no time to leave the kitchen. And once she'd finished making the sides for dinner, she promptly retreated to the apartment to get off her feet. She'd found herself dozing several times and had to force herself to get up or she would disrupt her sleep patterns. Although Kayana was not responsible for overseeing the kitchen for dinner, she passed the time going over the foodstuff inventory. It was a task she performed daily to ensure that they had the ingredients needed to prepare every dish on the menu. Soft-shell crabs were now a popular item, and they'd gone through two cases last week. Derrick had contracted with a Maryland-based fishery to clean and flash-freeze the crabs in dry ice and ship them to the restaurant within two days of removing the crustaceans from their traps.

"Of course. Please sit down." He was casually dressed in a pair of tan walking shorts, matching deck shoes, and a white, short-sleeved golf shirt. The scent of his cologne wafted to her nose as he sat opposite her. Streams of waning sunlight filtered through the screen behind Graeme, creating a halo around his head and making it difficult for her to read his expression.

"It's not often I see you at this time of day," Graeme said as he spread a napkin over his lap.

Kayana smiled. "That's because I rarely eat out here. I take most of my meals either in the kitchen or in my apartment."

"That must get boring."

"I'm used to it."

"Have you eaten?"

She nodded. "Yes." Kayana pointed to his plate. "I see you ordered the Korean barbecue."

"I ordered it for the first time last week, and I'm ashamed to admit I overindulged. I plan to eat half and take the rest of it home."

The Café had built its reputation on offering generous portions. "I must admit it's one of my favorite dishes on the menu."

"How did a basically seafood restaurant come to serve Korean barbecue?"

Kayana watched Graeme as he cut into the grilled soy and sesame short ribs. "I'd gone to New York City on vacation and visited several Asian restaurants because I'd heard people rave about Korean barbecue. The first time I ordered it, I was hooked, and I knew it was a dish that we had to add to the menu. The deliciousness comes from the marinade."

Graeme chewed and swallowed the meat. "Everything you and your brother serve here is deliciousness. I can't believe the two of you aren't professionally trained chefs. By the way, why did your folks decide to open a restaurant?"

"My grandmother wanted to go to college to become a teacher but knew that wasn't possible when my grandfather died from complications of diabetes. Meanwhile, her mother had started up a catering business in her home, making desserts for weddings and dinner parties. Grandma Cassie began writing down her mother's recipes, and once her mother passed, she used the money she'd received as the sole beneficiary from her insurance policy as a down payment on this place. My grandma put in eighteen-hour days to get the restaurant up and running, and once my mother was old enough to assist her, the Café had earned the reputation of serving some of the best soul and seafood dishes in the county."

"Did your father work in the restaurant, too?"

Kayana's expression changed, as a frown settled between her eyes. "My father didn't want anything to do with the restaurant. He made his living as a housepainter, and when he didn't have a job lined up, he would refuse to come in and help. My grandmother never liked her son-in-law. She felt he was lazy because he was content to earn just enough money to keep a roof over his family's head. Grandma Cassie was superstitious about everything, including not marrying someone with the same last name."

Graeme's fork halted in midair. "Your mother and father are both named Johnson?"

She smothered a laugh when seeing Graeme's eyebrows lift questioningly. "Yes. There was a running joke in the family that Mom did not have to change her name when she married Kenneth Johnson." She sobered quickly when recalling her parents' arguments. "Mom was the stronger of the two in the marriage and made more money than Dad, which became a source of contention between them. He claimed it made him feel like less of a man. He was so insecure that he'd pick a fight with my mother just to try and intimidate her. Apparently, he'd forgotten who he'd married, because Mom wasn't taking it. They finally divorced the year I celebrated my eleventh birthday, and it was as if everyone in the house could finally exhale."

"Did he or your mother ever remarry?"

"Dad did, but my mother claimed once was enough. Now that she's hung up her apron and spatula, she lives for her grandbabies, who can do no wrong."

A hint of a smile lifted the corners of Graeme's mouth. "Are your children included in her spoiler fest?"

A cold knot formed in Kayana's stomach as she met Graeme's steady gaze. Those in her and James's Atlanta's social circle were aware of her inability to have a baby, and there were occasions when she'd imagined their silent pity whenever she had to interact with those who had children.

"No," she said after an uncomfortable pause. "I can't have children, and please don't look at me like that."

Graeme set down his fork, touched the napkin to his mouth, and then leaned back in the chair and crossed his arms over his chest. "What are you talking about?"

"You were looking at me like poor little Kayana."

"Do you have the ability to read minds?"

"No. But—"

"But nothing," he said, cutting her off. "You don't know what I'm thinking, and if you did, then you'd know it's not pity or even sympathy. Do you think because you can't have children that you're less of a woman?"

"No."

"If that's the case, then why are you so defensive?"

"I wasn't being defensive, Graeme, and I resent you saying that I am."

Pushing back his chair, Graeme stood and picked up his plate and place setting. "I'm sorry I intruded on you. Have a good night."

Kayana watched as he turned on his heel and retreated inside the restaurant. She knew she hadn't imagined his expression when she'd revealed she couldn't have children. She'd heard Graeme's slight intake of breath at the same time he went completely still. Had her revelation hit a nerve, or had she reminded him of someone who had been unable to give him a child?

She sat at the table, watching the sun sink lower and lower beyond the horizon until it disappeared altogether, taking with it a display of orange and violent streaks against the darkening sky. She lost track of the time as diners left the patio, leaving her totally alone. Kayana blamed herself; she had broken her own promise not to get involved with any of the vacationers who frequented the restaurant. Long-time residents knew her, had watched her grow up and leave for college. She'd come back while on vacation to visit and to support her family whenever they buried a loved one. And when she came back the last time, it was to stay. She told those who'd asked that she was divorced and did not volunteer any additional details. The busboy came out to collect dishes and silverware at the same time she got up and went inside.

She hadn't taken more than three steps when her brother called her. "Hey, Kay, there's someone on the phone asking for you."

"Who is it?" She rarely received calls at the business number.

Derrick slung a towel over his shoulder. "I didn't ask."

Kayana gave him a withering glare. "Well, you should have," she said under her breath as she picked up the receiver. "Hello."

"I need to explain to you why I left."

She turned her back when she saw Derrick staring at her. She wasn't about to carry on a conversation with a man with her brother listening to every word that came out of her mouth. Picking up a pen, she reached for the pad where they jotted down takeout orders. "Please give me your number, and I'll call you back." Kayana wrote Graeme's number on the pad and then tore off the page. "I'll talk to you later."

"What was that all about?" Derrick asked.

"Nothing."

"It has to be something if the man's calling you, Kay."

She gave him a fixed stare. "Everything's okay, Derrick."

"If you say so."

"I do," Kayana said over her shoulder as she walked in the direction of the staircase leading to the second story. As far as she was concerned, there was no need for Graeme to explain his actions; however, she would be polite and listen to what he had to say.

When she opened the door to the apartment, she was met with a blast of frigid air. It hadn't taken the air conditioner long to dissipate the heat. Kayana adjusted the thermostat before going into the reading room and picking up her cellphone off a side table.

She'd missed a call from Jocelyn. She knew it wasn't an emergency, because her sister tended to either text her or call the restaurant's phone if she needed to contact her right away, and Kayana decided she would return the call after talking to Graeme.

Kayana sank down in her favorite chair and dialed his number; he picked up after the second ring. "I'm returning your call." Her voice was shaded in neutral tones.

"I'm calling to apologize if you thought I was being rude, but I thought it best that I leave before we began arguing."

"What makes you think our difference of opinion would have developed into an argument?"

"There was always the possibility that it may have escalated into one. The last memory I shared with my late wife was a nasty argument, and since then I've sworn an oath to walk away before I'd say something I would live to regret for the rest of my life."

Graeme's explanation rendered Kayana temporarily mute. The seconds ticked until they became a full minute. "I'm sorry, Graeme."

The apology sounded so clichéd that she was at a loss for words. When Derrick had said that Graeme wasn't married, she'd assumed he was probably divorced or a confirmed bachelor. His status as a widower had never entered her mind.

"You don't have to apologize. I just wanted you to know why I did what I did."

A smile found its way through Kayana's pained expression. "Now that we're into true confessions, I want you to know that I've made it a practice never to get involved with any of the restaurant's guests. Not only did I tell you about my family, but I've also committed to a summer book club discussion with two other seasonal visitors." When she'd told Leah and Cherie that she didn't have any children, they hadn't asked for an explanation, and for that she was grateful.

"Are you saying we're involved with each other?"

Pinpoints of heat flooded Kayana's face. It was obvious from Graeme's query that he'd misconstrued her use of the word *involved*. "Not in the romantic sense, Graeme."

A chuckle caressed her ear. She opened her mouth to ask him what was so funny, and then closed it just as quickly because she didn't want him to again accuse her of being defensive. But she had to admit that taking a defensive stance was something that had become second nature to her whenever she felt challenged. Her mother asked her why she'd let James have the house after she'd spent years decorating it so his slut could move in. Jocelyn had been just as relentless when she accused her of being a coward for not confronting the woman who'd been sleeping with her husband. At that time, it had been easier for her to walk away with her dignity intact than to stay and fight. What her family did not know was that she'd held all the cards because James hadn't wanted a scandal to besmirch his family's good name. When he'd asked her what she wanted, Kayana quoted a settlement figure she'd assumed would shock him, and much to her surprise, he'd agreed to her request. She didn't know where he'd been able to come up with that amount of money, but it hadn't been her concern.

"Okay. What about friends?"

She smiled. "Friends who discuss books?"

Graeme chuckled again. "Of course."

"By the way, our book club selected *Kindred* for our first discussion, and *Pride and Prejudice* the following week."

"You like Jane Austen?" Graeme asked.

"I love Jane Austen."

"Are you familiar with the movie theater in Shelby?"

"Of course. They feature a lot of black-and-white and classic movies," Kayana said.

"A couple of days ago, I picked up one of their flyers. This summer they're showing films that are adapted from books. They're showing the original *Les Misérables* with Frederic March, *The Hunchback of Notre Dame* with Charles Laughton, Dumas's *The Count of Monte Cristo*, several Jane Austen films, and Emily Brontë's *Wuthering Heights*, just to name a few."

"I can't believe they're showing all of my favorites."

"Would you like to go with me when they're showing one you'd like to see? Afterward, we can critique it to see if it's as good the book."

Kayana couldn't believe her good luck. She'd spent more than half her life in Atlanta and at no time had she met anyone who liked books as much as she did; now, within the span of a week, she'd encountered three people who were avid readers. "Can you take a photo of the flyer and send it to my cellphone? Once I look it over, I'll let you know."

"Consider it done."

"Thanks." She paused. "I'm going to ring off now because I have to be up early tomorrow morning."

"Good night, Kayana."

"Good night, Graeme."

She ended the call and palmed the phone. Kayana did not think of his asking her to accompany him to the movie theater in Shelby as a date, because it wasn't. With Cherie and Leah, she would read and discuss books, while with Graeme, she would view a film and subsequently compare it to the book. This was her third summer since she'd moved back to Coates Island, and she predicted it was to become quite memorable.

Chapter 6

Kayana opened the door at the rear of the restaurant for Cherie and Leah. Both were wearing rain slickers. It had been raining steadily for three days, and the dreary weather appeared to affect everyone who came into or worked in the restaurant. Those who did come in lingered longer than necessary.

"Come on in," she urged, stepping back to keep from getting wet. A tropical storm was parked off the coast, and the increase in wind velocity blew the rain sideways.

Leah slipped out of her rain gear and hung it on a wall hook, and then handed Kayana a canvas tote. "This is definitely weather for ducks."

Cherie set a bag with several bottles of wine on the floor before shrugging off a candy-apple-red slicker. "I like rain, but this is a bit much for me. I hope it doesn't rain so much that the island floods and we are forced to evacuate."

"We're in tropical storm and hurricane season, and being so close to the ocean, we can get a lot of rain. Fortunately, many hurricanes don't make landfall near here. Although we have the dunes, most of the structures located closer to the beach are erected above the ground," Kayana explained as she led them into the kitchen.

Leah sniffed the air. "Something smells good."

"I told you not to buy the ingredients for a charcuterie, because with this weather we need something hot and more substantial."

"What did you make?" Cherie asked as she set bottles of red, white, and rosé on a butcher block table.

"Chili with corn muffins."

Cherie pumped her fist. "Hot damn! I may have to check out of the boardinghouse and move in with you just to eat. And I don't mind working for my keep," she said, smiling.

Lifting the lid on the pot on the stove, Kayana slowly stirred the chili with a wooden spoon. "My apartment has two bedrooms, and I've turned the extra one into a reading room."

"Is that where we're going to hold our book discussion tonight?" Leah asked.

Kayana was slightly taken aback by Leah's query. She'd planned for them to eat in the restaurant's dining room, followed by talking about the book. But when she thought about it, the room was the perfect place for a small gathering. "Yes."

Resting a hip against a countertop, Cherie met Kayana's eyes. "Are you looking for a roommate? There're some folks at the boardinghouse that bug the hell out of me. Whenever we sit down for breakfast, there's a couple who can't stop arguing. I'm so tempted to tell them to shut the hell up, but I know that would start something, and I'd probably get evicted."

"I'm sorry, Cherie, but I'm not looking for a roommate."

The young woman shrugged her shoulders. "I had to ask."

Kayana had been forthcoming when she told Cherie she didn't want a roommate, because she had come to value her privacy. She got up and went to bed whenever she wanted, and she loved not having any intrusions or distractions when reading or watching television.

"I have an extra bedroom in my bungalow," Leah said, "so if you really get tired of staying at the boardinghouse, you're welcome to it."

Cherie gave the redhead a smile that did not reach her eyes. "Thanks for offering, but I believe I can put up with their bitchin' a little while longer. If they truly get on my last nerve, I'll let you know."

Kayana hoped she wasn't imagining it, but she still detected a modicum of hostility between the two women. "I already set up the table in the dining room . . ."

Her words trailed off when the rear door opened and her brother walked in. Derrick rarely returned to the restaurant after they closed on Sundays. That was his time to stay home, kick back, and watch his favorite sports teams. After living in New York, he'd become an avid Mets fan, because North Carolina did not have a professional baseball team. However, he'd refused to switch his loyalty from the Carolina Panthers and Hornets to New York football and basketball teams.

"Did you forget something?" she asked Derrick.

Derrick slipped off the rain poncho and hung it on the wall hook with the other rain gear. "No. I came in to get a jump on prepping some meat for the smoker because the Mets game was rained out."

Kayana saw Leah and Cherie staring at Derrick, and realized it was something she'd noticed whenever women looked at her brother. However, Derrick always appeared totally oblivious to the opposite sex, even though many women were drawn to his tall, toned body and his premature cropped gray hair, which contrasted with a smooth mahogany complexion. And once he smiled, the overall effect was mesmerizing, as a matched set of dimples creased his lean jaw.

The one time she'd asked Derrick if he was ready to date

again after he'd been widowed for a couple of years, he'd claimed his plate was full working at the restaurant and taking care of Deandra, and she wondered if his excuse would be the same when his daughter went off to college. And he'd talked about Graeme staring at her with his tongue hanging out, but it was no different with Leah. The woman was married with two adult sons, yet she couldn't take her eyes off Derrick.

"Leah, Cherie, I don't know if you've met my brother, but—"

"We've met," Leah said, cutting her off.

Derrick nodded. "Ladies, I promise not to get in your way, so please don't mind me."

"I'm almost finished here, and we're going into the dining room to eat before going upstairs for our book discussion," Kayana said.

"Is there anything I can help you with?" Leah asked.

Kayana opened the oven to check on the mini corn muffins. They were golden brown. She took the pan out of the oven. "These are done." She made quick work of removing the muffins from the tin, gave the plate to Leah, and then ladled chili into a large soup tureen and handed that off to Cherie.

Ten minutes later, they sat at a cloth-covered table, eating buttery corn muffins and a thick rich chili topped with chopped raw onions and shredded sharp cheddar cheese; it had just enough heat to tantalize their palates. They'd decided the red wine would go better with the meal, and between sips of the merlot, the three women concentrated on eating rather than talking. There would be time later to talk ad nauseum about their chosen title.

Leah reached for another muffin. "I grew up eating cornbread and muffins, but these are better than the ones my mama made."

Kayana smiled at her across the table. "I thought I'd change it up with the muffins because we usually serve hush puppies with chili." Earlier that afternoon she'd chopped onions and grated cheese as toppings for the chili, though it would take her a while to become familiar with the food preferences of her book club buddies. She'd also seasoned the ground meat with finely minced jalapeño peppers to add a dash of heat to the dish.

Cherie touched the napkin to the corners of her mouth. "Damn, Kayana, you really can burn some pots."

"Should I take that to mean she's a good cook?" Leah asked.

Cherie stared at Leah as if she'd spoken a language she didn't understand. "You've never heard that expression?"

A slight flush darkened Leah's pale face. "Not really."

"When you talk about someone burning pots, you're giving them a compliment that they're a good cook."

Leah nodded. "Now I know."

Cherie chuckled softly. "Hang out with us homegirls and you'll become more familiar with a lot of our vernacular."

Leah took a sip of her wine. "I'm of the belief that you never get too old to learn new things."

"How many girls are enrolled at your school?" Kayana asked Leah.

"Last count we had an enrollment of two hundred eighty-six."

"How many of them are black?" Cherie questioned.

"Twenty-two."

Cherie exchanged a glance with Kayana. "That's less than ten percent."

"That's only because the yearly tuition is comparable to some private colleges," Leah explained. "However, we do offer scholarships, but there is a lengthy wait-list. Most of our girls who graduate go on to many of the top colleges in the country."

Kayana noticed Leah said "our girls" as if she'd claimed them as her own. "That's because their daddies pay the big bucks to get them in."

Leah lowered her eyes. "I'm not going to lie and say endowments don't play a major factor, but they still have to have the grades."

"That's bullshit and you know it, Leah," Cherie spat out. "It's the ones on scholarship who have to maintain the grades."

Leah went completely still as she glared at Cherie. "That's why they're on scholarship. Because it's all about the grades."

"Tell me about it," Cherie said under her breath.

Kayana immediately picked up on Cherie's statement. "Did you attend college on scholarship?"

Cherie took a long sip of her wine, staring at Kayana over the rim. "Yes. I attended an elite prep school on scholarship and then went to a private college on a full academic scholarship."

Sitting back in her chair, Leah angled her head as she met Cherie's eyes. "You must be very smart."

"If you say so."

Kayana frowned. "Why are you downplaying your intelligence, Cherie? If you've got it, then flaunt the hell out of it."

Touching the napkin to the corners of her mouth, Cherie flashed a wry smile. "I was a lot smarter than many of the kids in my graduating class, but it didn't matter. They still related to me as the poor little black girl from public housing."

"Being black and living in public housing didn't appear to hold you back," Kayana said.

A beat passed before Cherie said, "It took me a while to realize that it didn't matter how smart I was. I would always be an outsider."

"I don't think race had anything to do with you being an outsider," Leah countered.

"How would you know?" Cherie snapped angrily.

"I know, because I was one of those outsiders. I was the first one in my family to go to college, and the girls at Vanderbilt avoided me as if I was carrying a communicable disease once they found out that I'd spent the first nine years of my life living in a trailer park before my folks saved enough money to rent a small apartment. It didn't matter to them that I'd graduated high school at fifteen and was on full academic scholarship with a 4.0 grade-point average, because to them I'd never be more than white trash."

"Boo hoo, Leah," Cherie drawled facetiously. "Don't expect me to start playing a violin because you grew up in a trailer park. The difference between us is that I had two strikes against me—race and poverty, while you only had the latter. And judging from the diamonds on your hand, you appear to have done quite well for yourself."

Splaying her left hand on the tablecloth, Leah stared at the diamond-encrusted eternity band on her finger. "Marrying well isn't everything."

"Amen," Kayana whispered.

She had married a prominent Atlanta-based surgeon and had a glamorous life, but if she had to do it all over again, she wouldn't have given Dr. James Hudson a passing glance. However, James wasn't one to accept rejection when he'd embarked on a scheme to wear her down. He'd had flowers delivered to her office, along with greeting cards that made her laugh until she finally agreed to go out to dinner with him. There was one thing James did not lack, and that was charm, and after a while he'd literally charmed her out of her panties. The first time she slept with him, she knew she wanted him to be the last man in her life. Less than a year after their first date, Kayana married James in what had been billed as the wedding of the season for Atlanta's black elite.

"Are you saying you didn't marry well?" Cherie asked Leah.

"I'm not saying that," the redhead countered, "but you should be careful what you wish for. I didn't want a repeat of what my mother had with my father, pinching pennies and going to thrift shops to buy clothes for her kids, but I've had to put up with bullshit from my mother-in-law for years; she's reminded me every day since I married her son that I wasn't her first choice as a daughter-in-law."

"Is she still alive?"

Leah nodded. "She just celebrated her eighty-sixth birthday. Last year, she moved into an upscale assisted-living facility several miles from Richmond, so thankfully I don't get to see her as often as I did in the past."

"Why haven't you told the old crow to fuck herself?" Cherie drawled.

Leah laughed softly. "I would have a long time ago, but her grandsons worship the very ground she walks on."

Kayana's laughter joined Leah's. "It does make a difference when you have children. There was a time when I couldn't wait to become a mother, but when it didn't happen, I realized I'd been given a pass."

Cherie gave her a wide-eyed stare. "You didn't want kids?"

Kayana shook her head. "I couldn't have any."

"Are you sure it wasn't your husband that couldn't make a baby?" Leah asked.

She paused, contemplating how much she wanted to disclose to the two women she still regarded more as strangers than acquaintances. But then, when she thought of it, she realized she'd revealed things about her family to Graeme that she hadn't to any other restaurant guest. Why, she mused, had she felt the need to open up to strangers when she'd never done it in the past? However, she had to remember that the women in her Atlanta social circle weren't ones she felt comfortable enough to relate to as confidants. Many of them were friends of James who'd become her so-called associates. They were native Atlantans who'd grown up together, many attending private historically black colleges, while she was a North Carolina transplant who'd attended and graduated from Spelman College and the University of Georgia.

"I got pregnant early in my marriage but lost the baby in

the first trimester. The doctors couldn't stop the bleeding, so when I woke up in the recovery room, I was told that I would never be able to have another child."

"Why didn't you adopt?" Cherie asked.

A wry smile twisted Kayana's mouth. "Initially my ex and I talked about adoption, but after a while we decided having a child or children didn't prevent us from being a family."

Leah's eyelids fluttered. "How long were you married before your divorce?"

"It was several months before our nineteenth anniversary when I discovered he was sleeping with another woman and gotten her pregnant."

Cherie's jaw dropped. "Did you know who she was?"

Kayana nodded. "Yes. She was one of his colleagues."

"It doesn't bother you that your husband cheated on you with another woman?" Leah asked.

"It bothered me that I didn't find out about the two-faced heifer sooner than I did," Kayana countered. "As they say, the wife is always the last to know."

Resting her elbows on the table, Leah leaned closer. "Did you confront her?"

Kayana shook her head. "Hell no! I wouldn't give her the satisfaction of lowering my standards to fight over a man. My grandmother told me, when I was a little girl, that a man is like a train—there is always one leaving the station. The only thing I'm going to say is that if he cheated on me, then he will cheat on her."

Cherie breathed out an audible sigh. "I suppose I should count myself lucky that I'm not married."

"Not all cheating ends in divorce." Leah's voice rose slightly with her fervent declaration.

Kayana wondered if the redhead was gloating or overcompensating, hoping it was the former, because as an intern she'd counseled many women who'd professed to having perfect marriages or relationships, while their husbands and partners were either cheating or verbally or physically abusing them. "True," she said. "But I don't believe in staying in what I think of as a toxic relationship, because I refuse to allow myself to be diminished."

Cherie applauded. "Good for you. No man on the face of the earth is worth a woman losing her self-respect."

Leah peered over the rim of her wineglass at Cherie. "It sounds as if you're speaking from experience."

"I am. I gave a man more years of my life than he deserved, and in the end, I wound up the loser."

"He married someone else?" Leah questioned.

Cherie nodded. "Yes, but I don't want to talk about it."

"Maybe you need to talk about it, if only to get it off your chest."

"Let it go, Leah," Kayana cautioned her. "We're supposed to be talking about books and not discussing our personal lives."

Leah lowered her eyes. "You're right." She pantomimed zipping her lips. "From now on, it's all about books. I have to confess that I didn't know what to expect when I first started rereading *Kindred*."

"Did you enjoy it?" Kayana asked Leah.

"I found it disturbing."

"You found it disturbing, while I hated it," Cherie countered.

Kayana's eyebrows lifted slightly. "Well, it looks as if we're going to have an interesting discussion. Once we finish eating, we can go upstairs and have our first official book club meeting."

Pushing back her chair, Leah stood up. "I need to stop eating or I'll blow up and won't be able to fit into my clothes." She went completely still when the other two women stared at her. "I used to have a weight problem. I'd gained more than seventy pounds when pregnant with the twins. Instead of losing the weight after they were born, I gained even more, tipping the scale at two hundred and eighteen pounds."

Rising, Cherie picked up bowls and serving pieces. "How did you lose it?"

"I began with hypnosis and a nutritionist. Then I hired a personal chef who prepared pre-cooked meals for me. The first six months I managed to lose thirty-five pounds, and then when I appeared to plateau, I joined a health club to kickstart my metabolism. It took more than a year for me to lose seventy pounds. I now weigh one thirty-five and feel better than I have in a very long time. But I must confess that bread is my weakness."

Kayana stood and began clearing the table. "Desserts are my weakness, and that's why I steer clear of them." She smiled at Cherie. "You definitely don't look as if you have a weight problem." The young woman's slender body did not appear to have an ounce of fat.

Cherie rolled her eyes upward. "Whenever I am ovulating, it's salty snacks, which causes me to retain fluid."

"I'll definitely keep in mind to cut down on the carbs and sodium whenever we get together for our meetings," Kayana said, as she walked in the direction of the kitchen. She hadn't had a weight problem like Leah, but as she grew older, she'd discovered it had become more and more difficult to lose a few extra pounds. If bread was Leah's weakness, then it was sugary desserts for her. And now that she didn't have access to exercise equipment, she tended to limit her intake of cake, pie, and ice cream.

Chapter 7

Kayana opened the door to the apartment and was met with a blast of frigid air. When she'd gone down to the restaurant earlier that afternoon, she had forgotten to adjust the thermostat.

"Whoa! It feels like Siberia up here," Cherie said.

"I'm going to turn off the air conditioning until it warms up." She tapped a button on the thermostat, shutting off the cool air.

Leah walked into the living room and set her tote on the floor next to a side table. "This place is charming."

Kayana felt a rush of pride. Other than family members, Leah was the first person to compliment her for turning the space that had been used for storage into a comfortable apartment. "Thank you. I really like it."

"What's not to like?" Cherie said, as she strolled over to the wood-burning fireplace. "If I had a place like this, I'd never think about going on vacation. Do you mind if I look around?"

"Not at all."

Kayana smiled. Leah thought the apartment charming, while Cherie liked it enough to want to move in. Kayana wanted to tell the two women it was a far cry from the house with all the amenities she wanted and needed at her fingertips, yet when she looked back, she realized it hadn't been a home but a showplace. And, not for the first time, she reflected that she had been relieved to uncover her ex-husband's infidelity, because it had given her a reason to end their sham of a marriage.

To the public, she and James had been the perfect couple, while behind closed doors, they had begun to grow further apart. They'd continued to share a bedroom and a bed, but their lovemaking had decreased dramatically from three to four times a week to once. As a woman in her early forties and without the concern of possibly becoming pregnant, Kayana wanted and needed physical fulfillment from her husband. Other than falling in love with James, she had agreed to marry him because they had been so well matched sexually.

Leah ran her fingertips over the needlepoint throw pillow on the sofa. "Have you ever thought about renting this apartment during the tourist season?"

Leah's query broke into her musings as Kayana gave her an incredulous look. "Rent my home?"

"People around here do it all the time."

"And where would I live, Leah?"

"Couldn't you stay with your brother?"

"My brother has his life, and I have mine," Kayana countered.

"Are you saying you don't get along with your sister-in-law?"

Kayana successfully hid a grin at the same time she turned her head. What she'd suspected was suddenly manifested. Leah was attracted to her brother and wanted to know about him. "I don't have a sister-in-law. Derrick is a widower with a seventeen-year-old daughter."

Leah sank down to the sofa in slow motion, one hand pressed to her throat. "Oh, I'm so sorry. Please forgive me for being insensitive."

"There's nothing to forgive. You had no way of knowing my brother lost his wife four years ago." Kayana held up a hand. "And before you ask, Derrick is not seeing anyone."

"Why would you, a supposedly happily married woman, be interested in another man?" Cherie asked, as she strolled back into the living room.

Leah sprang up, her face flushed with high color. "Maybe it's because I'm not *that* happily married."

"Damn," Cherie said under her breath.

"Yes, damn!" Leah spat out. "I've had to work my ass off for the past twenty-eight years to be the perfect wife and mother to my sons, but it is never enough for Mrs. Adele Stephens Kent." She paused. "My mother-in-law had planned for her son to marry another woman, so when I came onto the scene, she blamed me for ruining her life and her standing in society in Richmond, Virginia." She pressed her palms together in a prayerful gesture. "Enough talk about me. I'm ready to discuss *Kindred*."

Kayana was ready to discuss the book, but she was also intrigued by the woman who'd professed that "not all cheating ends in divorce." An inner voice told her that not all of Leah's problems were the result of her mother-in-law's disapproval. The older woman's son had to have been complicit for the hostility to have endured for nearly three decades. It was only their second meeting, and Kayana knew that before summer's end, she would come to learn more than she needed to know about her book club companions.

"Let's go into the reading room, where we'll be a lot more comfortable."

Leah's eyes grew wide as she glanced around the space; two of the four walls were covered with floor-to-ceiling built-in shelves filled with hardcover and paperback books. "I thought I had a lot of books, but you've got me beat."

"It's more like a library than a reading room," Cherie chimed in.

Kayana smiled. "It's my favorite spot in the entire apartment."

Cherie walked over to the window and peered out. "I can understand why. You have everything you need here to kick back and relax." And she turned and smiled at Kayana. "I like the prints."

"Thanks. I have a few more I need to frame and put up." She pointed to a trio of tubes in a corner. "I like them because they're unabridged works of literature on one page."

"Which ones do you have?" Leah asked.

"*Othello*, *Beauty and the Beast*, and *Romeo and Juliet*." Kayana crossed the room, opened one of the tubes, and handed the single sheet of paper to Cherie. "The print is small, but it still can be read."

Cherie nodded, smiling. "This is better than downloading a book because everything is on one page."

"The selections are limited, but Shakespeare's plays are the most available."

Leah folded her body down onto the love seat. "Have you read all of these books?"

Kayana took her favorite chair, while Cherie slipped the page back into the tube and then sat on an armchair with a footstool. "Most of them. However, after a few years I tend to reread some of my favorites."

"Speaking of reading, we should begin our book discussion before it gets too late," Leah suggested as she reached into the pocket of her slacks and unfolded a sheet of paper. "I took down some notes," she explained when Kayana and Cherie looked at her.

Kayana bit back a smile. "If that's the case, then why don't you start?"

Leah exhaled an audible sigh. "I loved the writing and the evocative storytelling, but the subject of slavery really disturbed me."

"Did it disturb you because you're white, and some of your ancestors may have been slaveowners, or because you live in the city that was once the capital of the Confederacy?" Cherie asked her.

Kayana knew Cherie had struck a nerve with Leah when a large vein became clearly visible in Leah's forehead. When she read the novel, she knew the subject matter would be controversial and provocative. Cherie didn't like it, Leah had found it disturbing, while she'd come away with mixed emotions of frustration with the characters, but was left in awe at the author's vivid depiction of slavery in America.

"It has nothing to do with my race," Leah said, between clenched teeth, "because none of my ancestors ever owned human beings."

"Did your husband's folks own slaves?"

"Whether Leah's husband's folks owned slaves is irrelevant," Kayana interjected, when she realized Cherie was going off topic.

"I think it's very relevant," Cherie countered, "because Leah is coming from a different place than me. She has to ask herself whether she is disturbed by slavery because perhaps she's harboring some guilt that her race is responsible for not only America's original sin, but also for the genocide of the native people and the fact that they were robbed of their lands because of a phony-ass claim to so-called Manifest Destiny."

Closing her eyes, Kayana slowly counted to five. "Cherie, I know where you're coming from, but I thought we could discuss this book without getting personal. I don't know where you're from, but I was born, raised, and lived in the South all my life. I'm aware of racism, even though it's not as overt as it was in prior generations. What I refuse to do is let it bog me down to the point where I get up every morning angry and looking for a confrontation with a white person for what they've done to our people. And I don't need to know what went on with you and the man who hurt you, but take it from someone older and wiser—you have to let it go before it eats you alive."

"Was he a white man?" Leah asked, after a strained silence. Cherie closed her eyes and nodded. "Have you taken a good look at yourself? You're young, beautiful, and smart, and you could have any man want, but what you have to do is learn to choose wisely and understand that it doesn't matter who or what he is. There are SOBs in every race, and I'm here to tell you because I'm married to one."

Cherie's shock was apparent from her stunned expression. "You're kidding."

"No, my dear. I wish I was."

"If he's an SOB, why do you stay with him?"

"Because he's never flaunted his affairs. And it doesn't bother me if he sleeps with other women as long as he's discreet."

"Are you saying it's all about money?"

Leah smiled. "Not for me, because I earn enough to take care of myself. But for Alan, it's money, reputation, and family honor. My husband is a judge, as were his father and many others in the family before him. The Kents are old-money Virginians who trace their roots back to before the American Revolution. And they were slaveowners. In fact, they owned hundreds of them until the Civil War. None of the Kent boys fought for the Confederacy because they paid others to fight for them, which perpetuates the theory that it's always a rich man's war and a poor man's fight. After the war, they went into politics and slowly rebuilt their reputation as one of Richmond's leading families. And what no one could understand was how an eighteen-year-old girl from a trailer park had managed to ensnare one of the city's most eligible bachelors who was seventeen years older than her."

Kayana covered her mouth with her hand in an attempt to smother a gasp. She never would've guessed that Leah's husband was that much older than her. "Were you his first wife?"

"Yes. Alan belonged to an exclusive club of very eligible bachelors who had an unwritten rule to date but not marry until they turned thirty-five. Then they would select a woman within their social circle who on average was ten years younger than their prominent wealthy suitor. Alan was engaged to the daughter of one of his father's colleagues, but he was forced to break the engagement once I told him I was pregnant with his baby."

With wide eyes, Cherie stared at Leah. "How did you meet?"

Crossing her feet at the ankles, Leah sank lower on the love seat. "It was my last year at Vanderbilt, and I'd come home during winter break. A couple of months before, my parents had moved out of the apartment and into a rental house after my father was promoted to head mechanic at a used-car dealership. It was the first time I'd had a bedroom and didn't have to share with my younger brother. I'd driven to Dillard's in downtown Richmond to buy a Christmas gift for my mother. I bought her a nice blouse and perfume. When I walked out of the store, I ran headlong into a man and dropped the bag, shattering the bottle. At first, I didn't recognize him as Alan Kent, but he apologized and offered to replace the bottle because it was his fault; he hadn't looked where he was going. The salespeople were fawning over him because they were more than familiar with the Kent name. He bought not only a larger bottle, but also the matching body lotion, and paid for it to be gift-wrapped.

"He invited me to have lunch with him, but I turned him down with the excuse that I had to get home to help my mother get the house together for the holiday. He asked me what I did, and I told him I was a senior at Vanderbilt. And because I didn't tell him I was eighteen, he probably assumed I was at least twenty-one or twenty-two because I was a senior. That's when Alan asked if I would see him before I went back to Nashville, and again I said that wasn't possible, but I promised we could get together after I graduated for a celebratory meal. What I didn't count on was his showing up at my graduation ceremony. That's when I introduced him to my parents, who were shocked that a Kent was interested in their daughter.

"Once I returned home, Alan reminded me of my promise to have lunch with him, and although I knew he was engaged to another woman, I rationalized it would only be the one time. He took me to a small hotel with a wonderful restaurant thirty miles outside of Richmond, and for an eighteen-year-old young woman being wined and dined by a worldly, thirtysomething handsome man, it was nothing short of magical. Years later, I discovered it was a place where most of his friends had conducted their clandestine affairs."

A knowing smile parted Kayana's lips. "And it was where he seduced you."

"Yes," Leah whispered. "I'd had only one lover before sleeping with Alan. We met several more times over the next two months, and when I didn't get my period, I knew I was pregnant. The one time we had unprotected sex, he got me pregnant. When I called Alan and told him I needed to see him, he must have heard something in my voice and asked me if I was carrying his baby. I told him I'd taken a home pregnancy test, and the results were positive for pregnancy. He said not to worry and that he would pay for the abortion. Things got really testy when I told him I was not going to get rid of my baby, and he didn't have to worry about me naming him as the father. It was apparent he didn't believe me, and to protect his family's name, we were married in a private ceremony at his parents' house with his uncle as the officiate. That's when Adele told me if she'd known I was sneaking around with her son, she would've offered me enough money to leave the state and never come back.

"It was a less than joyous occasion, with the Kents dressed in haute couture, while the Berkleys, in their Sunday best from JC Penney, looked as if they were attending a funeral. Adele was very vocal that she hadn't approved of her son marrying me after Daddy told her that I was much too good for him. Meanwhile, I saw the nasty side of Alan whenever he accused me of tricking him into marriage while refusing to accept any blame for getting me pregnant. Adele was his cheerleader, and she got into his head that I didn't have the social breeding or home training befitting a Kent woman. She'd been widowed several years before I married Alan, and she convinced him to move into the family mansion because he was going to need more room once a sonogram indicated that I was having twins."

Cherie had pulled her lip between her teeth during Leah's monologue. "Where were you living before that?"

"Alan owned a two-bedroom condo in a trendy section of the city. The family mansion, known to the locals as Kent House, is listed on the national register of historic homes. From the day I moved in, my life was no longer my own to control. Adele hired a nanny to look after the twins and insisted I go back to college to earn a graduate degree. Meanwhile, she also had a life coach give me lessons on how to host formal and informal dinner parties and select the appropriate attire for different social occasions. The few times I'd complained to Alan that his mother was controlling my life, he said she was only trying to make certain I wouldn't embarrass the family, because, after all, I was a Kent and, as such, needed to keep up appearances."

Kayana could not believe what she was hearing, because there was no way she would have permitted someone to regulate and control her life as Leah's mother-in-law had done. "Didn't you get tired of being manipulated while the puppeteer pulled the strings?"

"I put up with it until my boys left for college. That's when I moved out of our bedroom and into one in the opposite wing of the house. From the day we married, we never agreed on anything that didn't have to do with our sons."

"You're a better woman than I am," Kayana said under her breath, "because I would've cussed the hell out of my mother-in-law and left my husband so long ago that he would've forgotten what I looked like."

"Would you, Kayana," Leah questioned, "if you'd had children?"

Leah's query gave her pause, because whenever children were a part of the equation, it wouldn't be that easy to pick up and walk away. "It would all depend on the circumstances. If I'd been in a verbal or physically abusive relationship, then yes, because I wouldn't want my children to witness that type of behavior."

"Alan made certain never to argue with me in front of Adele or our kids."

Cherie emitted an unladylike snort. "What the hell did you argue about?"

"Things."

"Things?" Cherie and Kayana said in unison.

Leah blinked slowly. "Yes. It could be what he wanted me to wear to an event, or what I planned to serve his friends and associates for a dinner party."

"Did you ever have any good times together?" Cherie had asked another question.

Leah smiled. "Yes, but only when it involved our sons." Resting her head against the back of the love seat, she closed her eyes for several seconds. "I can't believe I've been telling y'all my business when I've never even talked to Mama about it."

Kayana met Leah's steady stare. "That's because mothers aren't known to be objective when it comes to their children."

"I said it before, and I'll say it again. Thank goodness I'm not married," Cherie drawled.

Leah didn't appear to be bothered by Cherie's taunt when she said, "If you were, then you'd realize there are times when you have to make sacrifices to protect your children. I'm certain you've had to make sacrifices in your life you hadn't thought possible. Look at Dana in *Kindred*, a young black woman in the seventies who endures unspeakable, inhuman torture when she travels back in time to save a small white child's life at the risk of losing her own freedom."

"I understand the writer's motivation—why she had Dana time-travel back to the eighteen hundreds in the pre–Civil War South, but I can't reconcile a few of the decisions she made," Cherie stated, as she glared at Leah.

Kayana was still trying to process Leah's revelation of her marriage to the son of one of Richmond's prominent families, when she forced herself to focus on the book discussion. "I was frustrated with Dana time-traveling back to the antebellum South whenever Rufus's life was in jeopardy, and then returning to the twentieth century whenever her life was at risk. But I realize she had to save his life because she was to become a direct descendant of a depraved and evil individual."

"I know that," Cherie said, "but what good did her white husband do time-traveling with Dana when he did little to protect her?"

"I have to agree with Cherie," Kayana said. "Kevin's assessment of the slaves on the Weylin plantation really bothered me when he told Dana it wasn't what he would have imagined it would be because there was no overseer, and no more work than the people could manage. What he failed to realize was that these people were slaves with no rights, and they could be beaten or sold away at the whim of their owner. To him, as long as they appeared content in their plight, it really wasn't that bad, but as a reader, I saw him as being insensitive, especially since he was married to a black woman in America whose ancestors had been enslaved for centuries."

The discussion continued for the next forty-five minutes as the three women agreed they were hooked from the first sentence and unable to put the book down until they finished it. Kayana thought of it as psychological horror, while Leah regarded it as a commentary on the disturbing and ugly history of slavery in America. However, Cherie was still ambivalent about liking the novel, despite finding it brilliantly written and thought-provoking.

It was after nine o'clock when Kayana led Cherie and Leah to her SUV. The rain had slacked off to a steady drizzle by the time she left Leah at her bungalow and Cherie at the boardinghouse. When she'd suggested a book club, and invited Leah Kent to join her, Kayana hadn't expected Leah to be that forthcoming about her marriage. Tapping a button and decreasing the speed of the windshield wipers, she maneuvered onto the road leading back to the restaurant.

She'd always thought of herself as a good judge of character, but Leah definitely had her fooled, just like the woman who'd been sleeping with James. Kayana wasn't certain whether she was losing her edge, or if her focus had switched from attempting to solve other people's problems to concentrating on herself. She parked under the raised structure next to the restaurant, shut off the engine, and walked to the rear door of the Seaside Café. She unlocked the door, disarmed the alarm, and reset it before taking the staircase to the apartment.

Kayana removed her cellphone from her wristlet, checked it for calls and messages, and then placed it on the bedside table. It wasn't until after she'd brushed her teeth and changed into a nightgown that she remembered the flyer Graeme had sent her about the movies at the Shelby theater.

"Tomorrow," she whispered. She would contact him then to let him know which film she wanted to see.

Chapter 8

Graeme saved what he'd typed when the ringtone on his cellphone indicated he had a text message. He smiled when he saw who'd contacted him.

Kayana: *I looked over the flyer, and I would like to see The Count of Monte Cristo.*

Graeme: *I'm glad you selected that one, because now I can compare it to the two TV mini-series with Richard Chamberlain and Gérard Depardieu.*

Kayana: *I haven't seen those, but I happen to like Jim Caviezel.*

Graeme: *Should I assume you've watched Person of Interest?*

Kayana: *You assume right. I rarely watch a program for more than one or two seasons, but I must admit that I did follow this one until its final episode, because it was an intelligent adult drama that never deviated from its original premise.*

Graeme smiled, although Kayana couldn't see him. Her including *adult* and *intelligent* in the same sentence told him a lot about the woman who'd captivated him with her natural beauty and sophistication. He had never been one to accurately guess a person's age, but there was something about Kayana that silently told him she was mature enough not to engage in head games, unlike a few of the women he'd dated since becoming a widower.

Graeme: *I'll pick you up at the Café at 7.*

Kayana: *I'll be ready.*

He smiled again when she posted a smiley emoji. They seemed to have gotten off on the wrong foot when she felt he'd pitied her because she couldn't have children, but she wasn't aware that he too hadn't had kids. Graeme knew he'd turned a corner in his life when he called to apologize to her; that wasn't something he'd done in the past. He'd been raised spoiled and pampered by his wealthy and extremely intellectual adoptive parents, who had given him a sense of entitlement that had been ingrained in his personality throughout his adulthood.

However, the death of his wife had shattered his confidence and reminded him of his own mortality, causing him to embark on a journey of self-examination. He discovered there were things about himself that he did not like, and after countless hours spent on a therapist's couch, he sought to change. Graeme liked to think of himself as the new and very improved version of his former self, and at fifty-two, he looked forward to enjoying whatever life offered him.

Setting down the cellphone, he leaned back in his chair and propped his bare feet on the corner of the workstation. Text messaging with Kayana had shattered his concentration, and he knew his writing session was over for a while. Barley ambled out of his bed, stretched and shook himself, and then came over to look up at him.

"Hello, sleepyhead. Are you ready to go out?" Barley barked as if he understood what he'd been asked.

Graeme walked the active little dog twice a day to release some of his energy. When he first brought the puppy home, he'd had to puppy-proof baseboards and furniture legs to keep him from chewing on them. It had become a period of adjustment for the poodle mix when he went from the house in Newburyport to the bungalow on Coates Island. He'd had to be coaxed from the crate to explore his new surroundings, and it was a week before Barley felt comfortable enough to wander in and out of rooms and navigate the stairs to the second story.

Slipping his feet into a pair of sandals, Graeme left the study, Barley following close behind. He took the dog's leash and harness off the hook in the alcove outside the kitchen. Kayana's text had come at the right time; he'd been writing for more than three hours and needed a break.

The rain had stopped earlier that morning, and the sun had broken through watery clouds to dispel the dampness that appeared to cloak the entire island. The weather had forced Graeme to remain indoors, eat leftovers, and write as if his editor were looking over his shoulder to chart his progress.

The instant Aviva Campbell appeared on the page, he knew he'd made the right decision to include her. Not only was Zack intrigued with her presence, but as the writer, Graeme had portrayed her as a woman of mystery. Aside from the hero, Aviva was the only character he heard speak to him. It was as if he'd become their alter ego, seeing what they saw and feeling what they felt.

Picking up a set of house keys, he slipped them into the pocket of his walking shorts. He was aware that many of the locals did not lock their doors or their cars, but Graeme hadn't lived on the island long enough to become that trusting. And it wasn't as if Coates Island was crime-free because deputies from the mainland's sheriff's department conducted regular patrols to check on residents and businesses.

"Slow down, boy," he said to the poodle as he pulled on the leash in an attempt to run. Graeme knew Barley wanted to visit with another dog at the end of the street. Miss Donaldson, the owner of a Jack Russell terrier, had asked if he could bring Barley over for a doggy playdate, but he'd declined the invitation because the poodle had just gotten his shots and was lethargic. The retired schoolteacher appeared insulted and never asked him again, but that didn't stop Barley from stopping in front of her house and barking for Lulu to come out.

Graeme groaned under his breath when he saw Miss Donaldson walking Lulu. The woman was the first person to welcome him to the island once he took up long-term residence. She'd brought over a houseplant and an assortment of cookies from the local bakery. He'd invited her in, and within an hour she'd revealed not only her life story, but also those of other permanent residents. This was when he'd learned that Kayana had grown up on the island, left to attend college, and after a divorce, returned to work in the family-owned restaurant. Knowing she was single served to buoy his curiosity about the woman who unknowingly had enthralled him.

"Good morning, Miss Donaldson." The tall, slender, never-married woman's rosy complexion, bright blue eyes, and silver-blond hair cut into a stylish bob belied her age.

"That it is," she said, smiling. "After all this rain, it's good to see the sun."

Graeme nodded, although he didn't agree with her. The rain had forced him indoors, where he had been more than productive with his writing project. Now that he was ahead of his self-created schedule for completion, he was looking forward to taking in a movie with Kayana.

"The sun does feel good," he said truthfully.

"It's too bad Barley has been neutered; otherwise, I would have asked you if he could mate with my Lulu."

"Wouldn't you want to mate her with another Jack Russell?"

"I would if she were purebred."

Graeme glanced down to find Barley and Lulu smelling and nipping at each other. Not only was the terrier larger and heavier, but she was also more hyper than the four-pound poodle. Barley let out a yelp when Lulu bit his tail, and then he retaliated by biting the terrier's ear. Tightening his grip on the leash, Graeme leaned down to pick up his dog.

"Playtime is over."

Miss Donaldson shortened her dog's leash. "I've never known her to be so aggressive."

He gave the woman a look that said he didn't believe her and wanted to tell her that Lulu was always aggressive, and it was one of the reasons why he didn't want his dog to interact with the forceful bitch. Barley exhibited periods when he wanted to play, but most times he preferred lounging in his bed.

Turning on his heel, Graeme retraced his steps, leaving the woman and her canine staring at his back. It was more than apparent that Lulu needed obedience training. And the last thing he wanted was for Barley to mimic the terrier's behavior, in which case he wouldn't have a minute of peace. Miss Donaldson had admitted that Lulu was very needy and she had to give her a lot of attention.

He held the poodle closer to his chest. "I'm sorry, Barley, but you can't spend time with Lulu. I don't want you to get into a fight with her and possibly get injured." Lowering his head, Graeme dropped a kiss on the puppy's curly head.

He returned to the house and let Barley have the run of the fenced-in backyard. Picking up a tennis ball, Graeme tossed it, watching as the dog took off after it. Fencing in the yard and having it landscaped not only provided him with privacy from his closest neighbors; it was also where he would sit and unwind at the end of the day. After ten minutes of playing catch with the puppy, he coaxed him into the house. Barley retreated to the alcove in the kitchen to find his bowl of water. Making certain the poodle did not need to return outside to relieve himself, Graeme returned to the study to pick up where he'd left off before getting the text from Kayana.

Kayana was looking forward to a couple of hours away from the Café as she descended the staircase and went out to the parking lot to meet Graeme. Three days of nonstop rain had kept a lot of customers indoors; however, Monday morning they were back for breakfast, lunch, and dinner. She'd had to fill in to assist Derrick and the retired short-order cook in the kitchen when they were unable to keep up with the number of orders. Not only were they serving tourists and locals; there was also an influx of customers from the mainland. And it was the first time in a long time that they'd run out of several menu items.

She didn't think of going to the movies with Graeme as a date, despite taking special care when choosing what to wear; the slim-fitting, polished-cotton, royal blue and white striped dress, ending at her knees, and navy-blue ballet-type flats were a welcome change from her loose-fitting chef pants and tunic, or the shorts and T-shirts she generally wore when her shift ended.

She waved her hand to get Graeme's attention as he pulled into the parking lot and came to a complete stop. A slow smile parted her lips when he stared at her as if seeing a stranger. It was apparent he hadn't recognized her. She'd missed seeing him, like so many of the other regulars who hadn't come into the restaurant during the three-day torrential rainfall. Even Cherie and Leah were among the missing until they showed up for their book club meeting. The rain had stopped completely Monday morning, but he still hadn't shown up—until now.

Graeme blinked slowly as if coming out of a trance when he saw Kayana in the dress that hugged every curve of her body and revealed an expanse of smooth skin on her shoulders, arms, and legs. Galvanized into action, he got out and approached her. The subtle scent of her perfume wafted to his nostrils, enveloping him in a spell of longing that reminded him how long it had been since he'd asked a woman out.

It had taken him more than a year to realize Jillian was gone and wasn't coming back when he'd accepted an invitation from one of his colleagues to stand in as her date at a faculty function after her boyfriend decided to reconcile with his ex-wife. The woman spent the entire time talking about how much she hated the man who'd used her while wooing his ex in order to get back into her life, and Graeme couldn't wait for the evening to end so he could take her home. She subsequently apologized to him about going on incessantly about another man, but Graeme reassured her he understood and then was forthcoming when he told her he was in mourning and not ready to begin dating again.

That was then, and this was now. He was a fifty-two-year-old former high school math and economics teacher who had become a reclusive, best-selling author; he had buried his wife eight years ago, and for the first time in a very long time, he'd found himself enthralled with a woman who related to him as she did with countless other patrons who dined at her family's restaurant.

"You look incredible." Graeme said the first thing that came to mind. However, he hadn't lied. Her dress, her subtle makeup, and the mass of shiny curls framing her beautiful face made it impossible for him to avert his gaze.

Kayana smiled. "Thank you."

Cupping her elbow, Graeme led her to the passenger side of the SUV, opened the door, and cradling Kayana's waist with both hands, lifted her effortlessly until she was seated. He hadn't missed her gasp of surprise when her feet left the ground. "I doubted you would've been able to get up without hiking your dress halfway up your thighs."

She glanced down at the hem of the dress riding inches above her knees. "You're right about that. The next time I go out with you, I'll make certain to wear something less restricting."

"Will there be a next time, Kayana?"

"Of course. That is, if we're going to see more than one movie. Better yet, we can take my vehicle, which isn't as high as yours."

Graeme closed the door, rounded the SUV, and slipped in

behind the wheel. He'd assisted Kayana up because he doubted whether he would've been able to remain in control if she displayed too much leg in the revealing dress. As it was, it was all he could do to control an onslaught of normal physical urges whenever they occupied the same space. There were mornings when he woke up with an erection, and those were the times when he'd masturbate to relieve a buildup of sexual frustration. As a middle-aged man, he was fortunate to still be able to achieve and sustain an erection, though he wondered for how much longer.

Alma was right, but there was no way he was going to agree with her when she'd talked about his protagonist jerking off, because he'd made certain readers were left to draw their own conclusions about how Zack dealt with his sexual frustrations. But that was going to change now that Graeme had introduced his hero to Aviva Campbell. He hadn't planned for his protagonists to sleep together in the current manuscript; his intent was to establish enough sexual tension for readers to demand they have an intimate relationship.

Waiting until Kayana was belted in, Graeme backed out of the parking lot and headed in the direction of the road and bridge leading to the mainland. Sitting next to Kayana and enjoying the sensual scent of her perfume, Graeme was suddenly struck with the realization that he'd become his fictional character's alter ego. When Zack wasn't playing superhero, he'd become a recluse, existing in a world where he got up and went to bed whenever he wanted and controlled who he interacted with. And, like Zack, there was no woman in his life, and he wondered if Kayana would become his Aviva.

"How did you survive our mini monsoon?" Kayana asked after a comfortable silence. She'd taken a surreptitious glance at Graeme as he drove, wondering what he was thinking about when she noticed a hint of a smile lifting the corners of his mouth. Other than his eyes, she'd found his mouth to be his most attractive feature. It wasn't too full or thin, but strong and what she thought of as masculine—if a man's mouth could be considered masculine or feminine.

"Just barely," Graeme said when his smirk became a full smile. "I ran out of perishables and nearly depleted my pantry."

"Why didn't you come into the restaurant? We hadn't closed because of the weather."

"The rain gave me an excuse to stay in and work on a project."

"Is the project work-related?"

Graeme shrugged a shoulder under a pale-blue shirt he'd paired with navy-blue linen slacks and black leather slip-ons. "Somewhat."

Kayana shifted on her seat, until she was able to look directly at him. "Can you define somewhat?"

"I am attempting to write and complete a novel."

"Do you find it difficult?" She didn't want to ask him what it was about because aspiring writers tended to be secretive and protective about their works in progress.

"Yes and no. I'm able to get the words down, but there are times when the characters fight with me because they refuse to do what I'd planned for them."

She nodded. "I've met a few people who are aspiring writers, and they tell me it's very frustrating to be faced with writer's block; there were times when they'd wanted to give up completely."

"Are any of them published?" Graeme asked her.

"Only one. And she self-published her book because she couldn't get a publisher to accept her manuscript."

"I know you love books, but have you ever considered writing one?"

Kayana laughed. "Thank goodness, no. I don't have the patience or temperament to be a writer."

"Talking about patience. I've watched you interact with a few very difficult customers, and you always seem to defuse what could blow up into something that could become quite ugly."

"That's when I go into psychiatric social worker mode."

"You're a social worker?"

"Why does that shock you?" she asked him.

Graeme met her eyes when he stopped at a four-way flashing red light. "I don't know. Somehow I figured you for a teacher."

Kayana smiled. "My younger sister is the teacher in the family. But if I'd remained in social work for another ten years, I probably would've considered teaching a few courses as an adjunct."

"Do you mind if I ask what made you give it up?"

"No, I don't mind." She paused. "My husband and I worked at the same hospital, so once our divorce was finalized, I decided to move back here and help my brother run the restaurant."

"Where did you live before?"

"Atlanta."

"I like the city, but I don't believe I could ever get used to the downtown traffic."

"It is quite challenging, and I must admit that I don't miss it."

Graeme wanted to ask Kayana if she missed being married, but decided it was too personal and sensitive a subject for her. And given that she and her ex-husband worked at the same hospital, it must have been very uncomfortable for her.

"Traffic jams are definitely not a problem here on the island," he said instead.

"They would be if tourists were able to drive their cars. There was a time before I left to attend college that vacationers were able to drive on the local roads. But a single incident changed everything when a vehicular accident escalated into road rage. The drivers refused to move their cars off the road until sheriff deputies arrived. Curses and fists were thrown, and both drivers were arrested for disorderly conduct. The locals were enraged they had to wait for tow trucks to come, hook the cars up, and drive them away before they had access to their homes on the dead-end street. The city officials got an earful at the next city council meeting, and that's when they instituted the law banning driving on local roads for vacationers during the summer season."

Nodding his head, Graeme smiled. "As a first-year local, I really appreciate not having to deal with getting stuck in traffic."

"What about when you go back north?"

"I rarely encounter a lot of traffic in Newburyport. I have less than a ten-minute drive from my house to the high school."

"You don't live in Boston?"

Graeme waited for the light to change from red to green before turning onto the road leading to Shelby. "No. I grew up in Boston but spent my summers in Newburyport."

"How far is it from Boston?"

"It's about thirty-five miles away. There's something about Coates Island that reminds me of Newburyport; it's a historic seaport with a bustling tourist industry."

"Why come here when you could stay home?" Kayana asked.

"Spending the summers in Newburyport is not what I think of as a vacation. I know most of the people who've lived there all their lives, and I know practically every kid who attended the high school. Here I have the anonymity I need to come and go and work without someone recognizing me."

"Have you met any of your neighbors?"

"Only Miss Donaldson. And that's because she wanted her Jack Russell bitch to mate with my dog, but I had to disappoint her when I told her Barley has been neutered."

"Is Barley a Jack Russell?"

"No. He's a toy poodle mix. I got him nine months ago. He's a rescue from a puppy mill." Graeme hid a grin when he heard a gasp slip past Kayana's parted lips.

"I love poodles."

Kayana had just given Graeme the opening he needed to see her beyond going to the movies. "Maybe one of these days you can come over and meet the spoiled little pup."

"Do you have a photo of him?"

"No."

"What kind of puppy parent are you, Graeme? You're supposed to take pictures of Barley and use it as a screen saver on your phone and computer."

Graeme chuckled under his breath. "You can tell that I don't have any children."

"That's why you should have photos of your dog."

"I'm totally inept when it comes to using my camera phone."

"Maybe one of these days when I meet Barley, I'll take the photos for you so you can upload them to your computer."

"You have to let me know beforehand when you want to photograph him, because I'd like to take him to be groomed."

Kayana gave him an incredulous stare. "You're really something."

Graeme met her eyes for a brief moment. "What are you talking about?"

"First, you don't have photos of your dog, and now you're acting like a proud pet parent who wants to make certain his puppy doesn't come off looking scruffy during a photo shoot."

"I can't have my boy not looking his best."

"He's probably adorable with or without a cut."

"He is," Graeme said in agreement. "The movie ends at nine-thirty, and we should get back to the island before ten. If it's not a problem for you, I'll stop by the house, where you can meet Barley Ogden before I drop you home."

"I'd love to meet him."

Graeme felt as if he'd hit a walk-off home run. Not only had he gotten Kayana to go to the movies with him, but she'd also agreed to come to his home to meet his pet. He'd heard stories about men attracting women when walking dogs, yet that hadn't been his intent.

He was much too old to play games or use ulterior motives when interacting with a woman to whom he was attracted. And if he did approach her and she did not seem remotely interested in engaging in conversation, then he would retreat without a blow to his ego.

Graeme would be the first to admit that he wasn't perfect, that he had personality flaws, but he was cognizant of his shortcomings and sought to overcome them. He'd walked away from Kayana rather than stay and verbally spar with her. That would not have happened before he'd become a widower. It wasn't that he was argumentative by nature; he simply believed in verbalizing his beliefs.

Graeme knew he had to be careful—very, very careful—with Kayana not to become confrontational; he did not want anything to impact what he hoped would become an easygoing friendship. He knew they would not agree on everything, yet he was willing to hear her out and, if necessary, also compromise.

Chapter 9

Kayana stared out the windshield at the passing land-scape. She was trying to understand why she'd agreed to go with Graeme to his home; it was something she would never have done with any man in the past when going out with him for the first time. Even as a college student, she'd made it a practice never to find herself alone with a boy in his dorm room, and even before dating and marrying James, she still resisted going to his home until she'd felt she could trust him.

She knew her reluctance had come from a high school incident when a boy in her study group invited her to his house. She'd been unaware that his parents weren't home for the weekend. Within minutes of walking through the door, he'd attempted to sexually assault her. Kayana managed to escape by kneeing him in the groin; she got into her car and drove as if the hounds were chasing her back to Coates Island. He didn't attend classes the following week, and when he did show up, he avoided her as if she were carrying a communicable disease. And judging from his gait, Kayana knew her kneeing him had caused him obvious discomfort.

"How was your book club discussion?"

Graeme's question broke into her musings. "It was very thought-provoking because of the subject matter."

"Slavery in America is never an easy subject to talk about."

"You're right, because not only did our discussion get rather heated, it also became personal. I have to admit the novel was masterfully written to have evoked so many different reactions from the three of us."

"*Pride and Prejudice* will probably be less controversial."

"Yes and no," Kayana countered. "It depends if you're looking at it based on societal mores or a behavioral analysis."

Graeme whistled softly. "That sounds heavy."

"Maybe since you're a mathematician and you deal with what can be proven, you view things differently from the women in our group. Leah is an English lit teacher, so she's really the expert when it comes to analyzing books and authors, and Cherie has a degree in early-childhood development."

"I'm glad I declined your invitation to join the group because there's no way I'd be able to hold my own against you intellectual heavyweights."

Kayana gave him a *You've got to be kidding me* look. "Don't play yourself, Graeme. If you teach high school math and economics, then you're definitely no slouch when it comes to intelligence."

"I just happen to be good with numbers."

"Yeah, right," she drawled. "I'm willing to bet you can compute equations in your head. The only thing I remember about math is the quadratic equation, and not much beyond that."

"How about science courses?" he asked.

"I managed to get high marks in biology, but I did not do as well with chemistry. Having to memorize the periodic table kept me up more nights than I care to remember."

"It sounds as if you were an overachiever."

"I was," Kayana admitted, "until I realized I could never

compete with my brother. Derrick was a straight-A student, even without studying."

"I think you're being modest, Kayana. Average students don't become psychiatric social workers."

"Average students have to study hard in order not to be categorized as average."

"Where did you attend college?"

A beat passed. "I went to Spelman as an undergraduate and the University of Georgia for grad school."

Graeme wanted to ask Kayana why she tended to downplay her intelligence when she'd graduated from a historically black liberal arts college for women. "That's quite impressive."

"And where did you go?" she asked, as if he hadn't commented on her being accepted into the elite college.

"Harvard."

"All right, Mr. Ivy Leaguer."

"I wanted to go to MIT, but chose Harvard because my father was a professor and alumnus."

"Was your father also a mathematician?"

"No. He taught bioengineering."

"And your mother?"

"Mom was a linguistics professor at Boston College."

"How was it growing up in a family of intellectual heavy-weights?"

"They were exceptional parents, and I still miss them. Once they left the classroom or lecture hall, they were like kids at the circus. Dad once confessed that he always wanted to be a standup comedian, while my mother believed she was the second coming of Julia Child."

Kayana laughed. "Did she teach you to cook?"

"Nah. Mom's kitchen was off-limits to everyone. I know if she'd allowed me to watch her, I'd know much more than just how to boil eggs, grill steaks and corn, and bake potatoes."

"What about chicken?"

Graeme slowly shook his head. "I've tried roasting chicken, and each time it ends up in the garbage."

"It's not that difficult, Graeme."

"It's not difficult because you're an expert. I love chicken, and would eat a lot more of it if I knew how to prepare it without coming down with salmonella."

"Have you thought about using a meat thermometer?"

Graeme slowed as he neared Shelby's downtown business district. "No, because I'm done with trying to cook chicken."

"What if I write out a recipe, step-by-step, which will include how to truss the wings and legs, and send it to you."

He shook his head again. "No. I've followed a number of recipes, and the result is always the same."

"Would you agree to me walking you through the entire process?"

Graeme smiled as he pulled into the parking lot behind a row of stores. "That will definitely work. What size chicken should I buy?"

"Look for a three- to four-pound roaster. Not only will it have more meat, but you'll be able to use the leftovers for soup and salads. Is there anything else you want to learn to cook?"

"Rice."

"I can also walk you through that," Kayana volunteered.

He found an empty space, maneuvered into it, and shut off the engine. Resting his right arm over the back of Kayana's seat, he met her eyes. "What if I paid you for cooking lessons?"

Kayana undid her seat belt. "You don't have to pay me, Graeme. Let me know what you want to prepare, and I'll let you know when I'll be able to make time for you."

"No pressure. After all, I'm the one with nothing but time on my hands," Graeme half-lied.

He could not reveal to Kayana that he was *New York Times* best-selling author Brendan Andersen, and if she did elect to give him lessons, he would have to rearrange his writing schedule. He also didn't tell her that learning to cook was on his bucket list, along with penning a nonfiction book on the definitive history of music. After teaching for twenty years, he now had the luxury of indulging in whatever he chose.

Graeme knew if he hadn't been financially solvent, he would've continued to teach until he was at least sixty-five. He still could recall the look on the principal's face when he'd submitted his resignation letter the day before the end of the school year. Despite making the decision months before, Graeme had waited because he didn't want a retirement party or his colleagues questioning his reason for giving up his teaching career; most of them believed he was still grieving the loss of his wife.

He released his seat belt. "Don't move. I'll help you down."

Kayana moved closer to Graeme when he reached for her hand as he led her out of the Bijou des Artes. The theater's seating capacity of one hundred and eight had been sold out, and she discovered that Graeme had purchased their tickets in advance online and just had to scan them at the box office. A crowd had gathered in front of the theater for the late-night showing. The warm nighttime air felt good on her exposed skin after sitting for two hours in the air-cooled building.

"Did you like it?" she asked him.

"Very much."

She gave him a sidelong glance. "Watching it has me thinking about reading the book again."

Graeme released her hand and put his arm around her waist as they navigated their way through the throng lingering in the parking lot. "When was the last time you read it?"

"It had to be high school, because I don't remember reading it in college."

"I also read it in high school, which now seems like another lifetime." Graeme stopped beside the Range Rover and opened the passenger-side door for Kayana.

"I think I'm going to recommend it for our book club," Kayana said when he slipped behind the wheel beside her."

Graeme punched the START ENGINE button. "Now that discussion should be very interesting, with all the themes of treachery, vengeance, self-indulgence, jealousy, and infidelity."

"It sounds as if Dumas wanted to highlight some of the deadly sins," Graeme remarked, checking the side mirrors before shifting into reverse.

"And he did," she confirmed. "The Dantès character was so fixated on revenge that it nearly destroyed him."

"Don't you think he was justified seeking revenge once he realized his best friend had not only deceived him but also, with the assistance of the chief prosecutor, had him exiled to a prison where he would spend the remainder of his life? And the love he'd felt for his fiancée, Mercédès, also died once he learned she'd married his betrayer a month after he'd been exiled."

"I'll admit thirteen years spent in solitary confinement, eating slop and being beaten every year on the anniversary of his imprisonment, is enough to change a man into someone subhuman," Kayana said, rationalizing the change in Edmond Dantès's personality.

"So you agree with his plan to enact revenge on those he deemed his enemies."

"It's not that I agree, Graeme, but I understand his motivation to right the wrongs. Armed with the knowledge given him by the imprisoned priest in the Château d'If and the treasure he found on the Isle of Monte Cristo, he had the resources and, more importantly, the power needed to bring those to justice."

"He could've been like Michael Corleone in *The Godfather*, who settled all his debts with murder."

"He could have, but Edmond Dantès as the Count of Monte Cristo was much more skillful, because he used his victim's flaws to strip them of what they valued most. Everyone and everything had become a means to an end for Dantès once he executed his plan for revenge.

At what cost, Graeme? Do you really believe exacting revenge on his enemies brought him happiness?"

"No. But he did derive satisfaction knowing he had power over them."

"Why are men always fixated on power?"

"Not all men, Kayana. When Dumas recognized that Dantès's thirst for vengeance and absolute power was going to corrupt him absolutely—to the point where his moral sense threatened to destroy him—he had Mercédès admit that she had been pregnant with his child before he was imprisoned, and it was the reason she'd rushed to marry Mondego. And the instant he discovers Albert is his son and not Mondego's, everything changes for Edmond, and he is ready to forgive even Mondego for his treachery."

"Are you saying he redeemed himself because he was ready to offer Mondego mercy?" she questioned Graeme.

"Yes, but Mondego didn't want mercy because he couldn't live knowing someone he deemed beneath him when it came to social status had everything he'd always wanted. Engaging in a duel with Edmond and hopefully killing him would assuage his jealousy, but in the end, he had become the loser."

Kayana recalled the book ending differently and knew she would have to read it again to familiarize herself with characters and scenes that did not appear in the film. "I find it amazing that plays, novels, and poems written thousands of years ago are still being read today. The *Iliad* is purported to have been written around the eighth century B.C."

"There is nothing more powerful than the written word. It has imprisoned and freed men."

Kayana shifted slightly, staring at Graeme's profile as he focused on the road. "If Edmond Dantès hadn't been illiterate, he wouldn't have been imprisoned in the Château d'If for thirteen years. And slaves would've gained their freedom long before the Emancipation Proclamation if they hadn't been prohibited from learning to read."

"How true, Kayana."

Graeme's voice seemed to have come from a long way off, despite his sitting less than a foot away from her, and the return trip to Coates Island was completed in complete silence, with each person lost in their own thoughts. However, Kayana had to admit she'd enjoyed the time they had spent together. Graeme's disclosure that his parents were college professors was a clear indication that he'd had a life of privilege growing up in Boston and summering in Newburyport. And he wasn't impoverished, as evidenced by the fact that he drove a state-of-the art luxury SUV with a starting price of just under one hundred thousand dollars. Rumors swirled around the island that not only had he offered cash for the elderly widow's house, but he had also paid a contractor to gut and update it with monies he would've had to save for years from his teacher's salary.

"Which movie would you like to see next?" he asked.

"Probably *Les Misérables*."

"That's not showing for three weeks."

"I'll be ready for another movie by that time. Don't forget I work every day, and I have only a week to finish reading a book before the book club meets on Sundays."

"I won't buy the tickets until you let me know whether you're able to go."

Kayana didn't want to consciously compare Graeme to her ex-husband when it came to compromise. If she'd told James that she didn't want to host a small gathering at the house, he'd invariably ignore her, and their home would resemble a sports bar or an airport terminal, depending on the number of invitees. All she'd wanted was at least two weekends a month when she could enjoy her home without playing hostess to a group of what she deemed strangers because they weren't her friends and family members, but James's.

Graeme eschewed arguments like the one he'd had with

his wife before her death, while Kayana avoided verbal confrontation because of what she'd witnessed and overheard between her parents. Most times, she was able to escape between the pages of a book until they called a truce. Derrick would leave the house and shoot baskets into the hoop at the back of the house, while Jocelyn spent more time with their grandmother than she did with her mother. Even at an early age, Kayana had promised herself she would never fight with her husband, as her mother had done with hers, and the result was that James had taken her acquiescence for weakness. Early on when they were dating, she'd warned him that cheating would abruptly end their relationship; however, he must have forgotten or totally disregarded it as an idle threat when sleeping with a woman other than his wife.

"If you want to see it, then please don't wait for me if I'm unable to go."

"I'd rather wait for you, because if I go alone, I won't have you to talk about it with."

"Aren't there other women you could ask to be your date?"

"No."

"Why not, Graeme? You're a decent guy, so I'm certain quite a few women would love hanging out with you."

Throwing back his head, Graeme laughed loudly. "That's the nicest backhanded compliment I've ever had."

"I didn't mean for it to sound backhanded. You *are* a nice guy."

He inclined his head. "Well, thank you."

"No, Graeme. Thank you for an enjoyable evening."

"It's not over yet. Not until you meet Barley. I'd like to ask you something, and you don't have to answer if you choose not to."

A shiver of apprehension nagged at Kayana; at the same time, she wondered what Graeme was going to ask her that could possibly ruin the evening, with her telling him it would be the first and last time she would agree to go out with him.

She hadn't had an actual male friend in years. The last one was a fellow grad student. Since interacting with Graeme, she had begun to think of him as a friend. And despite Derrick's assessment that Graeme was staring at her with his tongue hanging out, not once had he demonstrated he wanted more from her than friendship.

"What is it?" she asked, her voice barely above a whisper.

"Am I the first man you've gone out with since your divorce?"

The tense lines ringing her mouth relaxed at the same time she exhaled an inaudible breath. "Yes. Why did you ask?"

"I need to know if you intend to punish me for the sins of another man."

Reaching over, Kayana covered his hand gripping the steering wheel with hers. "No. I know very little about you, and from what I've seen, I can honestly say you're not anything like my ex-husband."

She wanted to tell Graeme that he and James were as different as night and day in physical appearance and temperament. James becoming a renowned Atlanta-based trauma surgeon wasn't enough for him. He had to surrounded himself with people who made him the center of attention, and his beautiful home and intelligent, talented wife were tangible symbols of his so-called perfect life.

"Thank, you," Graeme said, reversing their hands and giving Kayana's fingers a gentle squeeze.

He hadn't realized he'd been holding his breath until he'd felt the constriction in his chest. It had taken all of his resolve to conduct himself like the quintessential perfect gentleman; he hadn't come on to her and therefore ruined a possible relationship before it could begin. After all, he wasn't a horny adolescent boy looking to score with a girl willing to put out. Been there. Done that. As a child and young adult, he'd traveled extensively with his parents, and as a college student, he'd sown his wild oats. As a bachelor, he continued to date different women until he woke up in bed with one whose name he could not remember. That's when he knew he had to become more discriminating.

Decelerating, he drove down the street leading to his home and came to a stop under the carport. He'd programmed lights to come on and go off at different times of the day. A security company had installed hidden cameras and motion detectors to protect the perimeter of the property and the contents of the house. The structure was far enough from the beachfront for it not to be erected on stilts, and he'd become accustomed to waking up in the two-story, two-bedroom, two-bath bungalow with a screened-in porch and second-story verandas with unrestricted views of the beach and ocean.

Graeme got out and came around to assist Kayana down. "Are you ready to meet the boss?"

"Yes."

A chime echoed throughout the house until he disarmed the security system, and Barley raced to the door, whining and going up on his hind legs for Graeme to pick him up. "Have you been a good boy?" he crooned. Barley barked as if he understood what he'd said. "I have a friend I'd like you to meet." Bending slightly, he scooped up the poodle, cradling him to his chest.

Kayana could not pull her gaze away from the tiny, curly, sand-colored puppy snuggling against Graeme's chest as he stared back at her. "What a bundle of cuteness. Will he let me hold him?"

"Hold out your hands and see if he'll come to you."

She extended her hands, and Barley sniffed her before her fingers closed around his chubby middle. Kayana luxuriated in his warmth and slight weight, and she lowered her head and kissed an ear. "Hey, baby boy. Do you want to come home with me tonight?"

"No, he doesn't," Graeme snapped.

Her head popped up. "Chill, Graeme. I was just kidding."
She glared at him until he lowered his eyes.

"I'm sorry. I didn't mean for it to come out like that."

"I can understand you being possessive, because this little
guy is definitely precious."

Graeme managed to look sheepish. "I suppose I overacted
because he normally won't let anyone other than myself hold
him. Usually he's squirming and nipping until they put him
down."

Kayana rocked him gently as if attempting to console a
fretful child. "He knows that I'm partial to poodles. I got a
poodle–bichon mix puppy for my tenth birthday, and we
were inseparable. He howled every morning when I left to go
to school and greeted me with somersaults once I got home.
After I left for college, my sister took him for a walk, and he
must have eaten something that made him sick. He didn't
survive the night, and I didn't find out that my baby was
gone until a week later when I came home for the Christmas
break. Not having him there to greet me when I walked
through the door ruined the entire holiday for me. That's
when I said I never wanted another pet."

Crossing his arms over his chest, Graeme's expression
grew serious. "It's never easy losing something you love."

Kayana wanted to ask if he meant someone and not something, and she wondered if he hadn't gotten over the loss of
his wife. "Everyone and everything with breath has an expi-
ration date."

He blinked as if coming out of a trance. "You're right."
He forced a smile. "It's getting late, and I know you usually
get up early, so I'd better take you home."

She set Barley on the shiny wood floor. The entryway with
a staircase leading to the second story opened out into an
open continuous floor plan with living/family/dining rooms
and a spacious stainless-steel kitchen with top-of-the-line ap-
pliances. She wondered if Graeme had selected the furnishings or had hired a professional decorator.

"The next time you come over, I promise to give you a tour of the house," he said, as if he had read her mind.

She smiled. "I'm going to hold you to that promise."

It took less than three minutes for Graeme to drive from his house to the restaurant. He got out and waited with her as she unlocked the rear door and disabled the alarm. An overhead light at the bottom of the staircase threw shadows over his face.

Kayana extended her hand. "Thank you for a most enjoyable evening."

Graeme stared at her hand before taking it, bringing it to his mouth, and pressing a kiss on her inner wrist. "The pleasure has been all mine. Good night, Kay."

She felt a shiver of awareness snake up her arm with the slight pressure of his mouth on her skin. "Good night, Graeme."

He released her hand, and she closed the door, shutting out the image of the man who had her wanting to see him again because of their shared passion: books.

Graeme returned home and walked Barley for the final time that day. The puppy trotted after him as he walked into his bedroom and changed into a pair of shorts and a T-shirt. "I'm not ready to go to bed," he said when the dog looked up at him. "I'm going to do a little writing before I turn in for the night. By the way, should I be concerned that you have something going with Miss Johnson?" He smiled when Barley tilted his head from side to side. "I know she's pretty and smells good, but I want you to remember that I saw her first."

Graeme knew if someone had overheard him talking to his dog, they would've thought he'd taken leave of his senses. But he would be the first one to admit that there was something about Kayana that kept him slightly off balance, although she hadn't given him the slightest indication she wanted more than friendship, while he was more interested in her because at this time in his life he craved companion-ship more than sex. He wanted to have a relationship with a woman with whom he could share similar interests and have spirited but intelligent conversations about a myriad of topics.

The year he'd summered on Coates Island, Graeme felt as if he'd come home. There was something about the quaint seaside town that offered him the peace he'd sought the year he celebrated his eighth birthday, when Patrick and Lauren Ogden revealed they weren't his biological parents. Unable to have children of their own, they'd gotten him through a private adoption. His birth mother was a linguistics major at Boston College who'd been sleeping with a married man. When she told Lauren about the affair and her plan to give birth and leave the baby in the hospital, Lauren offered to adopt the baby.

Graeme had spent years wondering about the woman who could carry him to term, then hand him over to someone else to raise, but as he matured, he knew she had done the right thing because Patrick and Lauren were the best parents a child could wish for. His mother tended to be overindulgent, while his father was more the disciplinarian who'd insisted on setting up boundaries he was forbidden to cross. The few times he did challenge Patrick, he was forced to give up his car for a month and take public transportation to and from the campus.

Coates Island also permitted him distance from Newbury-port—where the good, and some bad, memories of what he'd shared with Jillian still lingered. She reminded him of a cat who would permit him to stroke her and then, without warn-ing, would turn on him, hissing, spitting, her luminous green eyes giving off angry sparks that left him wondering why he had fallen in love with and married her.

Within his first two weeks on the island, he'd stopped wondering who his birth mother was, and why he'd married Jillian. Walking along the sand while inhaling the distinctive smell of saltwater and returning to the bungalow to write were better than sitting on a therapist's couch and baring his soul.

Fast-forward a year; he'd retired from teaching and had become a permanent resident, and he now had the option of staying on the island once the vacationers left when the summer season ended. By that time, he would've completed his current manuscript, the Seaside Café would resume their regular off-season hours, and hopefully he and Kayana would be able to spend more time together.

Chapter 10

Kayana had just finished chopping the ingredients for the trays of potato, macaroni, and pasta salads when the rear door opened and Derrick walked into the kitchen. He attempted to conceal a yawn with his hand. "Late night, brother love?" she teased.

"Yeah. The game was in San Francisco and went into extra innings."

"What time did it finally end?"

"It was after three on the East Coast."

"Why didn't you DVR the game and watch it later?"

Derrick washed his hands in one of the prep sinks, dried them on a bar towel, and covered his head with the cap he only wore when cooking. "That's no fun because I'd already know the score. I need to see it live."

"I can't believe you're still a sports junkie."

Derrick narrowed his eyes at her as he slipped a bibbed apron over his head and secured the ties around his waist. "I could be addicted to worse things."

"True." Some of the boys she'd gone to high school with on the mainland had dabbled in drugs before becoming full-blown addicts. A few had overdosed, and others had resorted to a life of crime to support their habit, while the lucky ones went into treatment to regain control of their lives.

"By the way, how was your date with Graeme last night?"

Kayana wasn't going to debate with Derrick whether her going to the movies with Graeme was a date, because he'd spotted her coming down the staircase wearing a dress and makeup. His expression was impassive when he mentioned Graeme's name, and she nodded.

"It was nice."

"Are you going to see him again?"

Reaching for a large aluminum bowl with cooked elbow macaroni, she added chopped celery, fresh dill, red bell pepper, red onion, and frozen green peas. "Probably."

"You like him, don't you?"

"I like him because he's a nice guy."

"Nicer than James?"

She halted, picking up a small dish with Dijon mustard. "What's up with the interrogation, Derrick?"

"I just want to know if my sister has finally gotten over her divorce and will start dating again."

"Graeme and I are not dating in the traditional sense. We love to read, and when he told me the theater in Shelby was featuring films this summer based on books, I agreed to go with him. Last night we saw *The Count of Monte Cristo*, and the next one we plan to see together three weeks from now is *Les Misérables*."

"So, it's just about books and movies?"

She smiled. "Yes. Did you want me to admit that it's more?"

"Yes."

Her smile vanished. "Why?"

"Because I don't believe you'll get over James until you become involved with another man."

"I'm over James."

"If you say so," Derrick drawled.

"You don't believe me?"

"No, Kay, I don't believe you. Men come in here every day, and some of them flirt with you, yet to you they may as well be invisible."

"I've been single for two years, compared to the nineteen I gave James, so don't begrudge me if I'd like to remain unencumbered. What do you plan for tonight's special?" she asked, smoothly veering the topic of conversation away from her.

"I'm going to use the rest of the tomato sauce that's in the freezer for lasagna."

Kayana loved her brother's lasagna, because of his homemade pasta and the tomato sauce and sweet Italian sausage and lean ground beef he used. Whenever it was featured as the dinner special, it sold out completely. "Remember to put aside a portion for me."

Derrick opened the walk-in refrigerator/freezer and took out several quart containers of tomato sauce. "What you need to do is learn how to make it."

"I could say the same about you learning to make the sides."

"Nah, Kay. That's not happening, because we don't want to lose customers when they complain about the potato salad and mac and cheese tasting funny. I don't mind taking care of the meat and main dishes, but I want nothing to do with the sides."

"Miss Johnson, this came for you."

Corey handed her a jade succulent plant wrapped in clear cellophane. Asian calligraphy covered the porcelain, handpainted pot. The attached card indicated it had come from a florist on the mainland. "Is the delivery person still here?"

"No, ma'am. He said his tip was taken care of."

"Thank you, Corey." Kayana set the plant on a table, removed her disposable gloves, and dropped them in a trash bin. She'd celebrated her forty-sixth birthday in early May, and maybe someone was sending her a belated gift. Plucking the envelope off the cellophane, she removed the card: Thank you for a wonderful evening—GNO.

Derrick met her eyes. "Graeme?"

She nodded. "Yes. He's thanking me for last night."

Her brother's eyebrows lifted slightly. "Nice. He's a keeper, Kay."

Kayana had to agree with Derrick. Graeme was the only man who'd sent her a token of his appreciation to celebrate their first date. "I suppose I'll keep him for the summer." She told herself that she had nothing to lose dating Graeme.

Kayana waited until late afternoon to call Graeme to thank him for the plant. She'd set it on a table with potted echeveria 'blue prince,' hens and chicks, and donkey tails. She favored succulents. Once she watered them, she allowed the soil to dry slightly before watering again. And the table was positioned under a window for them to take advantage of a full day of sunlight.

"How did you know I like succulents?" she asked when he answered the call after the second ring.

"I didn't. I would've sent you flowers, but they only last for a few days. I'm partial to succulents; that's what I had the landscaper plant in my garden."

"We have something in common because your jade plant will make my fourth succulent."

"Two out of three isn't bad."

A slight frown furrowed Kayana's forehead. "Two out of three what?"

"We both like books and the same types of plants. What's next, Kay?"

She noticed that he'd begun to shorten her name. "I don't know. You tell me."

He laughed softly. "Give me time, and I'll come up with something. I went to the butcher and bought a roaster. What do I need to season it with?"

Kayana settled back in the chaise and crossed her bare feet at the ankles. "Don't worry about it. If you're not busy on Friday afternoon, I'll come over after I'm finished here and walk you through everything."

"What about rice?"

"I'll bring the rice. What else would you like to eat with the chicken?"

"A Caesar salad. Your salad is the best I've ever eaten."

"That's because we make our own dressing. All gravies, stock, salad dressings, and mayonnaise are made in-house," she explained. "It's a tradition established by my Grandma Cassie, and it has continued to the present day."

"I suppose that's what makes the dishes at the Café so exceptional."

"I always believed my grandmama would come back and haunt me if I attempted to change or reveal the ingredients used to make her mac and cheese and honeyed fried chicken. And there's also my mother's creole chicken with buttermilk waffles."

"Are you saying they're family secrets?"

"Yes. What's the expression? If I tell you, then I'll have to kill you."

Graeme laughed again. "I don't need to know."

Kayana heard a beep indicating she had another call. "I have someone on the other line. I'll call you Friday to set a time when I'll be over. And thank you again for the plant."

"You're welcome."

She tapped a button, connecting her to the caller. "Hi, Leah."

"Hey, honey. I'm calling to ask if I can host this Sunday's meeting at my place? It's not fair that you do all the cooking while Cherie and I sit around and eat."

Kayana wanted to tell Leah that she didn't mind cooking because it was what she did seven days a week during the summer season. "I don't mind at all. Just let me know what you want me to bring."

"Nothing. Cherie has offered to make the libation and bring dessert."

"You're on. Don't forget to text me your address."

She ended the call, and seconds later, Leah's address appeared as a text message. She'd rented a bungalow within walking distance of the beach. Kayana picked up the book containing the complete works of Jane Austen and opened to the bookmarked page in *Pride and Prejudice*. It was her second time reading the novel, though she'd watched the films and PBS miniseries several times, which helped her to better understand the characters' personalities. Cherie had chosen *Pride and Prejudice* when Kayana's choice would've been *Mansfield Park*, because in that book Austen's characters were not only more complex, but she had also explored the issues of slavery and adultery. However, she never tired reading or watching movies about the five Bennet sisters' searches for wealthy husbands not based on love but for economic and social prestige.

Afternoon shadows lengthened, forcing her to flick on the table lamp, and she continued to turn pages until she got a text from Derrick telling her he had set aside a serving of lasagna for her dinner. Closing the book, Kayana went down the staircase to the kitchen to get a bowl of mixed greens tossed with vinaigrette and a plate with lasagna. The minifridge in the apartment was stocked with bottled water, juice, and wine. Once she'd transformed the second-story space from storage to living quarters, she'd thought about installing a kitchen, but changed her mind when she realized she always had access to the restaurant's kitchen. The tub was removed from the bathroom to make space for a washer and dryer.

Flicking on the television, she settled down to eat dinner and watch an all-news cable channel. Derrick hadn't lost his touch. The lasagna was delicious.

Kayana alighted from her car, carrying an oversized shopping bag filled with the items Graeme needed for his cooking lesson. She smiled when she saw him standing in the doorway awaiting her arrival. His hair had grown out of the military cut; the gray-flecked ends were beginning to curl over the tops of his ears, while he appeared totally relaxed in a pair of jeans, a gray faded Harvard T-shirt, and running shoes.

He lowered his head and pressed a kiss to her cheek. "Please come in."

Kayana smiled up at him. "Thank you." She handed him the shopping bag. "Everything you'll need for your lesson is in that bag." She'd called him before leaving the restaurant to tell him to take the chicken out of the fridge to bring it to room temperature.

Graeme closed and locked the door. "Do you plan to grade me?"

"Of course." She glanced around her. "Where's Barley?"

"He's upstairs napping. The minute he realizes there's someone else in the house he'll be down. But he won't approach you if you're the in kitchen."

"Is he allowed in the kitchen?"

"No, because I don't want him to get into the habit of begging for table food. The kitchen and my bedroom are off-limits. Otherwise, he has the run of the house."

Kayana followed Graeme across the open floor plan to the kitchen. The carefully chosen furnishings reminded her of layouts in decorating magazines with monochromatic colors of gray and blue. Off-white and navy-blue area rugs in the living and family rooms complemented the dark-gray plank flooring.

"Your home is beautiful."

Graeme glanced over his shoulder. "Thank you, but I can't take credit for anything you see. I hired a decorator and told her I didn't want the space to appear overcrowded with a lot of furniture."

The woman had done an incredible job creating a minimalist ambience that allowed the space to appear larger than it actually was. A large flat-screen TV above a working fire-place was the focal point in the family room. There wasn't a speck of dust anywhere, and Kayana wondered if Graeme had someone clean his house; if not, he was a neat freak.

Graeme set the bag on a stool at the cooking island, and then picked up his cellphone and tapped a button. The melodious sound of a classical guitar filled the space. "If you don't like the music choice, I can always change it to something more upbeat."

"Please don't," she said quickly. "It's very soothing."

"I don't believe you brought this for me," he said when he removed an apron with COOK IN TRAINING stamped on the bib. "Where did you find this?" He smiled and a network of fine lines fanned out around his gray eyes.

"I ordered it online and indicated next-day shipping."

"Thank you. I really like it." Reaching into the bag, he took out a roasting pan with a rack, a box of disposable gloves, jars of herbs and spices, a plastic bag of cubed white bread, a yellow onion, several cloves of garlic, a ball of butcher twine, and a jar of chicken stock. "I feel like Santa with a magic bag that never gets empty," he teased as he removed a bag of romaine, bottles of olive oil, red wine vinegar, lemon juice, Worcestershire sauce, a jar of anchovy paste, a container of sour cream, grated Parmesan cheese, and a bag of rice. "This is a lot of stuff for one chicken."

"Chicken dinner," Kayana countered, correcting him. "Your first attempt will be a chicken with herb stuffing. Once you master this, you should be able to roast a turkey."

"Do you really think I'll be able to roast a turkey?"

"Of course, Graeme. The bird may be larger, but the preparation is the same. By the way, do you like stuffing or dressing?"

"What's the difference?"

"Stuffing is cooked inside the bird, and dressing is outside."

"I prefer stuffing."

Kayana pointed to the roaster in a platter on the granite countertop. "I'm going to wash the chicken and remove the giblets. Then I'll show you how to stuff, truss, and season the bird. Meanwhile, I'd like you to preheat the oven to three-fifty."

"Should I also program the timer?"

"The roaster looks to be between four and five pounds, so set it for seventy-five minutes."

Graeme gave her an incredulous stare. "You can tell how large the chicken is just by looking at it?"

She removed a pair of gloves from the box and slipped them on. "When you've seen as many chickens as I have over the years, you'll be able to estimate their weight just by eye-balling them."

Kayana sat across the table from Graeme in the dining area, enjoying the meal they'd prepared together. She'd found him a quick study and complimented him when he was able to follow and duplicate her instructions. Her gaze lingered on Barley, who lay on the area rug in the family room.

"You're a natural when it comes to cooking rice," she said. "The first time I attempted it, the grains were so sticky they could've been used for sushi."

Graeme chewed and swallowed a mouthful of salad. "How long did it take for you to perfect cooking it?"

The skin around her eyes crinkled in a smile. "Too long. My mother warned me if I ruined one more pot of rice, she was going to ban me from the kitchen. The next time was the charm once I was able to gauge the tenderness of the grains before draining the water, lowering the flame, covering the pot, and just letting it steam until fluffy. Different cultures prepare rice differently, but I've never been able to cook a pot of rice where I don't drain the water."

Graeme touched the corners of his mouth with a napkin. "I wasn't much of a rice eater until I traveled to countries where rice was a staple. I'm even surprised that Southerners prefer it to potatoes."

"That's because African slaves had the knowledge to drain swamps and cultivate the crop that has come to be known as Carolina gold. Rice planters were able to become as wealthy as cotton planters."

"It's unconscionable that people felt it was their right to own another human being."

Kayana was slightly taken aback when she registered derision in Graeme's voice. "You say that because you're a Northerner. There are still some Southerners who believe there was nothing wrong with slavery because the Bible says the darker race will be their slaves."

"That's bullshit, Kayana! They swear to love God, whom they've never seen, yet hate their fellowman whom they see every day. I'm just not buying it."

Her expression did not change with his explosive outburst. "You sound as if you're a descendant from a family of Yankee abolitionists."

Graeme lowered his eyes as lines of tension tightened his mouth. "I can't say who my ancestors were," he said so softly she had to strain to hear.

"You were adopted." The query came out as a statement.

He nodded. "Yes. My birth mother was a college student who'd had an affair with a married man and decided to give me up for adoption."

Kayana listened, transfixed, as Graeme told her about how his fortysomething, college-professor parents, who were unable to have children of their own, adopted him with the proviso they would never reveal the name of the birth mother. His adopted mother took a break from teaching until he was of school age and then returned as an adjunct. His childhood was remarkable, with his parents taking him with them when they went abroad every summer. By the time he was twelve, he'd traveled to six of the seven continents. His father, who had come from working-class Bostonians, met and married a fellow student, unaware that she was an heiress. Her family had made its fortune shipping goods from the States to Europe, before they diversified and invested in railroad travel.

"Her Brahman family would not have approved of her marrying someone who was not only not of their social class but also a Catholic, so they eloped. Patrick Ogden had no idea how much his bride was worth until she took him to Newburyport to meet his in-laws. While in college, she'd shared a cramped apartment with two other girls."

"How did Patrick react to discovering he'd married a wealthy woman?"

"He was very angry and wanted to annul the marriage, but Lauren lied and told him she was pregnant."

Resting her elbow on the table, she cradled her chin on the palm of her hand. "I thought you said they couldn't have children."

A hint of a smile lifted the corners of Graeme's mouth for the first time since talking about his parents. "Mother was the one who couldn't have a child. After she passed away, I found her diaries and read that she'd had an affair with the family chauffeur and gotten pregnant. The man took her to someone who performed illegal abortions, and she wound up with an infection that left her with scarring on her fallopian tubes. Her parents never suspected that their very precocious daughter had undergone an abortion or had a penchant for blue-collar men. Her parents finally came around when they believed they were going to become grandparents and welcomed Patrick into the family."

"It's not that easy to fake a pregnancy, Graeme."

"Lauren was aware of that. She waited until she was supposedly two months along to announce it was a false alarm, and that she and Patrick would put off having a family until after they completed their graduate studies."

Kayana's eyebrows lifted slightly. "To say your mother was a shrewd woman is an understatement."

"She was more devious, if you ask me, because she went

after whatever she wanted and damn the consequences. She wanted Patrick Ogden, and she got him. She wanted a child, and she adopted me. As her parents' sole heir, she inherited the house in Newburyport, its contents, and their assets. And as my parents' only child, I am the recipient of everything they owned."

"You're wealthy."

He smiled. "I'm comfortable."

"Comfortably rich," she countered.

"Just say I don't have to rely on my teacher's salary to make ends meet."

"Not only are you wealthy, but you grew up privileged."

"I'll admit we had a live-in chef, housekeepers, and a caretaker, but that didn't make me any different from the other kids I grew up with."

Her smile matched his. "Don't be so modest, Graeme. Either you are or you aren't."

"I am."

"Now, was that so difficult to admit?"

"No. But it's not something I advertise."

"Is it because you don't want women coming on to you for your money?"

Graeme pressed his palms together, bringing them to his mouth. The seconds ticked as he gave her a direct, lingering stare. "Lately, I haven't had much time for romance."

Kayana did not know what to make of his admission as to his involvement with women. "Oh, I see."

"Do you really, Kay?"

"What are you talking about?

"I don't have time for any woman except for the one sitting across from me. What's the matter?" he taunted. "Cat's got your tongue."

She recovered quickly from his jibe. "What if I tell you that I'm not interested. I don't want or need your money because I managed to do quite well when I divorced my wealthy trauma-surgeon husband."

Graeme blinked slowly. "Why did you divorce him?"

Kayana's eyes hardened, as did her expression. "He cheated on me with one of his colleagues."

"That's tacky. I don't believe in shitting where I have to eat."

"I'm of the same belief, but that didn't stop my ex, who would invite her to our home whenever we hosted a gathering. The two-faced heifer smiled in my face, while at the same time she was sneaking around and sleeping with my husband."

"Well, damn!"

"I'm over it, Graeme. They can have each other."

"Are you really, Kay?"

A shiver of annoyance eddied through her when she realized Graeme didn't believe her. "Yes. I'm a forty-six-year-old divorcée with a postgraduate degree in social work and two decades of experience, which makes me a marketable prospect. I don't want to get married again after conceding twenty years of my life to a man who did not value my love or respect me as his wife and partner. Which leaves me with the option of sleeping with whatever man I want without the fear of becoming pregnant even if we happen to engage in unprotected sex. And even if I was able to have a child, I'm too old to even consider becoming a mother. I say all that to let you know that what happened in the past stays in the past."

Lowering his hands, Graeme inclined his head. "Good for you."

"How about you?" Kayana questioned. "Have you let go of your past?"

A beat passed. "It has taken a while—but yes."

"Good for you." Pushing back her chair, she stood, Graeme rising with her. "It's getting late, so I'm going to help you clean up before I leave."

"Don't bother, Kay. You've done enough. I'll clean up."

"Are you sure?"

"Of course, I'm sure. I do know how to keep house. My

father insisted I learn to make a bed and clean up after myself regardless of how much I had. Although he'd married a wealthy woman and was highly educated, he still couldn't rid himself of his blue-collar mentality."

"There's nothing wrong with being working-class, Graeme."

"If I thought there was, I never would've become a public high school math teacher."

Rounding the table, Kayana went on tiptoe and kissed Graeme's jaw. Startled by the gesture, he turned his head, and his mouth brushed hers. The joining was mere seconds, but it was long enough for her to acknowledge she'd missed being kissed by a man.

He pulled back as if stabbed by a sharp object. "I'm sorry about that."

A mysterious smile softened Kayana's mouth as she winked at him. "I'm not. Good night, Graeme." Turning on her heel, she walked to the door, Barley trotting after her. She stopped, leaned down, and scratched him behind the ears. "You be a good boy for your daddy."

"Wait, Kay!" Graeme called out. "I'll walk you to your car."

She waved a hand over her head without turning around. "It's okay. I don't believe I'll get lost between here and the driveway."

"Text me when you get home to let me know you're safe."

Kayana stopped. "No, Graeme. I stopped checking in the day I left this island to go to college. Good night."

Graeme cursed under his breath when Kayana closed the door, leaving him staring at where she'd been. He'd made a serious faux pas. How could he have forgotten that she was a mature, independent woman who only had to answer to herself, and not Jillian, who despite her age, had never matured. He had loved her so much that he'd overlooked how needy she'd been. He hadn't become her husband but her father. At first, the need to protect her fed his ego, but after a while, her childlike behavior had begun to emotionally wear him down.

Barley came over and sat at his feet. "Do you know what, buddy? I've been dealing with the wrong women for so long that I don't know how to relate to one who's not looking for or needs a man to take care of her." Barley barked loudly. "Yeah, I know. Sometimes we dudes can do and say some dumb things, but the solution is not to repeat it."

His confidence returned when he recalled his apologizing for inadvertently kissing her; however, she didn't seem remotely bothered by it. And he hoped beyond hope that she enjoyed it as much as he did.

"I'll take you out after I clean up," he told the puppy.

Graeme made quick work of clearing the table. His first cooking lesson was a rousing success because everything was scrumptious. And he had enough leftovers to last for several days, which meant he could stay in and write. He knew he wouldn't be able to exhale and relax until he'd completed and submitted the book. Then he planned to take a month off, doing absolutely nothing, before beginning the next one. What he had to decide was whether to remain on the island or return to Massachusetts for the winter. He wasn't a snowbird because he liked cold weather and the change of seasons, but he had time to finalize his plans before the end of the year.

Chapter 11

Kayana hadn't realized how tense she'd been since leaving Graeme's house until she walked into Leah's rental. Images of what they had discussed lingered with her during her waking moments. And his kissing her and her reaction to the pressure of his mouth on hers seeped into her erotic dreams, where her body betrayed her, and she woke gasping from the aftermath of multiple orgasms. She could not and did not want to sleep with Graeme and use him to assuage the dearth of sexual fulfillment she'd experienced since she'd decided to end her marriage.

She asked herself over and over why she had agreed to accompany him to the movies and what had possessed her to give him cooking lessons, and the same answer came up every time—empathy and gratitude.

Then, his sending her a plant to thank her for going out with him was something she hadn't experienced with any other man. The men she'd dated thought she should've been grateful that they'd asked her out, and some of them would send her flowers for her birthday or take her to dinner for a special occasion, but nothing beyond that. James had thought of her as a challenge, and once he married her, she had become his trophy. It wasn't the cost of the jade plant, but the thought behind it when Graeme thanked her for agreeing to go out with him.

And when he'd talked about his parents, she was able to put on the professional face she'd used when counseling patients. Her gaze never wavered when they disclosed events in their lives that made her want to weep with and for them. There was no doubt that Graeme's adopted mother was not only used to getting what she wanted; she was also quite manipulative, and Kayana wondered if it had been a trait her son had unconsciously adopted.

She could not fathom how a woman who knew she couldn't have children would fake a pregnancy and then concoct a story to get out of it. It was apparent that Graeme's father was either totally unaware of the flaw in his wife's devious personality or chose to ignore it. Graeme wasn't her patient, so she did not want to question him about his feelings once he read his mother's diaries. Had he thought ill of her, or did he forgive her because she'd afforded him a life he would not have had if other parents with more modest means had adopted him?

It had been a week since she last saw Leah, and she had to admit that the woman looked well. Her face was fuller, and it was obvious she had gotten some sun because her fair complexion had taken on a rosy hue. A profusion of freckles covered her bare arms under an orange tank top she'd paired with white slim jeans. Today she'd brushed her hair off her face and secured it in a ponytail.

Leah opened the door wider. "Please come in. Cherie is in the kitchen blending margaritas."

Kayana pressed her cheek to Leah's cool one. "It's a good thing we only meet once a week or I would be too tipsy to get up the next morning."

"I'm glad we decided to end the meeting at nine, because if it went on any longer, we wouldn't be able to get up the next day."

Kayana wanted to remind Leah that she could always sleep in late, while she had to get down to the kitchen at 5:00 a.m. to begin cooking in order to have everything ready for 7:00, when the restaurant opened for business. She sniffed the air. "I smell cilantro."

"You've got a good nose. We're having Mexican food today."

"You cooked?"

"Yes. And don't look so shocked. I do know how to cook."

"Okay, Martha Stewart," Kayana teased.

Looping her arm through Kayana's, Leah led her through the living/dining area to the rear of the house and a patio, where she'd set up a table with plates and bowls filled with spicy salsas, empanadas, hard and soft beef, chicken, and shrimp tacos, quesadillas, guacamole, and crispy tortilla chips.

"Wow!"

"That's what I said when I saw this spread," Cherie told Kayana as she emptied a blender of margaritas into a chilled pitcher. "It looks as if Red wants to give you a run for your money when it comes to burning pots."

Leah blushed. "That's not going to happen. There's no way I can begin to cook like Kayana."

"Don't sell yourself short, Leah. If you're good, then own it."

"Word!" drawled Cherie. "I'm not going to lie and say I can even come close to putting something like this together, so my contribution will have to be store-bought."

Kayana shook her head. "That's where I draw the line. I'm not going to buy food from deli or gourmet shops when I can make it myself."

"I agree," Leah said. "Come, let's eat and drink before we talk about the Bennet sisters and their quest to find husbands."

Cherie filled margarita glasses with the icy, pale-green concoction. "I'd like to make a toast to celebrate the second meeting of the Seaside Café book club." The women took turns touching glasses before taking a sip.

"Damn!"

"Shit!"

Kayana and Leah had chorused in unison.

"Don't tell me y'all going to punk out on me," Cherie said, laughing. "Y'all supposed to be grown folks, and so I decided to make a grown-folk drink. Now, if you want fruit punch, then I'll bring it the next time we get together."

Leah blew out a breath. "I am grown, but if I keep drinking this, then I doubt whether I won't be blind, crippled, or crazy tomorrow."

"Let it sit for a while so the ice can dilute it," Kayana suggested. She made a sucking sound with her tongue and teeth. "And I can't believe y'all were complaining about my sour apple martinis."

Leah pointed to the pitcher. "This stuff is as lethal as napalm."

"It's a good thing your husband isn't around, or you would jump his bones," Cherie teased.

"I'd rather cut his throat," Leah said under her breath. "Don't look at me like that," she said when Kayana and Cherie stared at her. "I can't wait for the son of a bitch to die so I can finally live my life."

Kayana took another sip of the cocktail, grimacing when the icy liquid slid down the back of her throat. "You do know that you have options other than murder."

Leah's blue eyes narrowed as she stared down at the contents in the glass. "He would never give me a divorce."

Cherie set her glass down on a coaster on the table. "How do you know that?"

"Alan would make certain to drag it out so long that I'd probably just give in and stay with him."

"Don't you have a brother or some thug trailer-park cousins who would be willing to fuck him up if you gave them money," Cherie said, deadpan. "That's what some of the thugs in my family would do for me if I told them some dude was abusing me."

The natural color drained from Leah's face, leaving it a sickly sallow shade. "I've never told anyone in my family what goes on between me and Alan."

A slight frown creased Kayana's forehead. "Why keep it a secret?"

"Because I don't give a fuck what Alan does as long as he doesn't bother me."

"What about your sons, Leah?" Cherie asked.

"Aron and Caleb worship the ground their father walks on, and I don't want to do anything to change their opinion of him."

Kayana went completely still. "You named your sons after John Steinbeck's twin characters from *East of Eden*?"

Leah nodded. "Yes. It's my overall favorite of Steinbeck's work, and when I discovered I was having twins, I knew what I wanted to name them."

"What did your husband say?" Cherie questioned.

"He thought I'd gotten them from the Bible and not from a book of fiction."

Cherie shook her head. "The poor dumb fuck."

"That's what I said," Leah agreed, "when he told me they were good strong, masculine names for his sons. If I keep drinking this nitroglycerine and don't eat something, I'll wind up on my hind parts."

Kayana also reached for a plate and began filling it with tacos, an empanada, guacamole, and tortilla chips. After biting into the flaky dough of the empanada, she had to give Leah high marks on her cooking. The woman truly had skills in the culinary department. "If you come down here next year and want to help out in the restaurant, I'll put in a good word with Derrick for you."

Leah's eyes lit up like a child's on Christmas morning. "Really!"

"Yes, really."

Cherie emitted an unladylike snort. "Then she can ogle your brother all she wants until she goes blind."

Leah's eyes appeared abnormally large when she glared at Cherie. "You had no right to say that."

Kayana felt Leah's pain as if it was her own. "Cut the shit, Cherie. I'm not going to sit here and allow Leah to become your personal punching bag."

Cherie rounded on Kayana. "Why do you always feel you have to take up for her?"

Kayana clenched her teeth so tightly that her jaw ached. She liked Cherie, but she couldn't understand her resentment of Leah. "I'm sick and tired of your hostility because some white man did you wrong. You're not some teenage girl who can't get over the man who took her virginity and then married someone else."

"That's exactly what the bastard did!" Cherie spat out.

She fell back in the chair, slumping like a deflated balloon. If Cherie was in her early thirties, then she probably had had a long-term relationship with her lover. It was no wonder she was angry and resentful. "I'm sorry." Her apology sounded trite, even to Kayana's ears.

Leah stood up, rounded the table, and eased Cherie up to stand. Wrapping her arms around her shoulders, she pulled her close. "It's okay, baby girl," she whispered in Cherie's ear. "You're not going to feel better until you cry and let it all out."

Kayana watched the interchange between Leah and Cherie and knew instinctually Cherie wasn't ready to let go of her rage. Pain and anger couldn't be shrugged off like slipping out of a pair of too-tight shoes after standing in them for hours. It was a process—a very slow process—until one day you woke and decided you've had enough.

Cherie struggled out of Leah's embrace. "I'm okay."

Kayana wanted to tell her she wasn't okay and wouldn't be until she sought a professional to help her achieve closure.

"I'm okay, and I promise this is the last time I'll go off on you."

Leah smiled. "Not to worry. I'm not that thin-skinned."

Picking up her glass, Cherie took a long swallow. "I think I need to get laid."

"You're not the only one," Leah said in agreement. "I can't remember the last time I had a cock inside me."

Kayana's mouth gaped with Leah's pronouncement. She didn't expect her to be so explicit when talking about her sex life. She'd noticed the lowering of inhibitions once they'd begun drinking, in Cherie's case in particular. Perhaps she mused, at the next meeting they should serve mocktails.

Leah retook her seat. "What about you, Kayana? When was the last time you slept with a man?"

"More than a couple of years ago."

Cherie sat down and massaged the back of her neck. "It's been longer than that for me."

Kayana realized her friends were not interested in discussing *Pride and Prejudice* but wanted to air their personal gripes. She was willing to go along with them if it meant they would eventually focus on discussing books.

"What if we scrap today's book discussion and talk about whatever we want," she suggested.

"I'm game," Cherie said.

"So am I," Leah agreed. "Is there anything we can't talk about, Kayana?"

"No. After all, we are grown."

Not discussing the book appeared to take some pressure off everyone as they ate, drank, and talked about everything from their childhood, the time they lost their virginity, and the friends they'd made in college. Kayana ate more than she drank once she began to feel the effects of the tequila.

"Kayana, how did you meet your husband?" Leah asked.

"I was completing my internship at the hospital where he was a trauma surgeon when he asked me out. I gave him a hard time because I didn't believe in office romances. Needless to say, he wore me down, and I finally agreed to have dinner with him. The first time we slept together, I knew I wanted to spend the rest of my life with him."

"Was the sex that good?" Cherie asked.

Kayana smiled. "The only thing I'm going to say is it was the best I'd ever had at that time."

"Have you slept with anyone since you've been divorced?"

It was Leah's turn to question her love life, or lack of it. "No."

"Don't you get horny?"

"Not really."

She didn't want to tell Leah a recent erotic dream had kickstarted her libido, and she was unable to ignore the slight pulsing in her nether region that occurred when she least expected it. She did not want to believe that the slight brush of Graeme's mouth against hers had triggered a desire she'd thought long dead.

Cherie popped a tortilla chip with a glob of guacamole into her mouth, moaning under her breath as she chewed and then swallowed it. "Wow, that's so good. Leah, I know you told us your husband has had affairs, but did you ever have one?"

A mysterious smile tilted the corners of the redhead's mouth. "Yes. With my reliable vibrators. I have several in different colors, sizes, and speeds. My go-to one is the rabbit with a three-speed rotating shaft that's guaranteed to make me climax."

Cherie grimaced. "I can't imagine putting a foreign object in my body to pleasure myself."

"Don't knock it if you haven't tried it," Kayana said.

"You've used a vibrator?" Leah asked.

"A few times," she admitted. "I was in grad school and not dating anyone, so I bought one and tried it out. It was okay, but I prefer a real penis to a fake one. I've been celibate for more than two years, and right now, I'm on the fence about whether I should buy one." She didn't want to tell her friends that desire had resurfaced and she needed something to assuage it.

Leah smiled at Kayana. "Since you're not sleeping with

anyone, I'll text you the specs on my rabbit. You'll have to let me know if you like it. Better yet, I'll order one and give it to you as a gift." Leah turned to look at Cherie. "Should I order one for you, too?"

Cherie waved her hand. "No, thank you."

Leah shrugged her shoulders. "Suit yourself."

"Do you know what I don't understand about you, Leah?"

"What, Cherie?"

"You know your husband is or has been having affairs for years, yet you've remained faithful to his cheating ass."

"I symbolically divorced my husband a long time ago. And now that we've had separate bedrooms for ten years, I merely tolerate his wrinkled old ass. A couple of months ago, I saw him naked and I almost barfed. He needed to be fitted for a bra, his behind looked like cottage cheese, and his droopy balls were at least five inches lower than his shriveled little cock."

Clapping a hand over her mouth, Kayana laughed until tears rolled down her face at the same time Cherie doubled over in hysterics. She wanted to tell Leah it wasn't nice to talk about the man like that, but held her tongue. When she'd suggested they not discuss books, she hadn't known it was going to turn into a man-hating session.

Kayana didn't hate men, not even her ex. His cheating had given her the excuse she needed to get out of the marriage. There were a few times when she was tempted to send James's mistress a gift basket with a note thanking her for taking him off her hands.

Reaching over, she patted Cherie's back as she hiccuped. "Take a deep breath."

Pushing back her chair, Leah stood up. "I'm going inside to get some water."

"I think I'm all right now," Cherie whispered. She sounded as if she'd run a grueling race. "I'm a very visual person, and I almost lost my shit when Leah described her husband's body."

Kayana nodded. "Underneath her so-called prim and proper demeanor is a homegirl of a lighter hue."

Cherie nodded. "Leah and I have a lot in common. She lived in a trailer park, while I grew up in public housing."

"You both were luckier than a lot of folks because you were able to make it out. I've counseled a lot of women who are third- and even fourth-generation public housing because that's all they know. I once had a twenty-one-year-old client who was a single mother with six kids from four different men. She, her mother, grandmother, and great-grandmother all lived in public housing, and she loved it."

Cherie sobered. "That sounds familiar. My mother had my brother when she was fifteen and me at eighteen. She waited until she was thirty to give birth to twin boys, and whenever we ask who our fathers are, she turns deaf and mute. And what I find amazing is that no one has ever seen her with a man, so she had to be sleeping with someone in another town or city."

"Do you suspect you and your siblings have the same father?"

"No, because none of us look alike."

"Do you keep in touch with your mother?"

"Not in person. She'll call me and ask for money, and I usually send it to her. A couple of months ago, I sent her half of what she wanted because I knew I was going on leave without pay, and she cussed like I was a stranger in the street. I let her have her say, and then told her if she needed money, she should go and look for her baby daddies and hit them up. I hung up, and that was the last time we spoke to each other. Don't get me wrong, Kayana, I love my mother, but I refuse to support her when she refuses to help herself. My mother has a GED, is very articulate, but she's not motivated to improve herself. I've tried to get her to move out of the projects, but she claims she doesn't want to leave her friends."

"Change can be traumatic for some people, Cherie, because they fear the unknown."

"I know that firsthand from when I left the projects to enroll in prep school. It took months before I felt confident enough to speak up in class. I didn't have the pedigree of the other students, but I was able to hold my own academically."

"One of these days you'll learn that having money will not necessarily solve your problems."

Cherie laughed. "Now you sound like Biggie Smalls when he sang about 'Mo Money, Mo Problems.' "

"I'm a . . ." Kayana's words trailed off when Leah returned with a tray with glasses and a pitcher of ice-cold water.

"What did I miss?"

"Not much," Cherie said. "I managed to get over my laughing fit. Whether you know it or not, sometimes you're funny as hell."

Leah set the tray on the table and filled three goblets with water. "I've learned if I don't laugh, then I'll end up crying. And let me tell you that I cry really ugly. My face gets all red and blotchy, while my eyes swell and look like slits. Believe you me, it's not a good look."

Because this meeting was different from their first, when they'd discussed *Kindred*, Kayana was beginning to bond with Cherie and Leah beyond their love of books; now she realized they were more similar than dissimilar. And because they were willing to openly talk about any and everything without fear of being censored, they were confident about making their opinions known. The meeting concluded an hour early with a promise to meet the following Sunday, and *Pride and Prejudice* was still on the agenda for discussion.

Kayana dropped Cherie at the boardinghouse and then returned to the restaurant, where she put up a load of laundry before turning in for the night.

Blurry-eyed, Graeme walked out of his study on shaking legs to his bedroom and fell facedown across the bed. He couldn't believe he'd spent the past two days writing nonstop, though he had been forced to take a break to shower, change his clothes, let Barley out, and drink copious cups of black coffee to stay alert.

He was at least six weeks ahead of the contractual deadline, and if he stayed the course, he could expect to submit the manuscript in late August. He knew he'd pushed himself to keep from thinking about Kayana. He'd tried to convince himself that he didn't want to sleep with her, but that was a lie. Graeme had asked himself over and over what was there about Kayana that drew him to her, and he still hadn't come up with an answer.

Cooking with her was an experience he wanted to repeat again and again. Kayana was patient, and her tone never changed when she'd corrected him for failing to follow her instructions. Even when he'd attempted to apologize, she reassured him that he'd exceeded her expectations. Not only was she easy to work with; she was also easy to talk to. However, he'd found her to be an anomaly because of her directness. She was the first woman with whom he'd interacted who'd made it known she wasn't looking for a man to take care of her; she did not want to remarry; and she had relegated her past to the past.

Kayana had put her past behind her, while he was still struggling to come to terms with his. Discovering and reading his mother's diaries had dramatically changed his impression of her. He still loved Lauren Norris Ogden, but her entries allowed him to understand why she'd done or not done things that hadn't made sense to him. She'd grown up spoiled, privileged, and doted upon by her adoring father, and was used to getting whatever she desired.

Memories of his unconventional marriage continued to haunt him because he'd been willing to do anything and everything to save his marriage, despite the power struggle between him and his mother-in-law.

Groaning, he managed to get out of bed and undress. Every

bone in his body ached as if he'd run a marathon. Graeme had
lost track of time when he crawled into bed and fell into a
deep, dreamless sleep after showering and brushing his teeth.

A buzzing sound penetrated his foggy brain, and he'd believed an insect had gotten into the room when he'd opened
the sliding doors leading to the second-story veranda. But the
sound continued until he realized he'd programmed his cellphone to vibrate. He reached over and picked up the phone
without looking at the screen.

"Yes." His greeting came out in a croaking sound.

"Graeme?"

Pushing himself into a sitting position, he pressed his back
against the mound of pillows cradling his shoulders. He
swallowed a groan. Every bone in his body ached, probably
from sitting in the same position for hours hunched over a
keyboard.

"Kay."

"Are you all right?"

He registered a thread of concern in her voice. "I think so."

"You think so. You sound terrible."

He ran a hand over his mussed hair. "My throat feels a little raw."

"Who were you yelling at?"

Graeme smiled. "No one. Right now, I feel as if I've gone a
couple of rounds with an MMA fighter."

"Are you certain you're not coming down with something?"

"I never get sick."

"There's always the first time, Graeme."

Closing his eyes, he inhaled a deep breath, held it, let it out
slowly, and suddenly experienced a wave of light-headedness.
"You're right."

"What am I right about, Graeme?"

"That I'm coming down with something."

"Do have anything in the house for a cold or the flu?"

"No. I'll have to go out and buy something."

"Don't bother. I have some here. I'll be over in about fifteen minutes. Unlock your door and then get into bed."

"You don't have to do that, Kay."

"Don't argue with me, Graeme. I don't want you sick so you'll have an excuse not to take me to the movies."

He smiled. "Is that all you need me for?" Graeme teased. "To take you to the movies?"

"If not you, then I'll find another man."

His smile faded, his expression becoming a mask of stone. "That's not going to happen."

"Hang up, and unlock the door."

The phone went dead, and Graeme realized Kayana had abruptly hung up on him. Moving slowly, he managed to get out of bed, slip into a pair of briefs and shorts and make his way down the staircase. Barley met him as he walked to the front door. He disarmed the alarm, unlocked the door, and then opened the rear door to let the dog out. A light rain was beginning to fall, which prompted Barley not to linger, and he quickly raced back inside.

Holding onto the railing, Graeme pulled himself up the staircase to the second story. He'd just brushed his teeth and washed his face when he heard Barley's excited barking and assumed Kayana had arrived. An expletive slipped out when his knees nearly buckled as he returned to the bedroom, stepped out of the shorts, fell across the bed, and closed his eyes. What the hell had he contracted that made him as helpless as a newborn?

"You look like shit!"

Graeme opened his eyes to find Kayana looming over him. "Good morning, beautiful."

Chapter 12

Kayana managed to conceal her shock when she saw the dark circles under Graeme's sunken eyes. He hadn't shaved, and his hair looked as if he'd combed it with his fingers. She could not imagine what had triggered the change in his appearance since she last saw him.

"It's the afternoon. And I thought I told you to get into bed, not on it."

"I feel like shit."

"That's because you're sick, Graeme."

Setting her tote on the padded bench at the foot of the California-king bed, Kayana smoothed back the sheet, fluffed up pillows, and pulled the top sheet and lightweight blanket over Graeme's body. She suspected he'd either come down with a summer cold or a virus.

"I'm going to take your temperature before I give you something." She took a small case labeled FIRST AID out of the tote and placed a digital thermometer under his tongue until it emitted a beeping sound. Kayana removed the thermometer. "You have a slight fever," she said.

Graeme closed his eyes again. "I'm never sick."

"You have a fever of ninety-nine point eight, which means you're not well, Graeme. By the way, when was the last time you ate?"

"I don't remember."

"You don't remember? What have you been doing since I last saw you?"

"Writing."

Kayana could not believe what she'd just heard. She could not imagine Graeme writing so much that he'd forgotten to eat. "After I give you a dose of cold and flu medication, I'm going to see if I can put together something for you to eat."

Graeme opened his eyes, and she noticed they were dark and glassy. "Why are you doing this for me?"

She smiled. "Don't you know, Graeme?" she asked, answering his question with one of her own.

"No."

Kayana rested her hand against his graying stubble. "Because I like you." She hadn't lied to Graeme, because she'd come to like him more than she wanted to. He possessed qualities she'd looked for and admired in a man, but more importantly, she'd made Graeme aware that she wasn't interested in anything that would lead to a commitment. He would close up his house and leave Coates Island before the Labor Day weekend to return to Massachusetts to teach, while she would remain behind to work less, bond with her niece, and take time off to vacation at an all-inclusive resort.

She measured the recommended dose into the small plastic cup and watched as Graeme swallowed it as he screwed up his face. "That's nasty."

"I'll bring you some water and leave it by the bed. I'm also going to go through your refrigerator and see what I can make for you to eat." He caught her wrist as she turned to leave. "What is it?"

He attempted to smile, but it looked more like a grimace. "I like you, too."

Kayana patted the hand holding hers captive. "I've known that for a while."

Sandy-brown eyebrows shot up. "Really?"

She eased her hand from his loose grip. "Yes, really. You're not very subtle when you stare at me."

"That's because I happen to like what I'm staring at."

Shaking her head, she laughed softly. "I don't believe you."

"What don't you believe?"

"You attempting to sweet-talk me even though you can barely stand up."

"It's a good thing I can't stand up, because I want to do more to you than just sweet-talk."

Kayana knew he wanted to make love to her, and she also wanted the same thing. They were mature adults who did not have to play head games as to what they wanted. She'd consciously rejected every man who'd seemed remotely interested in her when she was married and after her divorce. Although she'd worn a wedding band, that hadn't stopped some men from coming on to her, because they knew she wasn't in a position to make demands on them. After all, she did have a husband, and what James failed to understand or realize was that she'd had more opportunities than he'd had to have affairs. First, she wasn't able to get pregnant, and second, she definitely would've been a lot more discreet than he could ever be. And unlike him, she would've never invited her lover to her home, even under the guise of a social gathering.

"That's something we'll deal with once you're better," she said, smiling.

"Is that a promise, Kay?"

She nodded. "Yes."

Graeme felt himself drift in and out of sleep, and when he was awake, he remembered Kayana sitting in bed with him while spooning chicken soup into his mouth. Then he recalled her waking him again to give him another dose of medication after he'd managed to make it to the bathroom on his own to relieve himself. The next time he woke, it was to find that night had blanketed the island.

"Feeling better?" Kayana's voice came from somewhere in the bedroom.

"Yes. What time is it?" His voice was still hoarse.

"It's after midnight."

"And you're still here?"

"Yes. I wanted to make certain your temperature didn't go any higher. It went down to ninety-nine."

"I don't remember you taking it."

"That's because you were sleeping."

"How long are you staying?"

"I'll leave around five. I have to get back to fix breakfast. I'll come back sometime in the afternoon to check in on you. Meanwhile, I've taken care of Barley. I'll let him out before I leave and give him clean water."

"How can I thank you for everything?"

"Just get well."

"Do you intend to sleep on that chaise for the rest of the night?"

"It's comfortable enough. And I found a throw in the linen closet, so I'm good."

Rising on an elbow, Graeme stared at the darkened corner where Kayana lay on the chaise. "There's enough room in the bed for the two of us to sleep side by side."

"No, Graeme. You're still contagious, and I can't afford to get sick at this time of the year."

"Can't your brother fill in for you if you do get sick?"

"He can, but it would be hard for him to put in sixteen hours a day for any extended length of time."

"How many hours do you work?"

"On average eight to nine. I begin preparing breakfast around five and shut down at ten. Then I stay to make the sides for lunch and dinner. Usually, I'm finished around one or two in the afternoon. Derrick will come in around ten and work until nine or ten at night. This summer he hired a retired short-order cook to help him."

"What about in the off-season?"

"We only serve one meal a day. A buffet lunch from ten a.m. to two p.m. Monday through Saturday. Sunday is our day off."

Graeme quickly computed the months. "So, you work long hours for three months, then you're able to relax for the next nine months of the year. That's a nice adjustment."

"I think so."

"Do you get many snowbirds during the winter months?"

"No. Many of the local residents look forward to the off-season to get their island back. They appreciate the money they can make renting their properties, but in reality, they resent having to share the beach with vacationers. You'll realize that once you decide to retire here permanently."

"That's something I'm looking forward to."

"How old are you, Graeme?"

"Fifty-two."

"You've got quite a few years ahead of you before you can think of retiring."

"I began teaching at twenty-two."

"Weren't you intimidated having to teach high school students?"

"No. I gave them the talk from the onset, emphasizing that I held the power over their passing and failing, so it behooved them to try and not act up in my class. Every once in a while, I'd get a few clowns that thought Mr. Ogden was just blowing smoke until they saw their grade. That's when we'd have a serious heart-to-heart about the importance of math if they wanted to get a decent score on the SAT or ACT so they could get into the college of their choice. On the other hand, I never had a problem with my students who planned to become economics majors in college." Graeme paused. "I've been running off at the mouth when you should be sleeping because five o'clock will be here before we know it."

"I'll take a nap when I come back this afternoon. I've grown quite fond of this chaise. In fact, it's spacious enough for two people."

"I doubt if you and I would be able to rest on it comfortably."

"We'll have to test it out and see," Kayana said.

"Good night. Or should I say good morning?"

"Go back to sleep, Graeme."

"Yes, ma'am."

Sliding down to the pillows under his head and shoulders, Graeme closed his eyes. He felt better than he had before but knew it would take a few more days before he could think of himself as fully recovered from whatever he had picked up. Not once during his writing marathon had he thought that he was running himself into the ground and therefore compromising his immune system. Subsisting on black coffee and not much else wasn't conducive to remaining healthy. Yet he knew his drive to complete the manuscript weeks before the deadline was based on wanting to set aside a lot more time to spend with Kayana.

And although something nagged at him to tell her that he'd retired from teaching and he planned to stay on the island after the summer season ended, he'd wanted to wait until they could take their friendship to another level where they could become lovers. His breathing deepened, and he soon fell asleep. Images of his making love to Kayana filled his dreams until the sun rose to herald the beginning of a new day.

"Rough night, Kay?"

Kayana refused to look at her brother as she sprinkled creole seasonings on the cut-up chicken in a large plastic bin. It was all she could do not to yawn. She'd slept fitfully in the chaise because she feared oversleeping and not making it back to the restaurant in time to start breakfast.

"Maybe I should tell Graeme not to keep my sister up all night because her day starts at dawn."

"Get your mind out of the gutter, Derrick. The only thing I did with Graeme was take care of him because he is sick."

Derrick stopped rolling and placing meatballs on a baking sheet. "I was teasing you about being with him, because I thought you were hanging out with your book club friends. I'm sorry to hear he's not feeling well."

"He's still running a low-grade fever, but says he's feeling better this morning than he did yesterday."

"You've always been good to your men."

"Graeme's not my man, Derrick."

"If he's not your man, then what is he?"

"A friend, my dear brother."

"Graeme's a lucky man to have you as his friend. Anyone you befriend is lucky, Kay. You chose the right profession when you decided to become a social worker. Mama always said you were her soft-hearted child who would give someone your last crumb even if you were starving."

"That's because Grandmama Cassie drummed it into my head that I was to always be kind, act like a lady, and never do anything to dishonor our ancestors."

"You always took everything our grandmother said literally."

"Being kind, Derrick, doesn't mean I'm willing to be a doormat for someone. I'll put up with a lot of things, but not a liar or a cheater."

"What about love, Kay?"

"Love means nothing if there's no trust."

A waitress stuck her head through the swinging doors leading to the kitchen. "Derrick, we have a situation out here."

His head popped up. "What's up, Jessica?"

"A guy gave me a credit card that wouldn't go through, and he claims he has no cash on him to pay his bill."

"I'm coming out." Stripping off his gloves, Derrick left the kitchen.

Kayana rarely had to deal with nonpaying customers. Most of the time, she was able to come to an agreement when a credit card was declined by keeping the card until the owner returned with the cash to pay the check. However, Derrick was more intimidating and a lot less diplomatic.

She finished making her salads, and once she seasoned the chicken and put it in the refrigerator to marinate overnight, her workday was over. Graeme had sent her a text message that he'd felt strong enough to get out of bed and sit on the veranda, where he'd fallen asleep. Kayana returned the text, saying she planned to come over around three to check on him. He responded with a smiley emoji.

"How did it go?" she asked Derrick when he returned.

"I asked to see his phone, and after he handed it over, I told him I'd give it back once he came back with the money. And I'd call the sheriff if he made a scene."

"Did it work?"

"Like a charm. He managed to find a couple of tens in his jeans, and all was forgiven."

"I don't understand why folks try to skip out without paying their bill. It's so embarrassing once they're caught."

Derrick slipped on a new pair of gloves. "I've known dudes who dine and dash, but that's impossible here because the law will be waiting for them before they can get off the island. And it's not worth it to get arrested and jailed for a paltry restaurant check."

"The jails and prisons are filled with dumb criminals."

"Tell me about it," Derrick said under his breath.

Kayana covered the tub of chicken with cellophane and left it on the prep table for her brother to put it in the refrigerator. She took off the apron and tossed it in a hamper with other soiled linens the laundry service would pick up.

"I'm done here, Derrick. I'll see you tomorrow."

"Don't forget to get some sleep."

"Okay." What Kayana hadn't told her brother was she planned to spend the night at Graeme's house; the love seat in the family room converted to a bed, and it was more comfortable than sleeping in the chaise.

Kayana had to admit that Graeme looked a lot better than he had the day before. He'd shaved and brushed his hair, and the purplish shadows under his light-gray eyes were fading. She eased back when he attempted to kiss her cheek.

"Hold up, cowboy. You can't afford to get me sick."

He managed to look sheepish. "Sorry about that," he said, reaching for her overnight bag.

Kayana felt his forehead. It was cool. "How are you feeling?"

"My head still hurts a little bit, but at least I can stay out of bed for longer periods of time."

"After I take your temperature, I'm going to change your bed."

Graeme held her hand. "You would've made an incredible nurse."

She scrunched up her nose. "No, I wouldn't. I don't like the sight of blood, and I'm not changing bedpans."

"But you have a wonderful bedside manner."

"That's because I shift into therapist mode." They climbed the staircase together, and she waited for Graeme to sit out on the veranda before she took his temperature. It was down to ninety-nine point one. Close, but still not within the range for normal.

Kayana suspected Graeme was putting on a brave face for her benefit. She'd noticed him massaging his temples when he believed she wasn't looking and wondered if he should see a doctor to diagnose why he had an elevated body temperature. She gave him another dose of the cold and flu medication, and then stripped and changed the bed.

Graeme was nodding when she returned to the veranda. She gently shook him. "Graeme, it's time for you to get into bed."

His eyes widened when he stared up at her as if seeing her for the first time. "Do you mind if I stay out here for a while?"

Kayana gave him a tender smile. He was asking her where he could stay in his own home. "Of course I don't mind." The sun had moved over to this side of the house, and with the shade and a light breeze coming off the ocean, the veranda was the perfect place to hang out and relax. "I'm going downstairs to prepare dinner. Do you still want shrimp and grits?" When she'd texted him, asking what he wanted for dinner, he'd requested the Low Country favorite.

Shifting into a more comfortable position on the cushioned lounger, Graeme closed his eyes again. "Yes."

She hesitated before walking off the veranda. "If you're not feeling any better tomorrow, I'm going to suggest you see a doctor."

"I'm already better."

Kayana wasn't about to argue with a grown man about whether he should go to the doctor if he had an elevated body temperature, which was an indication of an infection. "If you say so."

"I heard that, Kayana."

"I wanted you to hear it," she countered.

Graeme waited for Kayana to leave before he opened his eyes. She had become his angel of mercy because his ability to perform even the normal task of getting out of bed and taking a shower involved herculean effort. He'd sat on the side of the bed for at least three minutes before finding the momentum to stand because of dizziness. And it had taken an inordinate amount of time to shave, shower, and put on clothes.

Sitting on the veranda and doing absolutely nothing was something he'd missed. When he'd rented the bungalow the year before, it had been his favorite spot to begin and end the day, but since he'd purchased the property, his focus shifted from enjoying his vacation home to turning it into a work site.

Perhaps he needed something to remind him that, at fifty-two, he was no longer able to pull all-nighters as he had in college during finals week. Now that he was a month ahead of his deadline, Graeme decided to stick to a schedule of writing four hours a day, five days a week, and kicking back on the weekend. He'd retired from teaching to become a full-time writer, but not at the risk of compromising his health. And Kayana volunteering to take care of him had alleviated his apprehension about whether they would continue to go out together. He'd panicked after she said: "I stopped checking in the day I left this island to go to college" when he'd asked her to contact him to make certain she'd made it home safely, because he'd feared it would be the last time she would come to his home. In order to keep from calling her, he'd submerged himself in the manuscript. Writing had helped to purge the guilt of losing his wife, and it had also allowed him to escape and forget about the first woman with whom he'd been involved, and who did not need him—for anything.

Kayana had admitted that she wanted to take care of him because she liked him. Well, he liked her too. A lot. There was so much he wanted to share with her: books, movies, and vacationing in exotic and romantic places. He'd never visited Dubai, and the city in the desert was now on his bucket list. And there was taking a monthlong vacation to take in the sights in many of the world's capital cities. He had the time and the resources to indulge in most of his longings, yet he wanted and needed someone to share it with him.

The sound of the door sliding open captured his attention, and when he turned, he found Kayana balancing flatware on plates. He stood up and took the plates from her and set them on the glass-topped rattan table with two matching pull-up, cushioned chairs.

"Why didn't you ask me to come down and help you?"

She smiled at him. "I didn't ask because I don't want you moving around too much. I decided we'll eat up here tonight. I'll be back in a little while to set the table."

"Are you sure you don't need my help?" he asked.

"If you ask me the same thing next week this time, then maybe I'll say yes."

Graeme stared at Kayana's firm hips in her fitted white jeans as she walked. Was she sending him coded messages that she planned to return the following week and share a meal with him on the veranda, or had she said it just to pacify him?

Kayana made two more trips: one to spread a cloth on the table, set up the place settings, and light a quartet of votives, and another time to bring up bowls of creamy cheese grits topped with grilled shrimp, chopped green onion, and tiny pieces of andouille.

"I'll bring up the water after we eat," she said when he pulled out a chair to seat her.

Graeme lingered over her head, while resisting the urge to press a kiss on the strands, from which wafted the scent of coconut. He rounded the table and sat opposite Kayana, and everything around him ceased to exist as he stared at her. Kayana Johnson was the total package—looks, brains, and talent.

If asked why he'd been initially attracted to Kayana, Graeme would have to admit it was her round face. Her complexion, a flawless nut-brown, was the canvas for a pair of wide-set, large, dark-brown eyes, a pert nose, and a full, lush mouth. He'd found himself hypnotized when listening to her sultry drawl that indicated she had grown up in the South. The timbre of her voice never changed, even when she attempted to pacify an uncooperative customer. It had been impossible for him to imagine what her figure looked like under the chef's tunic and loose-fitting pants, but after encountering her at the bookstore and staring at her slender, compact body, his fantasy about the woman with chin-length black hair concealed under her bandana was complete.

Kayana Johnson was the second African American woman he'd found himself attracted to, but nothing came of it when he'd asked his former college classmate to go on a date with him. She'd rejected him, stating she only dated black men. Although her rejection stung, he respected her decision. The incident was a wake-up call for Graeme because, as someone of privilege and entitlement, used to getting whatever he wanted, there were things and people who would always be beyond his reach.

Graeme did not have a type when it came to the opposite sex, and he usually dated women not based on their physical attributes but their intellect and empathy. Those two qualities were the reasons he'd married Jillian. Her sole focus on empowering underrepresented and marginalized persons was what drew him to her. Sexual compatibility was important in a relationship, but not what he thought of as a deal breaker, yet it had become a cause of contention between him and his late wife.

"Is something wrong, Graeme?"

Kayana's voice shattered his musings. "No. Why?"

"You look as if you zoned out for a while."

"I was just thinking about something."

She raised a questioning eyebrow. "A penny for your thoughts."

"Only a penny, Kay?"

"Why? Do you want to wager more?" she said, smiling.

"If I'm thinking about you, then you have to know you're worth much more than a penny."

Kayana set down her fork and touched the napkin to the corners of her mouth. "How much?"

Graeme slowly shook his head. "It's impossible to put a price tag on someone who is the total package."

"Mr. Ogden, are you attempting to seduce me?"

He stared at Kayana for several seconds before dissolving into laughter. "Is that what you believe I'm attempting?"

"Yes."

Graeme could not discern from her expression whether she was teasing or serious. "Well, I'm not. You have to know that I like you in the way a man likes a woman. But when it comes to attempting to seduce you—no. Yes, I want you to sleep with me, but it's not about me, but you."

"Are you saying I'd have to make the first move?"

"No, Kay. I'm not going to put that responsibility on you. If we do share a bed, then it will be because both of us want it. I'm much too old to play head games, and I'm not going to apologize for being direct and up front when it comes to my feelings about you."

"Why me, Graeme, and not some other woman?"

"Why not you? Do you believe you're unworthy, that a man can't want you for yourself and not what you can give him?"

"I've never believed that I'm unworthy. Folks around here have always said that Johnson women have been blessed with an overabundance of confidence, and that's why men have always had a problem convincing them to become their wives. Do you realize how many men are intimidated by strong, independent women?"

"Too many, but I'm not one of them, Kay."

"It wouldn't bother you if I controlled our relationship?"

He chuckled softly. "Don't get me wrong, beautiful. I am not a punk!"

It was Kayana's turn to laugh. "You sound like Nixon when he claimed he was not a crook."

"But he was a crook."

"And you're not a punk."

"I'm definitely not a coward or a quitter," Graeme confirmed.

"So once you're in, you are all in."

"One hundred and ten percent."

"If your wife hadn't died, do you believe you still would've been married to her?"

Graeme went completely still. Kayana had asked him a question he wasn't able to answer, yet knew he owed it to her to be truthful if he hoped to have an open relationship with her.

"I can't answer that because we had been separated for five months at the time she was murdered." A slight gasp escaped Kayana with this revelation. She knew his wife was dead, but not how she'd died.

"That must have been very traumatic for you."

"It was more of a shock than traumatic," Graeme admitted. "She'd left me and moved back to Springfield to live with her mother. Her mother, who was a chain smoker, asked Jillian to go a convenience store to buy her a carton of cigarettes, where she'd walked in on a robbery. Jillian temporarily distracted the robbers, allowing the shopkeeper to pull his own gun from behind the counter, and gunshots were exchanged. What followed was a bloodbath. One of the robbers was struck in the chest, the shopkeeper lost an eye, and Jillian, shot in the head, died instantly." He saw Kayana's eyes well with unshed tears. He hadn't meant to upset her.

"I'm sorry for you and her mother that her life had to end like that."

Graeme ran a hand over his face. "I carried around a lot of guilt because I blamed myself for her leaving me."

"It wasn't the first time she'd left you."

"How did you know?"

"I've counseled women who've had issues with their boyfriends or husbands and will occasionally leave to check into a motel or stay with their girlfriends for a day or two, but they rarely travel distances to live with their mothers for five months unless they intend to end the marriage or relationship." A beat passed. "Had she filed for divorce, Graeme?"

"No."

"Why not?"

Suddenly Graeme felt as if he was on a therapist's couch answering questions about his volatile marriage. Then he remembered Kayana had been and by profession was still a therapist. "Jillian was a devout Catholic and didn't believe in divorce."

"Are you Catholic, Graeme?"

"Yes, but not a practicing one."

"How many times during your marriage did Jillian leave you and go back to her mother?"

"At least three or four times. But the last was the longest."

"That's because Mama finally got to her, Graeme. There had to be a reason your mother-in-law sought to control her daughter."

"Should I assume you've had cases that are similar to mine?"

"Yes. Your marriage mirrors the film *Now, Voyager*, in which a domineering mother turns her daughter into a neurotic. You probably would've never had a stable marriage as long as your mother-in-law was alive to control your wife."

Graeme was astounded that Kayana was that perceptive. He told her how his wife's death had so dramatically affected Susan Ellison that she finally had to be institutionalized after several suicide attempts, the last one of which resulted in her being declared brain-dead. "She was hooked up to a ventilator for more than a year, until her brother requested that she be taken off life support. Susan had lost her husband, son, and a daughter in a horrific vehicular traffic accident, which made her cling to Jillian because she feared losing her too. I believe Susan blamed me for depriving her of her last surviving child, and that was why she tried to destroy our marriage."

"What about children? Do you think Susan would've reacted differently if you'd made her a grandmother?"

"No. I didn't know until after we were married that Susan had brainwashed Jillian not to have children because the women in their family had been cursed and would invariably bury their children before they reached adulthood."

"That's crazy. Doesn't the Church want married couples to be fruitful and multiply?"

"Yes. But Susan was referring to prior generations where children died from diseases that now have been totally eradicated with vaccines. I dated Jillian for more than a year, and it wasn't until days before we were married that she introduced me to her mother. She must have known Susan would have done everything she could to prevent her from marrying me."

"Didn't you think it strange that you hadn't met your future mother-in-law before that?" Kayana questioned.

"No, because Jillian lied when she told me her mother had moved to a little town outside of London to live with her widowed sister and had promised to come to the States in time for our wedding."

"Meanwhile her mother was living in the States?" Graeme nodded. "That's some crazy . . ."

"You can say it," he urged, when her words trailed off. "Yes, it was some crazy shit, and I didn't know what I'd been caught up in until it was too late. But I'd married Jillian for better or worse, so I intended to stick it out. I'd tried to convince her to go into therapy, but she refused with the excuse that they were quacks out to change people into what they wanted them to be. After a while, I was grateful we didn't have children because she probably would've messed them up, as her mother had done with her."

"Did you think that maybe you could've been the voice of reason and the one to offset her neurosis?"

"I wasn't willing to take that risk once I met her mother. Susan's influence was just too strong to ignore, and the older Jillian got, the more she became her mother in looks and temperament."

"How long were you married?"

"Twelve years."

"That's a long time, Graeme."

He flashed a wry smile. He wanted to tell Kayana that it was a dozen years of craziness that he never wanted to experience again in his lifetime. No one at the hospital where Jillian was employed as an ER nurse was aware that the friendly, outgoing, empathic medical professional practiced rhythm as a means of contraception and would only permit her husband to make love to her during her safe cycle. After being denied his wife's body, Graeme tired of being put on a sex diet and stopped making love to her altogether, which seemed to please Jillian. He refused to sleep with other women and masturbated to assuage his sexual frustration.

"It is," he agreed after a pregnant pause. "I realize now that I should've been more forceful, but there was something about Jillian that was so emotionally fragile that I feared she would have an emotional breakdown."

"At least you recognized her fragility. She could have taken her own life, and that would have left you feeling guilty and perhaps even responsible."

"I did feel guilty about our last disagreement because I said things to her I could never retract. She was in a dark place when she began complaining about feeling trapped. I suggested she put in for a leave from the hospital, and I would take her away, but she said it wasn't her job but me. She hated me and resented the household staff because she claimed they looked down on her. A few times, I'd overhead her verbally abusing the housekeeper, and, of course, she held it against me when I warned her not to do it again. The argument escalated, and that's when I lost it and told her she'd made my life a living hell and that there was nothing in the world I could do that would ever make her happy. That's when she slapped me and would have hit me again if I hadn't held her wrists. I was so enraged that I told her the wrong girl had died when her father's car burst into flames after being hit in a head-on collision with a drunk driver who'd crossed the median, killing him, her brother, and sister. That was the last thing I'd said to her before she walked out and went to live with her mother. Five months later she was gone."

"We say a lot of things we don't mean when we're angry."

"I know. But I meant it at the time."

"Are you sorry?"

"Of course, I am. It has haunted me to this day." Graeme knew he would carry the hateful words to his grave.

Reaching across the table, Kayana rested her hand on his fisted one. "You have to let it go, Graeme, and go on living."

"So says the therapist."

A slight frown appeared between her eyes. "I'm not your therapist, and I don't want to be."

He sobered and tried making out her expression in the waning sunlight that left the veranda in shadows. "What is it you want to be to me?"

The seconds ticked into a full minute before she said, "A woman who will always be your equal, whatever comes of our relationship. And it's not about love but trust. If I can't trust you, then we're done."

"If I didn't cheat on my wife, then I won't cheat on you."

"The difference is I'm not and will not become your wife. And never lie to me, Graeme. I'd prefer you tell me something I probably won't like, and that's better than you lying to me." She waited, her gaze fixed on the flickering votives. "Let me know what you want from me."

"That's easy. I don't want you to change anything about you."

"That's it?"

Graeme's laugh was low and throaty. "Isn't that enough?"

Kayana offered him a demure smile. "I suppose it will have to be."

Chapter 13

Graeme lay in bed, his head resting on his arms feeling as if he'd experienced a rebirth once he'd revealed some details of his unhappy marriage. There were other intimate specifics he wanted to tell Kayana, but he did not want to kiss and tell as to what had or hadn't occurred in his bedroom while he'd been married to Jillian.

Kayana had insisted she wasn't his therapist, but he'd felt she was because she'd remained objective and nonjudgmental. But it had been so easy to open up to her and disclose things he'd only revealed to the therapist he'd paid to help him work through his lingering issues of guilt.

She had also set the ground rules if they were to have a relationship, while reminding him that she wasn't his wife and did not want to be. Graeme understood her reluctance to remarry after only being divorced for two years. Some of the men he knew who were divorced had remarried within two years, while he had been single for eight years. This was not to say he was opposed to marrying again but just that he hadn't found the woman with whom he wanted to spend the rest of his life. And he'd promised himself the next time he married, it had to be different from his first one. At his age, he felt too old to father a child; however, he wasn't opposed to marrying a woman with children or grandchildren.

Barley's barking echoed from the first floor. It was apparent his dog had quickly switched his loyalty from him to Kayana. She walked, cleaned up, and fed the puppy, who she said had become her constant companion. Graeme wanted to warn Kayana not to spoil his pet or Barley would become incorrigible, and he would be forced to enroll him in obedience school. Shifting on the bed, he stared at the screen on the sliding door. He hadn't bothered to draw the drapes, and the light of a full moon silvered the bedroom.

He shifted again in an attempt to get into a more comfortable position. Spending so much time in bed made him jittery, uneasy. And it wasn't about resuming writing but being able to take care of his basic needs without wondering whether he'd be able to stand for any period of time without falling. It was the dizziness that would come and go without warning that he feared most. Kayana had suggested he see a doctor, but he wanted to wait another day to see if the dizziness continued or abated before seeking medical attention.

A light tapping on the bedroom door got his attention. Kayana stood in the doorway, holding Barley, who was squirming to get out of her grasp. "He wanted to see if his daddy is okay."

Graeme pushed into a sitting position. "You can put him down." He smiled when his pet trotted over to his side of the bed and rose on his hind legs to be picked up. "Sorry, boy. You know you're not allowed on the bed." Barley let out a plaintive howl as if he was in pain. "Okay, just this one time," he said, and glared at Kayana before leaning over to pick up the dog. "Your foster mama knows my bedroom is off-limits to you."

"Who are you calling foster mama?"

"You, Miss Johnson. I should've warned you about spoiling my dog because once you leave, he's not going to listen to me."

"Then I'll take him," Kayana countered. "He's housebroken and obedient, and I'd never banish him from my bedroom."

"You are not taking my dog."

"This is the second time you've gone off on me about Barley. You don't have to worry, Graeme. I'm just teasing about taking your dog. First, I don't have a place where he can run free. And he's certainly won't be allowed in the restaurant, where we serve food, and it would be cruel to keep him cooped up in my apartment while I'm working."

Graeme felt properly chastised. Kayana was right. He tended to overreact when it came to Barley. He'd even changed his route for walking the dog because he didn't want Barley to encounter the aggressive Jack Russell terrier bitch.

"I'm sorry, and I want you to know that I really appreciate you taking care of him."

Kayana approached and sat down at the foot of the bed. Barley climbed over Graeme's chest to lie beside her. The puppy stayed outside the kitchen, watching her as she prepared meals, but shadowed her relentlessly in other areas of the house. Whenever she sat to read or watch television, Barley whined until she settled him on her lap, where he promptly went to sleep.

"He's really a good puppy, and lucky to live in a wonderful forever home."

"We adoptees have to stick together."

Kayana registered something in Graeme's voice that hadn't been there, even when he'd talked about his dysfunctional marriage—vulnerability. Did he still have unresolved issues about his adoption, despite his declaration that his adoptive parents had given him a wonderful life? Was he like many adoptees who ruminate about the woman who'd carried them to term and then handed them over to strangers with the hope their baby would have a better life? Had he spent years searching the faces of strangers, while looking for similarities between theirs and his; had he accessed AncestryDNA for a possible match to his biological parents? And had he resented Patrick and Lauren for telling him that he'd been adopted when it was something they could've elected not to disclose.

His adopted parents had rescued him from a college student who'd had an affair with a married man; if she'd kept her baby, there is no doubt his life would've turned out very differently. Graeme had rescued Barley from a shelter where, if he hadn't been adopted, he could have been put down.

"Maybe I should adopt you both," she said glibly.

Graeme chuckled. "Did you hear that, buddy? We're going to be adopted." He winked at Kayana. "When can we make it official?"

Kayana ran a fingertip down the tight curls on Barley's back. Smiling, she decided to go along with his playful bantering. "There is a thirty-day waiting period before we'll be able to finalize the paperwork."

"That's much too long. It's now mid-July, which means everything should be official on August eighteenth." Graeme paused. "What about ten days from now? You worked for bureaucrats, so you should have some juice at the agency."

Kayana laughed. "What do you know about juice?"

It was Graeme's turn to laugh. "Do you think I'm totally oblivious to today's vernacular? You forget I teach high school, and it's as if teenagers speak in code, so I'm forced to decipher what they're saying."

"I know what you're talking about, because I will occasionally see clients for a friend with a family counseling practice, and I must look like a deer in the headlights when some of the teenagers talk about their issues. It always takes me a while to translate what they are saying."

"Okay, then. Ten days it is."

Kayana lay with Barley, listening to Graeme recount some of the antics of his students until his voice trailed off and then stopped completely when he fell asleep. Getting off the bed, she closed the sliding doors and drew the drapes. Graeme was snoring lightly when she scooped up the puppy and descended the staircase.

"Your daddy's sleeping, and now it's time for us to turn in for the night. I must get up early and take care of you before I go to work." It hadn't taken Kayana long to grow attached to the puppy. It brought back memories of her childhood, when she'd been a pet parent. "But I promise," she said, continuing with her monologue, "to come back tomorrow afternoon."

Barley barked as if he understood what she was saying. She would stay overnight at Graeme's house until his temperature was normal, and then she planned to go home and sleep in her own bed.

Removing the seat cushions from the love seat, Kayana pulled out the collapsible bed and made it up. She'd enjoyed spending time at Graeme's home. It was a change from her apartment above the restaurant, and despite not being as large as the house where she'd grown up, she discovered it was spacious enough for at least two people. And it was more than apparent that Graeme had spared no expense when renovating his island home.

A trio of doors off the kitchen concealed a pantry, a laundry room with the latest, up-to-date washer/dryer, and a half-bath with a commode, vanity, and shower stall. One of the bedrooms on the second floor had become a home office, with a desktop computer and printer on an L-shaped workstation. Bookcases lined against one wall were half-filled, an alpaca rug covered the hardwood floor, and framed black-and-white and color photographs of the world's capital cities hung from the wall facing the doorway. She also noticed there were no photographs of Graeme with his parents in the study or in any of the rooms in the house. Although tempted to go inside and examine the spines of the books, Kayana had held back because she didn't want to be tempted to examine the loose sheets of paper stacked on the desk. Graeme had said he was attempting to write a novel, and when he hadn't been forthcoming as to what he was writing about, she hadn't asked.

She undressed and slipped into a pair of cotton pajamas, checked the doors for the last time, armed the security system, turned off the lights, and then got into bed. Graeme had given her an extra set of keys and the code to the alarm company. Barley whined for her to pick him up, but she ignored his whining until he finally walked over to the bed in the screened-in porch and settled down to go to sleep. If Graeme didn't want his dog to sleep in the bed with him, then she would adhere to the house rule.

Kayana slept fitfully throughout the night, and when the alarm on her cellphone went off at 4:30, she welcomed it, as it had banished the disturbing dream of a baby crying inconsolably. She'd found herself running in and out of rooms to find the child, but all of them were empty. The crying continued before growing faint and disappearing altogether. She didn't know if talking to Graeme about his adoption had triggered the strange dream. Was it about his birth mother trying to locate him? But the young woman had to know the legal names of his adopted parents, and even though they'd passed away, it would be easy enough for her to contact Graeme. Kayana took a shower, dressed, and put out fresh water for Barley. She walked him, waiting patiently for him to finish doing his business, then walked him back to the house, and closed and locked the door behind her. Now that Graeme was on the road to recovery, she planned to bring over enough food to last him several days.

"Good morning, Kayana."

Groaning under her breath, Kayana turned and smiled at the woman who'd been her third-grade teacher. Fortunately, she'd been able to leave Graeme's house without encountering anyone—until now.

"Good morning, Miss Donaldson."

The retired teacher must have discovered the Fountain of

Youth. Her blond hair had silvered, while her slender figure had remained virtually unchanged. Either she had inherited remarkable genes, or she'd gone another route where she had been nipped and tucked or used fillers to hold back the hands of time.

"How have you been?"

"Very well, Miss Donaldson."

The older woman angled her head, smiling. "I must say you're looking very well."

"So are you," Kayana countered. She wanted to ask the woman what her secret was for not aging.

"Twenty years ago, I decided to become a vegetarian, and it changed my life. Not only do I believe I look better, but I feel fantastic."

"It definitely shows. I'd love to stay and chat, but I have to get to work." Kayana had to get away from the talkative woman, who'd earned a reputation as an incurable gossip.

"Are you still reading?" Miss Donaldson asked as Kayana turned and walked to her vehicle.

"Of course," she said over her shoulder. Miss Donaldson had taught English and language arts at the local elementary school, and had been responsible for introducing her to the love of reading. Kayana started up her SUV and drove away from Graeme's house, peering up at the rearview mirror to find that her third-grade teacher hadn't moved from where she'd left her.

Kayana knew it wouldn't take long before the news of her involvement with Graeme, no matter how platonic, would spread throughout the island. Most of the locals tended to avoid Miss Donaldson or were careful about what they said to her if they didn't want it repeated. The retired former teacher was among a few older women—single or widowed—who were counting down to the time when they would sell their homes to strangers. Some of the kids with whom Kayana had grown up left the island as soon as they graduated high school, claiming there was no future for them on Coates Island.

The two-mile-long island was a summer paradise for the owners of the mom-and-pop novelty shops, but once the season ended, all activity slowed to a crawl. Students who attended the high school on the mainland tended to hang out there after classes or on the weekends. The mainland mall— with its movie theater, fast-food restaurants, game arcade, shops, and boutiques—offered discounts to repeat shoppers.

As the only eating establishment on the island, the Seaside Café could count on a steady stream of customers from the Memorial Day weekend to Labor Day, with enough of a profit to keep it viable for the next nine months. Kayana pulled into her reserved spot in the restaurant's parking lot and shut off the engine. The only other vehicle in the lot was a white panel van with the name of the restaurant stamped on the front doors. Derrick would occasionally drive the van when he needed to pick up restaurant equipment or supplies.

She unlocked the rear door, disarmed and then armed the security system. Climbing the staircase, she opened the door to her apartment and was met with a blast of hot air. Knowing she was going to spend the night at Graeme's place, to save on energy she'd shut off the air conditioner. Kayana left her overnight bag on the floor, closed the door, and retraced her steps to the kitchen. She changed out of her street clothes and into the uniform of a tunic, pants, and clogs before covering her head with a bandana from a stack on a shelf in the linen closet.

Six more weeks. That was how long she would be committed to getting up at dawn to prepare a buffet breakfast. After Labor Day, she and Derrick would alternate two weeks on and two off, Monday through Saturday, preparing a 10:00 a.m. to 2:00 p.m. buffet brunch. Sunday would become their day of rest.

Derrick had talked incessantly about missing his daughter,

while Kayana wanted to remind him that he needed to get used to missing her for more than the summer once she enrolled in college. Deandra had mentioned completing her senior year of high school in Florida in order to establish permanent residency because her intent was to attend one of their state colleges. Her niece's disclosure upset Derrick, and he'd gone into a funk for several days. Kayana had to remind him that at seventeen Deandra was growing up and becoming an independent young adult.

Kayana knew it wasn't easy for Derrick to let go of his daughter after losing his wife, but she promised she would always be there for him. And there was always the possibility that Deandra would someday take over running the Café like her father, aunt, grandmother, and great-grandmother before her.

Kayana stared intently as Cherie and Leah sampled the mai tai mocktail. The nonalcoholic drink was the perfect complement to the Asian-inspired menu for their third book club discussion meeting.

Cherie smiled. "This is delicious, and I don't miss the rum."

"I agree," Leah said. "What did you use to make it?"

"Almond syrup, grenadine, lime, orange, and pineapple juice, and sparkling water." Three maraschinos on toothpicks and an orange slice provided a vibrant garnish for the bubbly drink.

Cherie took another sip. "Next year, I plan to rent a bungalow way before the summer season begins so I'll have a kitchen."

Kayana removed the lids from serving dishes that held deep-fried pork garnished with chives with a soy dipping sauce, bite-size spareribs, shredded orange beef, and fluffy white rice. Cooking the rice was a reminder of the time she'd given Graeme a cooking lesson, while unaware she would sleep under his roof after he'd come down with what she suspected was a virus. After two days during which he registered a normal body temperature, she knew it was time for her to sleep in her own bed. She'd left containers of soup, salads, and steamed vegetables in his refrigerator for him to eat until he'd feel strong enough to venture outdoors.

She smiled at the younger woman. It was the first time she'd noticed Cherie wearing makeup. "You plan on coming back here next year?"

"Yes, but only for three weeks. I took off this summer without pay, so I won't lose my accrued vacation time."

Leah set down her glass. "Are we going to resume our book club discussions next summer?"

Kayana handed Leah a plate. "I'm game if you are."

"So am I," Leah said in agreement. "What about you, Cherie?"

"Count me in. I'd like to suggest we choose the books we want to discuss for next summer before we leave. That way we'll know what we're going to read."

"That's a good idea," Kayana said.

Leah filled her plate with rice and shredded beef. "If Cherie's only going to be here for three weeks, then each of us should select one of their favorites. My choice is *Memoirs of a Geisha*."

Kayana waited until Cherie filled her plate before serving herself. "That's one I haven't read. However, I did see the movie."

"The book is better than the movie," Leah countered, as she picked up a place setting. "Which one do you recommend?"

"*Love in the Time of Cholera* by Gabriel García Márquez." The novel rated high on Kayana's list of favorite books. "What about you, Cherie?"

"My choice is a little dark, but it is a masterpiece. *The Alienist* by Caleb Carr."

"Wasn't that a TV miniseries?" Kayana questioned.

Cherie nodded. "Yes, but the book goes more in depth. I believe you would like it because the protagonist is a psychologist—or alienist, as they called them at the time. The novel is set in New York City at the dawn of the twentieth century."

Kayana smiled. "Don't you think it's ironic that we've chosen period pieces?"

"That's because brilliant minds think alike," Leah quipped.

"Hear, hear!" Cherie and Kayana chorused.

"Before we rave about what we're going read next, are we going to discuss *Pride and Prejudice* today?" Leah asked.

"Of course," Cherie replied. "After rereading this novel, I realize today's so-called modern woman isn't that different from Austen's heroines."

"Why would you say that?" Leah asked.

"Because Mrs. Bennet's sole focus is making certain her daughters marry wealthy, eligible bachelors."

Kayana's fork halted in midair. "Not all modern women are looking to marry well. Sometimes it happens, and sometimes it doesn't." She thought about her own marriage to James Hudson and his family's status as members of Atlanta's black elite.

Leah nodded. "I have to agree with Cherie. Most of the girls at my school have coming-out parties where they're introduced to young boys in their same social class with the hope they will make suitable matches."

"The difference between the Bennet sisters and today's single woman is choice and options," Kayana said, after taking a sip of the punch. "We don't have to marry in order to support ourselves, and we have the choice of marrying or remaining single without being stigmatized. Charlotte Lucas, who happens to be Elizabeth's best friend, accepts Mr. Collins's proposal after he's rejected by Elizabeth because Charlotte doesn't have any suitors, and is nearly thirty and a spinster. For Charlotte, it's not about love but being mistress of her own home. And don't forget that Mr. Collins, who just happens to be a Bennet cousin, stood to inherit the Bennet estate upon the death of Mr. Bennet."

"And remember," Leah interjected, "at that time, a woman's

gender prohibited her from inheriting property. If there were no sons, then the next male heir in line would get everything. And if he chose, he could evict his female cousins, so it was incumbent upon a woman to marry well."

Kayana recalled the girls with whom she had attended college who had applied to Spelman because they were single-focused on marrying a Morehouse brother. "Women have come a long way when it comes to being self-sufficient, but not much has changed when it comes to Jane Austen's courtship and today's dating. Women have standards for what they want in a husband, and it's the same with men seeking a wife. In *Pride and Prejudice*, the elder Bennets are landed gentry, and they expect their daughters not to marry below their social status."

Cherie nodded. "It was the same with the girls at Yale. I got so sick of them preaching that they would only marry a man who graduated from an Ivy League college."

"That's so shallow," Leah said, wrinkling her nose as if she smelled something malodorous.

Cherie emitted an unladylike snort. "Shallow or not, that's who they are."

"I really like Elizabeth because she is one of Austen's strongest female characters," Kayana stated. "She meets Mr. Darcy again at Lady Catherine de Bourgh's home, and he asks her to marry him, and she refuses, despite his wealth and good looks, because Mr. Wickham told her how Darcy broke up the romance between Mr. Bingley and her sister Jane."

Cherie made a sucking sound with her tongue and teeth. "Wickham reminds me of a lot of boys I grew up with. Their only focus was using women for their own selfish needs. When Wickham convinced Lydia Bennet to run away with him, he had no intention of marrying her. He'd also attempted the same with Darcy's sister, who was even younger than Lydia at the time."

"Are you saying he took Darcy's sister's virginity?" Leah asked Cherie.

"I'm not certain. It may have been implied by Darcy."

"We do know that he took Lydia's," Kayana said. "If he'd been around today, he probably would've been a baby daddy many times over."

Holding a cherry by the stem, Leah popped it into her mouth. "Who's to say he wasn't? He did have a pattern of seducing young girls. I think Lydia was all of fifteen, which would make him a pedophile by today's standards."

Kayana was content to listen to Cherie and Leah analyze each of the Bennet sisters and the men they'd chosen as suitors. Cherie proved to be a hopeless romantic when she admitted she hated Wickham because he told Elizabeth that Darcy was responsible for Mr. Bingley breaking up with Jane.

"I rarely read romance," Kayana admitted, "but the novel has the same formula of boy meets girl, boy loses girl, boy finds girl, and they live happily ever after."

"And don't forget Wickham's the villain, and there's a meddling older woman who happens to be Lady Catherine de Bourgh, who believes Elizabeth isn't what she would approve of as a wife for Darcy," Leah added.

"Kayana, who were your favorite and least favorite characters?" Cherie questioned.

"I really like Elizabeth because she refused to be swayed by Darcy just because he proposed marriage. Her first impression is a lasting one when she overhears him refusing to dance with her. I also like Bingley. For him, it was love at first sight when he saw Jane. I'm ambivalent when it comes to Darcy because there were times when he was a complete ass. But he managed to redeem himself when he blackmailed Wickham into marrying Lydia by paying off his debts, while providing him with a substantial amount of money. Mrs. Bennet irked me because she was so anxious to get her daughters married that she never considered their feelings. The poor woman did have a hissy fit after Elizabeth turned down Mr. Collins's proposal. Mr. Bennet is what I think of as a cool dude. Lady de Bourgh is certainly on my shit list, along with

Wickham, when she demands that Elizabeth promise that she will never become engaged to Darcy. The manipulative heifer even has the audacity to tell Elizabeth that she can strip Darcy of his wealth if he goes against her wishes. What she fails to realize is that Lizzy is not one to be intimidated. We all know what Wickham is about. I'm willing to bet that if Austen had written a sequel, Wickham and Lydia would not be together. She'd end up with stairstep kids, while her husband would spend most of his time in a pub drinking, gambling, and praying he'll win enough money to buy some food for his family."

"What about you, Leah?" Cherie questioned.

The redhead pressed her palms in a prayerful gesture. "I like Charlotte because she didn't delude herself as to her status. She wanted a husband and her own household, and she got both once she married Mr. Collins. I too like Bingley because it was impossible for him to hide his affection for Jane. Lydia almost got what she deserved if Darcy hadn't bailed her out. She forgot that she was raised as a gentlewoman when she ran off to ho around with Wickham."

"No, you didn't say 'ho,' " Kayana said under her breath.

"Yes, I did." Leah stressed the three words. "That's what she was until Darcy forced Wickham to marry her. Darcy irked the hell out of me. First, he appears so unattainable, and then when Elizabeth rejects him, he views her as a challenge because she's the one controlling the courtship. My least favorite would have to be Lady Catherine de Bourgh. Everything about the pompous, malicious, manipulative bitch reminds me of my mother-in-law."

Kayana glanced at Cherie, who lowered her eyes with Leah's outburst. The animosity she felt for her husband's mother was palpable. Kayana knew from her initial meeting with her future mother-in-law that the woman did not approve of her for a number of reasons: She and her siblings were first-generation college graduates, her family were shopkeepers, and even if Kayana did marry her son, she would never be acceptable to those in her social circle. Her words were prophetic because Kayana was rarely invited to Hunter family gatherings, which prompted James to host, with annoying regularity, his own get-togethers where he'd become the center of attraction.

"I really enjoyed rereading *Pride and Prejudice*," Kayana said, shattering the pregnant pause after Leah's passionate outburst. "Thank you, Cherie, for suggesting and leading the discussion."

Cherie inclined her head in acknowledgment. "You're very welcome." She shifted her attention to Leah. "Well, Miss Lady, you're up next. What do you recommend for our next meeting?"

"Edith Wharton's *Ethan Frome*."

Kayana rubbed her hands together. "I love it!"

Cherie nodded in agreement. "Hell, yeah! We're going to have a field day with this one."

"I suggested Wharton because she's one of my favorite female writers."

"Didn't she write *The Buccaneers*?" Kayana asked. She recalled watching the miniseries on public television.

"Yes," Leah confirmed. "It was her last novel and unfinished at the time of her death. I taught a comparative literature class comparing *The Buccaneers* to *Pride and Prejudice*, because both authors focus on women looking to marry well. Austen's English girls want to marry wealthy titled men, while Wharton's American girls come from wealthy families and want to marry titled, landed, but impoverished Englishmen because, despite their beauty and wealth, they'd be considered new money and shunned by Old World society. The common theme between the two novels is ambitious families seeking elevated societal status for their daughters."

"I know we don't have too many more meetings before we disband our book club for the end of the season, but can we read *The Buccaneers* after *Ethan Frome* and have Leah lead the discussion?" Cherie suggested.

"I would love to read the novel," Kayana said.

Leah's smile was dazzling. "And I'm willing to moderate the discussion."

Kayana mentally counted how many more Sundays they had before suspending the book club until the following summer. It was the third Sunday in July, which meant they had, at best, three more meetings.

And it wasn't the first time that she had to acknowledge that she felt a growing kinship with Leah and Cherie that she hadn't felt with other women who weren't family members. The exception was Mariah Hinton.

She and Mariah met in graduate school and had become study partners. Kayana took an immediate liking to the Atlanta native because of her outspoken, in-your-face personality, which she'd struggled to suppress when counseling clients. They'd role-played situations in which Kayana was the client and her friend the therapist, and subsequently evaluated their improvised counseling sessions. It was only after she videotaped the session and played it back for her that Mariah was able to view her approach to counseling a client. She then admitted she hadn't exhibited enough empathy and made a concerted effort to change her tactics.

When she'd suggested the book club, Kayana had believed they would only talk about books, but somehow their private lives had become a part of their discussions, with Leah becoming the most forthcoming and vocal about her marriage.

Kayana did not understand why a woman whose adult children were out of the house and living independently had not left an unfaithful husband whose mother hated her. And she did not understand why Leah had resorted to using artificial devices to satisfy her sexual needs when she lived with a man who supposedly was capable of performing in their marriage bed.

The first time she'd discovered James was cheating on her, Kayana decided, no matter how long they'd been married, that it was over. Meanwhile, Leah had put up with cheating and verbal abuse for twenty-eight years in order to remain in a lifestyle she never could have imagined if she hadn't married Judge Alan Kent. Was it because she didn't want to give up the big house, the status as a judge's wife, and the diamonds in her ears and on her hand? Or did she not want to give her elderly mother-in-law the satisfaction that the marriage hadn't succeeded and she was no longer Mrs. Alan Kent.

The sun had set, and after Leah and Cherie helped her clear the table and stack the dishwasher, Kayana drove Cherie home before returning to her apartment to prepare for the next day.

Chapter 14

Graeme stroked Barley's back as he reclined on his lap. The puppy had whined incessantly from the moment Graeme had sat down until he picked him up and settled him down to sleep. It was apparent that Kayana had spoiled his dog.

Instead of sitting on the veranda outside his bedroom, he was on the screened-in porch, which had become his favorite space to greet and end the day. The sight of new saplings, potted ferns, and rows of succulents in the fenced-in, landscaped backyard had become his private oasis.

Not seeing Kayana exacerbated a loneliness Graeme had ignored for far too long, and it could not be assuaged by interacting with Barley or totally immersing himself in his writing. She'd become a wonderful friend, sacrificing her time and energy to care for him and his pet—something she did not have to do. He'd wanted to believe she felt something for him other than friendship, because he wanted more than that from her.

Graeme wanted to be able to call her and ask her to accompany him to out-of-the-way places where they could share a meal without being recognized or interrupted. If and when she spent the night, he didn't want her sleeping on the convertible love seat, but in his bed. And he wanted to go to bed and wake up with her beside him. He also wanted to make love with her and hold her long after their passions subsided. However, given her unorthodox work schedule, he knew what wouldn't be possible until after Labor Day.

He had recovered from whatever he'd come down with and had regained his appetite. Kayana had restocked his refrigerator and freezer with fresh dairy and prepared entrées he only had to reheat in the oven or microwave. It had been days since they'd last spoken, and he missed hearing her voice, layered with a slow, sultry drawl he found unforgettable. She'd claimed he talked funny when he'd accused her of the same. Graeme knew he sounded like a New Englander, and a Bostonian, in particular, whenever he said certain words, but it wasn't as apparent as Kayana's southern drawl.

"You miss her, don't you, buddy?" he asked the dog when Barley looked up at him. "I do too. But you have to admit that she took good care of you, even though you're pretending you're not spoiled," Graeme continued with his monologue. "I suspect she let you sleep in the bed with her, but that's not going to happen with me, Barley. The only other living thing that's going to share my bed is a woman, not a canine or a feline. And we don't have to wait much longer before we're adopted, so you must be certain you behave so we don't make Kayana regret that we're going to become a family." The dog stood up and turned around a couple of times before settling back down to rest his muzzle on his outstretched paws.

Graeme hoped Kayana wasn't teasing when she'd said, "Maybe I should adopt you both." Of course, her adopting him and Barley would be a merely symbolic gesture on her part. But the word meant so much more for Graeme. The year he'd celebrated his eighth birthday, his world as he'd known it was turned upside down. The man and woman he'd known as his mother and father were now his adopted parents—two people who'd chosen him when his birth mother made the decision not to raise him but give him away. He'd cried himself to sleep for two weeks before realizing his adopted parents had given him a life most kids could only fantasize about. They loved him unconditionally, and for a young boy, that was more than enough.

Reaching for the cellphone on the cushion beside him, he tapped Kayana's number. It rang three times before she picked up.

"Please don't tell me you had a relapse."

Graeme laughed. "No such luck. If I did, then could I count on you to take care of me again, Florence Nightingale?"

"I don't think so, sport," she teased, "because a hard head makes for a soft behind."

"I promise you I've been good. I'm eating and getting enough sleep. I also haven't ventured outdoors except to sit on the veranda."

"Good for you."

"How was your book club meeting?"

"It was awesome. We discussed *Pride and Prejudice*."

"I thought you discussed that last week."

"It was on the agenda, but we got off topic and decided to delay it until today. By the way, do you remember everything I tell you?"

"Yes, because I don't want you to accuse me of half-listening or ignoring you."

Kayana's sultry laugh came through the earpiece. "I'm not that vain, Graeme."

He smiled. "That's good to know. What's your next book club title?"

"*Ethan Frome*. And the following week it's another Wharton novel, *The Buccaneers*."

"I'm not familiar with *The Buccaneers*."

"It's about five American heiresses who marry cash-poor Englishmen with titles."

Graeme's eyebrows lifted slightly. "They're like Winston Churchill's mother and one of Princess Diana's ancestors, who become a part of British royalty because of their fortunes."

"Do I detect a hint of censure, Graeme?"

"Yes, because these men didn't love these women, but saw them as a means to an end. They used their money to save their land or pay off their gambling debts. I've read accounts where some of their husbands flaunted their mistresses and were unusually cruel to their American wives."

"Once the women married, they were stuck because they'd traded their fortunes to become a lady, a duchess, or the wife of an earl or marquise. Personally, I don't think it was worth it just to have a title."

"I'm certain it's still happening today," Graeme said. "Look how many girls were fantasizing about marrying Prince Harry until their hopes were dashed when he married Meghan Markle and she became the Duchess of Sussex."

Kayana let out a full-throated laugh. "Good for her. She succeeded where so many before her had failed."

"And she didn't have to give up the money she'd made acting to secure a title."

"You're preaching to the choir, Graeme. Thankfully, things and times have changed. Today people marry whoever the hell they want, and what others may think or believe be damned."

Graeme knew he was going to ask Kayana a question that might insult her, but he had to know if he was to further pursue her. "Would you be opposed to marrying someone outside your race?"

"No. It's not what a person looks like, but who they are inside. In other words, it's about character and not race. Why did you ask? Did you have a mixed-race marriage?"

"No."

"Have you ever dated a black woman?"

He smiled. "Yes. You."

There was a pause before Kayana said, "I suppose you can say it was a date when we went to the movies together."

"Trust me, Kay, it was, even though I don't believe in kissing on the first date."

"Neither do I. Because if it doesn't work out, then I don't want to give my date the impression that we can do it again."

"Are we going to do again, Kay?"

"Yes. Did you promise me we're going to see *Les Misérables*?"

"I did, and I will. By that time, I know I won't be contagious, so I'll be able to kiss you without getting you sick."

"Hang up, Graeme. I need to go bed and get some sleep before I have to arise with the chickens."

Throwing back his head, he laughed loudly, startling Barley. "I'm sorry, baby."

"Who are you talking to?"

"Barley. He's sleeping on my lap. And you're going to pay dearly for spoiling my dog to the point that he doesn't want his paws to hit the floor."

"Tell Barley Mama's going to come and see him in a few days. I can't believe how much I miss him."

Graeme wanted to tell Kayana that he also missed her. "Good night, my love."

Kayana stared at the phone until she heard a beeping sound indicating that the connection had ended. Graeme had hung up before she could react to his calling her his love. She'd found it wasn't easy analyzing Graeme Ogden, because most times she found him guarded, as if he was attempting to hide something. When she'd first noticed him coming to the restaurant the summer before, he'd basically stayed to himself, waiting for an empty table in lieu of joining others at a table with an empty seat. He'd come in for breakfast and lunch, but never dinner. This year, his routine changed, and he'd occasionally have breakfast and always dinner. He was solitary and reclusive, which had her wondering why he'd come to Coates Island in the first place, and why he'd elected to buy property on the island. Most teachers who summered on the island tended to rent in lieu of purchasing a vacation home. First, there weren't that many properties that were available for sale, and if someone did buy a house, chances were slim to none that they would not be able to rent it in the off-season. When she'd heard that Graeme had purchased the house and renovated it, Kayana wondered if he'd planned for a retired colleague to live in the house until he returned the following summer.

Despite not knowing much about Graeme, she knew he liked her and wanted more than friendship. What Kayana had to decide was whether she was willing to offer more than that. When she'd heard him on the phone and had hardly recognized his voice, her first reaction was to go to his house and check on him. Unconsciously, she reverted back to the time when she was in her office at the hospital and had to provide therapy or counseling services to a patient or help family members learn to deal with mental illness in the family. She'd trained herself to become attuned to changes in a person's voice or body language.

When Graeme had answered his phone and she'd asked him if he was all right and he said he thought so, Kayana knew he was not being truthful. She found men to be her worst patients, because they feared that showing weakness meant they weren't manly. So much for being manly when they were too sick to take care of their most basic needs. Thankfully, she hadn't had to help Graeme shave or shower because that would have crossed the line to an intimacy she hadn't been ready for.

Spending time at his house and talking to Graeme had

opened the door to his past; he'd felt comfortable enough to talk about his marriage and his estranged wife's death. Kayana could not imagine how he had lived with a woman for twelve years who definitely needed mental health therapy. He truly must have loved her to have stayed in the marriage, or perhaps it was pity that forced him to stay because he feared she would harm herself.

And when she compared her marriage to Graeme's and Leah's, Kayana considered herself fortunate that she had escaped unscathed. This is not to say she was unaffected when she'd discovered her husband had cheated on her with a woman she knew, but she realized she wasn't the first woman to have an unfaithful husband and definitely wouldn't be the last. In the end, she realized she loved herself more than she loved James, and she wasn't willing to look the other way in order to maintain her status as the wife of one of the city's leading trauma surgeons or forgive him for trampling on her trust. James had asked her to forgive him, but Kayana knew that, with his ego, he would cheat again because his father had cheated on his mother and his brothers on their wives. It was common knowledge in James's social circle that Hudson men were cheaters, but it wasn't something she was privy to until it happened to her. Although the phony-ass bougies treated her as if she had leprosy, Kayana knew herself and liked how she was.

She knew James was shocked when, served with divorce papers, he'd pleaded with her to talk it out with a marriage counselor. He did not want the stigma of being the first in his family to divorce, but she was beyond caring about his family's flawless reputation. However, she did agree to change the charge of adultery to irreconcilable differences, but for a price, considering the pain and suffering he'd put her through for almost twenty years. She would let him have the house and its contents in exchange for a huge settlement.

The house was worth half of what she'd requested, and

James had to take out a mortgage on the property and withdraw funds from his 401(k) to make up the balance. She deposited the bank check into the retirement account Derrick had set up for her, notified her attorney she was ready to finalize the divorce, and after shipping her books and personal items to Coates Island, left Atlanta for the last time.

Whenever she thought about Graeme, she did not want to compare him to James, but it was becoming difficult not to, the more time they spent together. James was brilliant, proud, boastful, and at times shameless, while Graeme, although wealthy, was modest, intelligent, and reclusive. She wasn't certain whether his need to spend time alone had come from his being an only child or resulted from being raised by parents who were older than those of his contemporaries. Then she recalled what he'd discovered in his mother's diaries, which was certain to have had an impact on what he thought of her. His mother had harbored secrets, and the woman he'd married had secrets of her own. Kayana had talked to him about trust, and she wondered if Graeme also had his own trust issues.

One thing she did not have was secrets. What he saw was what he got. He knew she was divorced and did not have children, had been a social worker in her former life, liked dogs, loved to read, and enjoyed cooking. She refused to divulge family recipes or her net worth, which she did not think of as secrets but just unavailable for public consumption.

Kayana checked her phone to make certain she'd set the alarm. She was counting down the days when she would have two weeks off each month and could sit up half the night reading, then sleep in late the following day. This year, she'd contemplated taking a cruise to the Caribbean or driving to the Florida Keys to sample their cuisine and take in the sights.

*　*　*

Kayana had just completed her shift, showered, and changed into street clothes when her cellphone rang. Picking it up, she saw the caller's name. "Good afternoon."

"Good afternoon to you too. I'm just calling to remind you that today the adoption should be finalized. Can you check on it for me?"

She struggled not to laugh. "Damn, Graeme, you don't forget anything do you?"

"Not when it concerns me and Barley. I must know if we're going to be adopted by someone who will love and take good care of us."

"Well, I have good news," she said, deciding to play along with him. This teasing, joking Graeme was someone she could get used to. "I got an e-mail earlier today to confirm it is final. I should get the official documents in the mail within the week."

"That's the best news I've heard since Barley came to live with me. This means we'll have to celebrate in grand style."

Kayana went completely still. "How grand are you talking about?'

"Dinner and drinks at a restaurant where someone other than you will do the cooking."

Folding her body down to the padded bench seat at the foot of the bed, she stared at a collection of crystal perfume bottles on a corner table. "When and where?"

"I'll leave that up to you."

Kayana closed her eyes for several seconds. In all the years she'd dated and been married to James, he'd never left anything up to her. And to keep peace in the house, she usually went along with him because she didn't want a repeat of her parents' increasing hostility toward each other.

"It's been a while since I've been to Carolina Beach, Oak Island, or Wilmington, so I'll go online and see what I can come up with."

"Just let me know where you want to go, and I'll make it happen."

She smiled. "You may come to regret saying that."

Graeme chuckled. "I doubt that. I'm coming to the Café for dinner. Would you mind if we eat together?"

Kayana's smile grew wider. "No, Graeme. I wouldn't mind. But what if we eat together at your place?"

"Is that what you really want?"

"Yes. We can cook together. What do you feel like eating?"

"Spaghetti and meatballs."

"That's easy enough to make."

"What time should I expect you?"

"Five."

"I'll be here."

"Later."

"Later, my love."

Kayana hung up. It was the second time Graeme had referred to her as his love. She wanted to tell him she wasn't his love, and she didn't want him to love her because he'd made it possible for her to like him more than she wanted to. There was never a time when they were together that she'd felt uncomfortable with him. She'd lain across his bed with him in it, slept under his roof, albeit he was sick, and was completely relaxed. Perhaps it was because he was the first man she'd gotten close to since her divorce that she was able to be open with without censuring herself.

But a quiet voice in Kayana's head reminded her that she wasn't twenty-six or even thirty-six, but a forty-six-year-old divorcée who could date or sleep with whomever she pleased, while her only commitment was to her brother, whom she'd promised to help run the Seaside Café. Pushing to her feet, she walked out of the bedroom and into the library to boot up her laptop. She'd just pulled up the website for several restaurants in Kitty Hawk when her cellphone rang again.

Tapping the screen, she activated the SPEAKER feature. "Hi, Leah."

"Hey, girl. I'm going online to order your vibrator. How long, and which color do you want?"

Kayana bit her lip to keep from laughing. She did not want to believe Leah was *that* serious about ordering a sex toy for her. "Forget it, Leah. I really don't need a vibrator."

"Are you getting some?"

"No," she said, laughing, "I'm not getting some."

"Are you sure, Kayana?"

"Yes."

"May I ask you a very personal question?"

Kayana wanted to tell Leah she'd already asked her a very personal question when she asked if she was having sexual relations. She'd learned quickly that her book club friends were not reticent and did not hold back from saying what came to mind.

"Yes, you may."

"You claim you haven't slept with a man in more than two years. Do you ever get horny? I'm older than you and experiencing the onset of menopause, but there are times when I'm as horny as a mink, and that's when I use my vibrator a couple of times a day."

Kayana did not understand Leah. She claimed she hadn't slept with her husband in years, was aware that he was sleeping with other women, yet she rationalized she didn't want to or couldn't divorce him because it would upset their boys. Was she aware that her boys weren't children but grown men who had gone on with their own lives? Yes, they might be disappointed that their parents were splitting up after so many years, but they would get over it more easily than if they were young children.

"I still feel desire, but if it gets to the point where I'm figuratively climbing the walls, then I'll do something about it."

"And what's that?"

She closed her eyes and groaned inwardly. "I'll find a man to sleep with."

"Are you talking about picking up a man?"

"No, Leah. That's not my style."

Kayana wanted to remind Leah that she wasn't so demoralized by her divorce that she was turned off when it came to men. She'd never had a problem with self-esteem, even when married to James or even before when the Hudsons had made known their resentment and hostility when James introduced her to his family as his fiancée. And no matter what they'd said or implied, she refused to succumb to their intimidation. Kayana knew that if she could survive being married to an egotistical man for almost twenty years and emerge unscathed, then she had the confidence to deal with any man.

"There's something else I'd like to ask you, Kayana."

"Why do I feel as if I've been summoned to your office for some school infraction?" she teased.

Leah's high-pitched laugh echoed from the speaker. "Not to worry, honey. I summon very few students to my office because I want to keep my position as headmistress. Kids will lie to their parents through their platinum-plated little asses, and yours truly will always come out looking like the villainess, so I ignore most stupid pranks unless one puts another student's life or safety in jeopardy."

Kayana knew what Leah was talking about. She knew social workers and psychologists who'd boasted they'd made enough money from helping their wealthy clients grapple with ongoing unresolved issues to pay for their children's college education without applying for student loans.

"What do you want to know?"

"Do you like men?"

A beat passed as she processed Leah's question. "You're joking, aren't you?"

"No, I'm not."

"Why would you ask me that, Leah?"

"I asked because I've seen the way men stare at you at the restaurant, and you look past them as if they don't exist."

"That's because I have a strict rule that I don't play in my own sandbox."

"In other words, you don't shit where you eat," Leah said.

"Exactly." She'd told Leah a half-truth because of her involvement with a man who was a customer at the Café.

"I really envy you, Kayana."

Shaking her head, Kayana did not want to believe what she'd just heard. Why would Leah envy her when she appeared to be content with her life? "Why do you envy me?"

"You can come and go whenever you want and see whatever man you want."

She bit her lip to keep from screaming at Leah. If she was unhappy with her so-called perfect life, then there was nothing stopping her from walking away. "And you can't, Leah? You and your husband have separate bedrooms, your sons are living their own lives, and if you lose your position at the school, you can always get another. So why can't you come and go and see whomever you want?"

"I don't want my boys . . ."

"Stop it right there, Leah," Kayana said, cutting her off. "How old do your sons have to be before they're no longer boys or your babies? They are men, Leah. Grown-ass men, and you have to stop using them as an excuse not to change your life."

"I think it's time I hang up. Good-bye."

Kayana did not want to believe that Leah had hung up on her because she didn't want to hear or face the truth. Well, she wasn't the woman's therapist, didn't want to be, and for that she was grateful. She'd counseled more women like Leah who had an excuse for everything to ensure they would not take control of their lives.

She forgot about her conversation with Leah as she searched for restaurants where she and Graeme could celebrate what had become a running joke between them. She had symbolically adopted him and his dog, and that would establish a bond for the rest of the summer season.

* * *

Graeme came out of the house and opened the driver's-side door when Kayana shut off the engine to her SUV. Since moving back to Coates Island, she rarely drove the vehicle, which was a welcome respite from the hour-long—sometimes longer, depending on traffic—daily commute to and from downtown Atlanta.

She smiled up at him when he helped her out, and she had to admit he looked a lot better than he had the last time she'd seen him. His face wasn't as gaunt, and it was apparent he'd sat in the sun because his former pallor was gone. The most noticeable difference was his longer, gray-flecked, light brown hair. The military cut had grown out, and she realized the texture wasn't straight, but curly.

Kayana did not want to believe she'd spent several days with Graeme at his house. It was as if she refused to acknowledge things about him she'd found attractive because she still wasn't ready to admit to herself that she was a normal woman with physical needs that only a man could satisfy. And despite admitting to Leah and Cherie that she at one time had resorted to using a sex toy, it wasn't something she wanted or needed as a substitute for foreplay and intercourse.

Unlike Mariah, she did not have a particular type when it came to a man. She'd gone out with men from different races and ethnic groups and had slept with one or two. But for Kayana, it was always about how she'd related to them and in turn how they'd treated her. However, she did have standards for behavior. She refused to date men who smoked, drank too much, or dabbled in illegal drugs. She'd had a hard-and-fast rule not to sleep with a man until they'd gone out for at least two months, because it would give her time to assess whether they would remain friends or take their relationship to the next level.

"You're looking well."

He smiled, and fine lines fanned out around his eyes. "Thanks to you, I feel wonderful."

She patted his arm. "All you needed was over-the-counter medication, chicken soup, and lots of rest."

Graeme looked at her under lowered lids. "I'll remember that the next time I run myself into the ground."

Kayana reached behind the driver's seat to pick up a large canvas tote. "What were you doing so you were that run-down?"

"Writing."

She handed Graeme the tote. "Books don't become best-sellers because the author writes nonstop until they exhaust their creativity. Why don't you complete a draft, and then go back and revise it?"

"What if I don't want to revise it?"

"Well, I don't have an answer for that. But at least you know what to expect if you decide to embark on another writing marathon."

Resting his hand at the small of her back, Graeme directed her to the door, where Barley stood, his tail wagging like a metronome. "Can I count on you to take care of me if I get sick again?"

Kayana slowly shook her head. "No. If you're intent on ruining your health, then don't look for me to take care of you."

"I thought we were family."

She patted Barley's head when he sniffed her leg. "We are not family, Graeme Ogden."

"What happened to you adopting me and Barley?"

Kayana stopped suddenly, causing Graeme to bump into her, and she would've lost her balance if he hadn't caught her upper arm to steady her. "You have to know I was just joking."

Steely gray eyes met a dark brown pair. "Really?"

She blinked once. "Yes, really. We're not a couple of kids playing jokes on each other. And you have to know that adoptions are a legal procedure that have to be finalized with a court proceeding."

Graeme continued to stare at Kayana, wondering if she was aware of how much he had come to depend on her, if only to remind him that he could perhaps have a normal relationship with a woman for the first time in his adult life. She made him smile—something he rarely did. And she made him laugh—something he hadn't done in a long time. There was something about her that was so natural and refreshing that he was allowed to be himself.

And he admired her maturity and independence. She wasn't needy and constantly seeking attention and/or compliments. He also had told her things about himself and his past that he hadn't revealed to anyone except his therapist. He'd trusted her just that much. There were other things he wanted to tell her, but he wanted to wait until he was certain he could share a future with her.

It had been four days since they had been together, and during that time Graeme had gone through mental and emotional calisthenics when he thought about Kayana. He'd carried on so many lengthy monologues with Barley that the dog had begun hiding under a chair on the porch as if to escape the sound of his voice. Their separation had allowed him to assess his life and what he wanted to do.

Graeme considered himself blessed that he'd been adopted by two people who'd not only wanted him, but also had loved him and given him a life most kids would fantasize about. They'd passed away within months of each other, his mother purportedly dying of a broken heart after his father lost his battle with colon cancer. At the age of twenty-six, and as their sole heir, he had become a wealthy young man.

Graeme had given up teaching after a twenty-year stint to concentrate on a second career as a fiction writer and had bought a house on an island off the coast of North Carolina to use as a vacation retreat, but he could not have anticipated falling in love with a woman whose presence afforded him the inner peace that had always eluded him. Talking to Kayana had allowed him to see his life differently. And when she'd said, "You have to let it go, Graeme, and go on living," he'd repeated that statement to himself until her words had become a permanent tattoo on his brain. He had let go and was looking forward to going on living—with her.

"What if we make it real?" Graeme knew he'd shocked Kayana when her jaw dropped. Seeing her indecision, he decided to press his point. "You have to know how I feel about you. And you know how I feel about playing head games."

Kayana recovered enough to ask, "What exactly do you want?"

"I want you to come and live with me. I promise not to put any pressure on you to sleep with me."

"Sleep with you or have sex with you?"

He flashed a sheepish smile. "Perhaps I should've said make love with each other."

"Do you actually believe we can share a bed and not make love?"

"Yes."

She gave him a look that said she didn't believe him. "Do you have ED?"

Graeme successfully curbed the urge to laugh in her face. "Not yet." A frown creased his forehead when she laughed until her eyes filled with tears.

"Do you actually expect me to share a bed with you and not ask you to make love to me whenever you wake up with a hard-on."

His eyebrows shot up. "So you're not opposed to letting me make love to you?"

Kayana gave him a smile he'd witnessed mothers giving his students when they attempted to placate them. "Let's not get ahead of ourselves. I need to see you a lot more often before

I decide on anything. And if we run out of time before you leave to go back to Massachusetts, then we can always continue this next summer."

Graeme opened his mouth to tell Kayana that he did not plan to leave at the end of the summer but changed his mind. He had time to prove to her that they could have a mature, ongoing relationship without the angst both had experienced with their exes.

He lowered his head and brushed a light kiss over her parted lips. "That sounds like a plan."

Chapter 15

Kayana felt as if she'd won a small victory when she got Graeme to agree not to fast-forward their relationship. She liked his gentleness, intellect, generosity, and dedication to a profession that did not get the respect it deserved. She was never able to reconcile why a professional athlete earned eight or nine figures for hitting, tossing, or kicking a ball, while teachers all over the country were striking for better wages.

Although she wanted to take her time to get to know him better, Kayana realized Graeme did not have that luxury. Most teachers left the island in August, depending upon when their district's school year was scheduled to begin. Others waited until just before the Labor Day weekend to depart.

And spending most of her free time with Graeme away from the restaurant would curtail gossip if he were seen leaving her apartment above the restaurant after closing hours. Coates Island was only two miles long but with the influx of vacationers, many of the locals were too distracted by the newcomers to pay much attention to their neighbors. The exception was Miss Donaldson, who could occasionally be seen sitting on her front porch or peering through her curtains to discern outside activity.

"Are you ready to learn how to make authentic Italian meatballs?" she asked Graeme.

"Lay on, Macduff."

Kayana glanced at him over her shoulder as she walked into the kitchen. "Should I assume you like the Bard?"

"I love Shakespeare. I have his complete works upstairs in the study."

"Your study reminded me of a man cave. In order words, enter at your own risk."

Graeme set the tote on a stool at the cooking island. "Nothing in the house is off-limits to you."

Anything connected to his writing was on thumb drives and stored in a fireproof safe on a shelf in the supply closet. One hardcover copy of each of his published novels was stacked on built-in shelves along with dozens of other books. Once the renovations to the bungalow were completed and he'd conferred with the decorator, Graeme had insisted she focus on simplicity when ordering tables, chairs, and accessories. Unlike the Newburyport mansion, there were no priceless Turkish and Aubusson carpets, porcelain vases, Baccarat chandeliers, Tiffany lamps, and vast collections of fragile bone china, silver, and crystal. He felt more at home on the island than in the house that was his permanent residence.

"Should I get my apron?" he asked when Kayana removed a chef's tunic from the tote.

"I'd advise you to, or you may end up with tomato sauce on your white clothes."

Graeme had paired a white, short-sleeved golf shirt with matching walking shorts. He opened a drawer under the countertop and took out the apron Kayana had given him before his first cooking lesson. He had remembered everything she'd taught him, and if called upon, he was certain he would be able to duplicate the dishes.

He watched as Kayana removed large cans of crushed tomatoes, plastic bags of fresh herbs, breadcrumbs, grated cheese, a plastic container of ground beef, and a bulb of garlic. "That tote is like Santa's magic bag that keeps on giving," Graeme teased. She added a loaf of ciabatta bread, another container of fresh spaghetti, a large bottle of extra-virgin olive oil, and a box of disposable gloves to the other items.

Kayana gave him bright smile. "I think that's it."

His eyebrows lifted slightly. "That's a lot for spaghetti and meatballs."

"You could've gone to the supermarket to buy a package of prepared meatballs and a box of spaghetti."

Graeme crossed his arms over his chest. "But it wouldn't taste the same as yours."

"Not mine, Graeme, but yours. I'm going to sit and watch you make the entire meal."

He went still. "Are you sure that's what you want?"

"Very sure, my love. You're a very bright man and an excellent student. And if I have to get up early to go to work, and then come home exhausted after standing on my feet for hours, I would really appreciate it if my boyfriend would occasionally fix dinner for us."

"So I'm your boyfriend and your love?"

Kayana winked at him. "You could be, but you're going have to work at it."

Graeme wanted to take Kayana in his arms and kiss her until he was forced to stop and catch his breath.

So many things in his life had changed in a year: He'd purchased a vacation home, retired from teaching, had finally met and interacted with Kayana Johnson. What he hadn't predicted was falling in love with her.

Graeme was more than aware that he'd come on strong when he'd asked Kayana to live with him, yet at fifty-two, he wasn't willing to become reticent when it came to his feelings about a woman. He knew he'd shocked Kayana when he'd asked her to live with him and had figuratively held his breath because he'd believed she was going to reject him outright. But she hadn't, and that permitted him to relax and to allow things to unfold naturally.

He washed his hands in one of the twin sinks, dried them on a paper towel, and slipped on a pair of disposable gloves. He'd learned early on that Kayana never handled food with her bare hands—meat, in particular, because she claimed it skeeved her out.

"I'm ready, Miss Johnson."

Graeme carefully followed Kayana's directions as she told him, step-by-step, what to put into the lean ground beef before forming it into balls and placing them on a baking sheet in a preheated oven. Even before he began cooking the meatballs, the scent of flavored breadcrumbs, grated cheese, garlic powder, and finely minced fresh oregano wafted to his nostrils. Twenty minutes later, the kitchen was filled with the mouth-watering aroma of the garlic-infused tomato sauce simmering in a large pot. He stirred the sauce with a wooden spoon before covering the pot with a lid.

"You can take the meatballs out of the oven now and, using a slotted spoon, put them into the sauce."

His head popped up when he looked directly at Kayana. "Don't you want to serve the meatballs on top of the spaghetti, and then cover them with sauce?"

She smiled. "No. Putting the meat in the sauce will enhance its flavor. Many Italians will make the sauce, which they refer to as gravy, with fresh San Marzano tomatoes and simmer them for hours with uncooked meatballs, sausage, and small pieces of spareribs. And the result is an incredible sauce that becomes even better days later."

"Why didn't we do that?"

"Do you want to eat tonight or tomorrow morning?" she asked him.

"Tonight, of course." He removed the meatballs from the oven and gently lifted them with a slotted spoon to drain off the excess grease and put them in the pot of sauce.

"That's why I had you use crushed canned tomatoes—to speed up the process."

Graeme, resting his elbows on the countertop, leaned closer to Kayana, who was sitting opposite him. "What other cooking shortcuts are you going to teach me?"

She smiled. "Everything but our secret family recipes."

"What would I have to do to get the secret recipe for your honeyed fried chicken and mac and cheese?"

Kayana scrunched up her nose. "You'd have to become family, and that's not happening."

"Why? Because you won't marry me."

Kayana stared at Graeme as if he'd taken leave of his senses. "That fever must have affected your brain, because how could you go from asking me to move in with you to now talking about me marrying you. I told you before I have no intention of ever marrying again. Not you or any man."

He recoiled as if she'd struck him across the face. "Do you find me that repulsive?"

She wanted to ask Graeme if he'd really taken a good look at himself. He wasn't what she would consider handsome in the traditional sense, but he was quite attractive. Tall and slender, he wore his clothes well. His features were unremarkable except for a pair of large, light gray eyes framed by long dark lashes and what she'd now come to think of as a sensual mouth.

Slipping off the stool, Kayana came around the cooking island, went on tiptoe, and brushed her mouth over Graeme's. She knew she'd shocked him when she heard his intake of breath before his arms circled her waist and pulled her closer until her breasts flattened against his chest. She felt the heat from his body and the strong, steady beating of his heart, and drank in the sweetness of his kiss, all which reminded her of what she'd missed since her divorce.

Kayana ended the kiss and bit her lip before she begged Graeme to take her upstairs and make love to her. Easing back, she smiled up at him. "No, Graeme. You are definitely not repulsive."

He inhaled a breath. "That's comforting to know."

A slight frown appeared between her eyes. "Now, where's the overly confident man who asked a woman whom he'd taken out once, and barely kissed, to cohabitate with him?"

Graeme smiled, exhibiting straight, white teeth. "He sometimes has to put a damper on his confidence with a woman who doesn't need to be taken care of and is emphatic about not remarrying."

"Is that what you want, Graeme? You want to get married again? So you can see if you can get it right the next time?"

His smile vanished, replaced by an expression of stone. "Is that what you believe? That I'm using you like a subject in an experiment? You talk about trust; well, I want you to trust me not to do to you what your ex did. Jillian denied me her body for weeks at a time, and not once did I ever consider cheating on her. I knew there was something special about you the first time I walked into the Seaside Café last summer and overheard you talking to the busboy, who was practically in tears. It was apparent he'd done something wrong, but it was the way you reassured him he still had his job that stayed with me. I finally figured it out when you took the time to come over and check on me when I was hardly able to get out of bed."

"What's that?"

"You are not only kind, but you are selfless. You could've stayed in Atlanta after your divorce, but you came back here to help your brother run the family business after your mother went to Florida to be with your sister and her children."

With wide eyes, Kayana asked, "How do you know all of this?"

"Miss Donaldson is quite the town crier. She told me that

you were once married to a trauma surgeon, your brother had lost his wife, and that your younger sister teaches school in Florida."

Kayana knew the woman was an incurable gossip, but she didn't think she would go into detail about her family's personal life. "Well, damn! What hasn't she told you?"

"I stopped her before she could tell me anything more or ask me my business."

"I'm glad you did, because there's an expression that a dog that takes a bone will carry a bone." Kayana paused. "But I do know your business."

"That's because I wanted you to know something about me if I hoped to continue to see you."

She pantomimed zipping her lips. "And it's safe with me, Graeme. Think of it as client-therapist confidentiality."

Graeme gave her a long, penetrating stare. "No, Kayana. I don't want or need any more therapy to figure out who I am and what I want for myself. I've lost count of the number of hours I spent in therapy trying to understand why my birth mother decided to give me up, and who was the married man she'd slept with and who got her pregnant. I was angry with my parents for telling me that I was adopted until I realized how much I loved them and they loved me. Then I went into therapy again because of the guilt I'd felt following Jillian's death. I'd looked forward to coming back here this summer because last year was the first time I was able to rid my mind of all the negativity that had prevented me from moving forward."

Kayana patted his chest. "Other than my mother relocating to Florida, it was the reason I decided to come back instead of staying in Atlanta. I had the time of my life growing up here, and unlike some kids who can't wait to move on from where they grew up, I didn't want to leave. But there was another world outside of Coates Island, and once I moved to Georgia to attend college, I knew that my vision of what I wanted to do couldn't be achieved here."

"But you returned here because this place is therapeutic. Waking up every morning to the sight of sun, sand, and ocean is restorative to anyone looking for healing."

"I never thought of the island like that."

Graeme winked at her. "That's because you took it for granted. Although I've always lived near the water, there's something special about living on a small island."

"Now you sound like Derrick. He claims he wasted too many years hustling in New York."

"I like your brother. He's even more of a sports fanatic than I am. When he found out I'd grown up in Boston, he asked if I was a Red Sox fan, and of course I said yes. And when he admitted that he rooted for the Mets and not the Yankees, I knew we would be able to have an intelligent conversation about baseball without going for each other's throats."

Kayana rolled her eyes upward. "Why do men get rabid when it comes to their teams?"

"Should I assume you're not into sports?" Graeme questioned.

"You assume right. I think it's unconscionable that athletes are paid obscene salaries, while teachers, folks in law enforcement, and first responders are forced to work overtime or take part-time jobs to make ends meet. And please don't get me started preaching about single mothers and poor families struggling to pay rent or a mortgage and buy food and clothes for their kids."

"You're preaching to the choir, Kay." Graeme didn't tell Kayana that for the past three years he'd donated half his teacher's salary to his favorite charities: St. Jude Children's Research Hospital, World Vision, and the Boys & Girls Clubs of America. He'd inherited a lot of money from his parents, and his current lifestyle did not involve reckless spending. The money from his book advances and royalties were deposited into a designated account from which he paid taxes, and he had invested in a startup that had realized a modest profit last year after he'd convinced the partners to reduce their overhead by not renewing their lease in a luxury glass-and-steel, high-rise office building; they had purchased an abandoned firehouse and then applied for a business loan for the renovations.

What he couldn't tell Kayana was that whenever he said something she misunderstood or disagreed with, he was forced to take a deep breath and think about what he was going to say because he didn't want a repeat of what he'd had with Jillian.

Kayana was strong and independent, which was compatible with his own personality, and although he'd found himself falling in love with her, he could as easily walk away and not look back before losing his temper and saying something he would come to regret.

He dropped his arms. "Are we going to have wine with dinner?" He'd stored bottles of wine on a shelf in the pantry.

"But of course," Kayana said, grinning. "An Italian meal would not be complete without wine."

"I still have to cook the spaghetti and warm up the bread."

Kayana took a backward step. "I'll help you cook the spaghetti. Because it's made fresh, you have to be careful not to overcook it.

Graeme felt as if he'd scaled a mountain and reached the summit when he sat down across the table from Kayana. The spaghetti was cooked al dente, the meatballs were flavorful, and a light coating of sauce on the freshly made pasta, the warmed garlic bread, and a bold dry merlot made him feel as if he was back in Rome dining alfresco under the stars.

"I know you work seven days a week during the summer, but do you ever go on vacation during the off-season?"

She peered at him over the rim of her wineglass. "Why?"

"I thought if you have some time, then whenever I'm off we can go somewhere and take in the sights."

"What sights are you considering?"

He lifted his shoulders. "Rome, Dubai, Paris. You pick the place, and I'll make it happen."

Kayana set down her glass. "You'd take me to Dubai?"

Graeme smiled. "Yes. In fact, it's on my bucket list."

"Do you have any other places on your bucket list?"

"Monaco and Tokyo."

Propping her elbow on the table, Kayana cupped her chin in the heel of her hand. "Those aren't weekend jaunts, Graeme."

"I know. That's why I asked if you get time off."

"Beginning in October, Derrick and I are two weeks on, two weeks off. How's that going to work for you with your teaching schedule?"

"I get a recess in December, February, and April." Graeme still wasn't ready to tell Kayana that he no longer had to prepare lesson plans, grade papers and exams, or punch a time clock.

"That's too far off for me to confirm anything. Once Derrick and I figure out our work schedules, I'll text you."

"Does this mean we're on for Dubai?"

"It means I'll let you know, Graeme."

There was a thread of hardness in Kayana's voice that told him to fall back and not attempt to put any pressure on her. Either she would accompany him or not, and he realized Kayana was right about them not having spent enough time together to get to know each other. And he also had to remind himself that she was nothing like any other woman he'd known. She was the personification of confidence; the only person he knew to match her confidence was his mother.

Born into wealth as an only child, Lauren had grown up pampered. But she was also generous to a fault. She was always cognizant of the less fortunate, which led her to be attracted to them. His father was the complete opposite; having come from a blue-collar, working-class family, Patrick coveted every dollar he earned. He didn't believe in spending his money frivolously but knew enough not to begrudge his wealthy wife the ability to spend hers, because she would turn on him like a rabid animal. Graeme knew his parents did not agree on everything, but he rarely witnessed their quarrels.

He noticed Kayana's eyelids drooping and her attempt to smother a yawn behind her napkin. "Why don't you go up-stairs and take a nap while I clean up here?"

"I'm okay."

"You're not okay, Kayana. Your eyes are nearly closed, and you can't stop yawning."

She flashed a lopsided grin. "I shouldn't have had that sec-ond glass of wine," she said around another yawn.

Pushing back his chair, Graeme rose to his feet, rounded the table, and bending slightly, swept her up in his arms. "There's no way I'm going to let you drive home in your con-dition."

Kayana pushed against his chest. "What are you doing?"

"I'm taking you upstairs, because I don't want you to fall and mess up that beautiful face."

She closed her eyes. "You think I'm beautiful?"

Graeme noticed she was slurring. He doubted she was under the influence with two glasses of wine, attributing her lethargy to exhaustion. He hadn't questioned why she pre-ferred to sit when she'd given him his first cooking lesson. It wasn't easy getting up before dawn seven days a week to begin the workday, especially if she'd stayed up late the night before.

Lowering his head, he pressed a kiss on her hair. "Yes. You're very beautiful. What time did you go to bed last night?"

"It's was around midnight. I stayed up late reading."

"Was it worth losing sleep?"

She gave him a mysterious smile as he climbed the stair-case. "Yes."

Graeme could identify with her. She had her books and he his manuscripts. On a number of occasions, he'd stayed up all night writing when he was scheduled to teach a first-period class. He was able to remain alert until mid-morning, then he would crash on a love seat in the teacher's lounge and take a power nap until it was time for his next class. Graeme had burned the candle at both ends one too many times; when he nearly crashed his car as he drove home, he was forced to access his priorities, teaching or writing, and it was a no-brainer. He'd taught for twenty years, and at fifty-two, he could realistically write for the next twenty years. Writing full-time would allow him more freedom than he'd ever had as a teacher.

Shifting Kayana's slight weight, Graeme placed her on the bed and removed her shoes. She was snoring lightly when he unbuttoned her tunic and untied the drawstring to the cropped slacks, leaving her clad in a bra under a white T-shirt and a pair of black, lacy bikini panties.

He stood there, motionless, staring at the perfection of her shapely legs and slender ankles. The only other time he'd seen her legs was when she'd worn a dress when they'd gone to the movies. Day after day, she sought to hide her incredibly toned body under loose-fitting, shapeless clothes.

Suddenly, he felt like a voyeur gawking at her in a state of half-undress and covered her with a sheet and lightweight blanket. Graeme drew the drapes and flicked on the bedside table lamp, turning it to the lowest setting. He walked out of the bedroom, smiling. Kayana giving him cooking lessons created an atmosphere of domesticity that lingered with Graeme long after she left; it was one of the reasons he'd asked her to move in with him. The other and more important reason was companionship.

Graeme thought about the direction his life had taken as he cleared the dining area table. He wasn't certain when he'd begun to become reclusive. When he looked back, he realized he had always been solitary, but that tendency was growing more and more evident since he'd become a widower.

As the only child of a couple who were unable to have children of their own and who were in their mid-forties when they adopted him, Graeme knew he would never have siblings. The summers they spent abroad or at his mother's family's estate in Newburyport further exacerbated his isolation from other children his age.

The year he entered college, his retired parents moved to Newburyport, while he took possession of the townhouse. But, unlike a lot of eighteen-year-olds who'd had a three-bedroom, two-bath house to themselves, Graeme refused to become a frat boy and allow other students to use his home as a hangout. Although not a virgin, he was very discriminating when he slept with a woman; there was never a time when he hadn't used a condom, because he didn't want a repeat of what had happened to his birth mother, who'd gotten pregnant as a college student.

He did well in college, quickly earning an undergraduate and a graduate degree, and when he applied and was accepted for a teaching position at the Newburyport high school, he convinced his parents to sell the Boston townhouse. His parents continued to travel, leaving him alone months at a time in the six-bedroom, eight-bath house that sat on an acre of land, along with a housekeeper suite and a renovated carriage house for the property's caretaker.

Graeme had a yearlong relationship with a woman he'd met at Harvard, but it ended after she accepted a position working for an insurance company with an overseas division. Three years later, he had another long-term relationship, this one lasting nearly two years, until his then girlfriend decided she didn't want marriage and children but a military career. He met Jillian and found himself in love for the first time. Six months later, he buried his mother, and he married Jillian a week after he celebrated his thirty-second birthday. Although he was married and shared a bed with Jillian, he felt as alone as someone marooned on a deserted island.

He kept hoping and praying his marriage would get better, but it didn't as his wife's behavior became more bizarre. Jillian had moved out of their bedroom when she was most fertile and returned during the safe period of her menstrual cycle. He'd become so enraged with her yo-yoing that he'd issued an ultimatum that the next time she slept in another bedroom she could stay there. She'd taken his threat seriously and never returned to their marriage bed.

Graeme had been married to a woman, lived with her under the same roof for twelve years, and existed as he had as a bachelor. His wife would leave the house without telling him where she was going and return days, and sometimes weeks, later, smiling and laughing as if she'd been there all the time.

He'd argue with Jillian about the responsibilities of being a wife, but it had fallen on deaf ears. He'd suggested she see a therapist to work through her fears and insecurities, but again she refused because she'd believed there was nothing wrong with her.

Once he buried Jillian and knew she was not coming back, Graeme continued to live in the big house with only the live-in housekeeper and the caretaker keeping him from being alone on the property. Not only was he living a more or less solitary existence; he'd also become more reclusive once he began writing. Cloistered in the room that was the mansion's library, he immersed himself in his fictional characters, breathing life into them as his protagonist became his alter ego.

He'd never invited his colleagues to his home and rarely visited theirs, and although approachable, he was considered somewhat eccentric. He'd earned the reputation of focusing solely on his students, coming in before and staying after classes to offer them extra help. When Graeme felt that loneliness was about to consume him whole, he decided to get a pet—not one from a breeder or pet shop, but from the pound. The first time he spied Barley staring through the bars of the cage, his large, liquid brown eyes pleading with him to take him home, he knew that he and the canine would save one another—him from loneliness, and Barley from being euthanized.

Graeme was aware that he'd become even more reclusive since moving to Coates Island, and he found himself talking to Barley as if the puppy was human; anyone who overheard him would've thought he was losing touch with reality.

When he'd reunited with his college buddies for their thirty-year reunion, he had attended alone. Many of them—also from well-to-do-families and some on their second or third marriages—teased him relentlessly. They called him a poor little rich boy who was unable to find a woman. A few had offered to hook him up with their sisters, their cousins, or their wives' friends, but Graeme did not want a hook up. He wanted a woman with whom he could share his interests and passions and she, hers.

Barley's barking caught his attention, and he walked into the porch to see what had disturbed his pet. Three birds were splashing in the marble birdbath. He scratched the pooch behind his ears. "It's all right, buddy. They're just taking a bath."

At the mention of bath, Barley took off like a shot, heading for the staircase and his bed in the study. It was the same whenever he took out the towels he used when giving the dog his weekly bath. A few times, Graeme wondered if the dog was part feline because he hated water and could be found sleeping on the floor wherever there was a spot of sunlight. He returned to the kitchen, turned on the dishwasher, and then swept the floor.

Going over to the family room, he flicked on the television and settled down to watch a cable channel featuring crime stories. It was never far from his mind that there was a woman upstairs, asleep in his bed. Graeme decided that if she didn't wake up, then he would bed down on the love seat. And as much as he wanted to share a bed with Kayana, he'd decided to wait for her invitation.

Chapter 16

Kayana woke, totally disoriented, and it took a full minute before she realized she wasn't in her apartment and her own bed. Then she recalled Graeme carrying her upstairs to his bed, but remembered nothing else once her head touched the pillow. There was no doubt she was more exhausted than she'd been in a long time.

She finished reading *Ethan Frome* and immediately began *The Buccaneers* and was unable to put it down until she'd read nearly half the novel. It had been close to midnight, her eyes were burning, and she had only four hours left to sleep before she had to get up at five. Cherie and Leah had time to read two novels in a week because they were on vacation, while she was responsible for preparing the restaurant's buffet breakfast.

Before forming the book club, she read at her leisure and could take as long as she wished to finish a book. But that changed dramatically when she'd committed to reading a book in a week while beginning her workday at five in the morning and ending around two in the afternoon; most of those hours were spent on her feet. Rising on an elbow, she peered at the clock on the bedside table, groaned, and fell back on the pillows. She couldn't believe she'd been asleep for hours. It was nearly ten.

Sweeping aside the sheet, Kayana went completely still once she realized Graeme had removed her slacks. Why, she mused, of all days had she decided to wear a pair of revealing lacy bikini panties? Then she remembered scrambling out of bed as soon her phone's alarm went off and selecting the first bra and panties she'd found in the lingerie drawer. At least he'd left her a modicum of modesty when he hadn't removed her T-shirt. Turning up the light on the lamp, she found her slacks and tunic neatly folded on the bench at the foot of the bed and her shoes near a chair.

After dressing, she entered the en suite bath to splash water on her face, patting it dry with a guest towel from a stack in a delicate dish on a side table. Kayana managed to tame her mussed hair with her fingers before she left the bathroom and headed for the staircase with Barley trotting after her. Bending over, she picked up the poodle and carried him down the stairs. She found Graeme in the family room sprawled across the love seat, watching an encore baseball game on the flat screen.

He sat up straight with her approach. "How was your nap?"

Kayana set Barley on the floor. "Restorative."

Graeme patted the cushion beside him. "Come and sit down."

She shook her head. "I think it's time I head home."

He stood. "I'll follow you in my car."

"I can assure you that I'm going straight home."

Graeme took a step and cradled her face in his hands. "Please indulge me, Kay. I'll feel a lot better if I know you made it home safely."

Kayana recalled the last time she'd snapped at him when he'd asked her to text him when she got home, and then chided herself for believing he was attempting to control her rather than being concerned for her safety. She wanted to tell

Graeme the drive from his house to the restaurant could be accomplished in minutes, but she decided to humor him.

"Okay. Just don't follow too closely or it will bring back nightmares of when I had to drive in Atlanta's downtown rush-hour traffic."

Graeme pressed a kiss on her forehead. "Okay."

She gathered her wristlet off a table and headed for the front door, as Graeme shut off the television and reached for his vehicle's key fob. He ordered Barley to stay before he armed the security system. She was behind the wheel, shifting into REVERSE, and had backed out of the driveway as Graeme made his way to his SUV.

Kayana drove slowly, keeping under the unofficial speed limit of twenty-five miles an hour on the unlit road. She pulled into the restaurant's lot and parked in her reserved spot. The lot was empty, and all of the lights in the restaurant were off, indicating that Derrick had closed up and gone home. Seconds later, Graeme maneuvered into a space next to her and lowered the driver's-side window.

"I'll walk you upstairs," he called out.

She knew nothing she could say to Graeme would get him to change his mind, although there was little to no risk of her being assaulted between the parking lot and the door leading to the second story. Coates Island wasn't exempt from crime; however, there hadn't been a reported murder in more than thirty years, while there was an occasional break-in in the downtown business district. She got out and waited for Graeme to join her as she unlocked the restaurant's door, disarmed the alarm, and led him up the staircase.

"You can get quite a workout if you go up and down these stairs several times a day."

She glanced at him over her shoulder. "There are exactly twenty-two steps, and when I first moved up here, I found myself stopping halfway until I could build up enough stamina to make it to the top without stopping."

"Where did you live before?"

"I stayed with my brother until I had the space renovated into an apartment."

"What was it before?"

Kayana heard that Graeme's breathing was heavier as she unlocked the door to her living quarters. She had made a practice to lock it whenever she was out of the building. And in the event of an emergency, Derrick had an extra set of keys.

"It was used to store everything but the kitchen sink. Sit down and catch your breath before you collapse."

Graeme gave Kayana a baleful look as he sucked in air before slowly letting it out. He didn't feel this winded when jogging along the beach. "I think I'm going to take you up on your offer to sit."

A floor lamp bathed the open space with soothing golden light as he made his way over to a sofa covered with a floral print in polished cotton. Stretching out bare legs, he studied the space Kayana called home. The first thing he noticed was that it was immaculate. There wasn't a speck of dust on the floor or on any flat surface. He stared at the antique clock and the collection of framed photos on the fireplace mantelpiece.

"Can I get you some water?"

Graeme stood. "No, thank you. I'm going to leave now so you can get some sleep."

Kayana gave him a bright smile. "I'm wide awake now."

"Please don't tell me you're going to stay up reading again?"

She took his hand, lacing their fingers together. "No. I don't want a repeat of last night—or should I say this morning. Are we on for tomorrow?"

Graeme's impassive expression belied his shock. He was the one who always asked when he was going to see her. "Yes"

"I'll text and let you know when to expect me."

Bringing her hand to his mouth, Graeme dropped a kiss on the knuckles. "I'll make dinner for us."

Kayana narrowed her eyes. "Really?"

"Yes, really. Didn't you say that if I have to get up early to go to work, and then come home exhausted after standing on my feet for hours, I would really appreciate it if my boyfriend would occasionally fix dinner for us? I've been practicing with a few recipes, and I believe I've perfected one that I hope you'll like."

"Do you want to give me a hint as to what it is?"

"Nah. You'll find out when you come over."

"Is there anything you'd like me to bring?" she asked.

"Yes. Just yourself."

Easing her fingers from his grip, Kayana rose on tiptoe and brushed a light kiss over his mouth. "I'll see you tomorrow."

Graeme stared at Kayana under lowered lids. Although her kisses were innocent enough, it was becoming more difficult for him to keep his hands off her. "Good night, babe. Come and lock the door behind me."

"The door is self-locking. I can set the alarm from up here."

Turning on his heel, he retraced his steps and walked into the cool night air. Graeme was in a quandary when it came to Kayana. Every time he saw her, his affection for her intensified until he'd wanted to blurt out that he was falling in love with her. It wasn't vanity, but Graeme hadn't had to work this hard to convince any woman to go out with him. He'd always heard that patience was a virtue, yet somehow he felt as if he was being tested.

He returned home, let Barley out for his last romp, and then sat down to search cooking sites for what he could prepare that did not require ingredients that weren't readily available. After forty minutes of scrolling through entrées, side dishes, and desserts, Graeme finalized his menu.

Whistling a nameless tune, he shut down the computer, left the study, and walked across the hall into the bedroom. He almost couldn't believe that Kayana had taken time to remake the bed. It appeared as if they had something in common: They were both neat freaks.

Graeme took a final look at the table, wondering if he had forgotten anything. He had opened a bottle of rosé to allow it to breathe and filled goblets with sparkling water. Suddenly, he wished he had paid more attention to his mother when she'd instructed the housekeepers how to set a table for her guests. Lauren loved entertaining, and during the summer months when they weren't traveling abroad, she hosted luncheons, garden parties, and even fund-raising gatherings at the estate in Newburyport. Whether these events were held under a tent in the garden, in the smaller and formal dining rooms, or the ballroom, Lauren was at the forefront of the activity, making certain silver and glassware were set correctly at each place setting. Graeme, like Patrick, generally left the house during such gatherings and only returned once their home had settled back to a normal routine.

Graeme knew his reluctance to invite friends and colleagues to his home was the result of his mother's constant need to entertain and surround herself with people, and as he aged, he'd come to acknowledge that he was more like his blue-collar father than his blue-blood mother. He'd preferred remaining in the background to standing in the spotlight.

He could not believe he'd turned into Lauren when he got up early and drove to the supermarket in Shelby and ordered Cornish game hens from the in-store butcher. He asked the man to remove the backbone so the hens would lie flat when cooked on the stovetop grill. The butcher recommended he thread two or three soaked wooden skewers through the birds to hold them flat while grilling.

Graeme felt like a kid in a candy shop when pushing the shopping cart up and down the aisles while examining fresh produce and searching for the items and ingredients for a salad and a marinade for the hens. He'd noticed both times he'd cooked with Kayana that they hadn't had dessert. He lingered in the bakery department, staring at the delicious-looking confections in the showcase. In the end, the salesperson made the decision for him, and when he checked out and stored his purchases in the cargo area of his vehicle, a silent voice told him, *You can do this.*

He did not want to believe he had to wait until he was over fifty to try and impress a woman. And it wasn't about taking her to a Michelin-starred restaurant for dinner or flying to exotic locales and checking into a private villa with a personal chef and housekeeper. She probably had experienced that and more when she was married to her physician husband, and Graeme hoped she would appreciate his uneasy attempt to make an impact on her, given her vast experience cooking for the public.

Graeme had removed the game hens from the marinade and slipped tablespoons of chilled herb butter under the loosened skin on the breasts and thigh, unaware that his hands were shaking because he feared tearing the thin flesh. He hadn't planned to grill the chicken until they finished the first course. He flicked on the tuner on a shelf in an overhead cabinet; it had an extensive playlist featuring his favorite recording artists and songs. He smiled when Adele, singing "All I Ask," flowed from hidden speakers throughout the first floor.

Barking excitedly, Barley ran to the front door and sniffed it. Wiping his hands on a terrycloth towel, Graeme left it on the countertop. "I know, boy. She's here."

Kayana knew she'd shocked Graeme when he opened the door and saw what she was wearing. If this dinner was to be special, then she had to wear something other than a T-shirt and cropped pants. She'd selected a quintessential little black dress and a pair of matching silk-covered, four-inch stilettos. The backless garment, with a high neckline and capped sleeves, ended at her knees.

"May I please come in?"

Graeme blinked as if coming out of a trance. "Please."

She handed him a colorful shopping bag but held onto a quilted weekender. He was also less casually dressed than he had been during their prior dinner dates. Tonight, he wore a pair of tailored slacks with a stark white shirt and Italian-made loafers. He'd protected his clothes with a black bibbed apron.

"There's wine, flowers, and candles for the table in that bag. I didn't know if you had a vase, so I brought one. I'm going to take this bag upstairs to the bedroom."

"You're planning to spend the night?"

Kayana gave him a saucy smile. "I will be forced to if I have more than one glass of wine." She sobered. "I don't know what it is, but wine always makes me sleepy, while I can drink at least two martinis or margaritas before feeling the effects of the alcohol."

Graeme met her eyes. "You know I want you to stay."

"And I want to stay."

Turning on her heel, Kayana made her way to the staircase, leaving Graeme staring at the bare skin on her back and legs. She was tired of denying what had been so obvious—she liked Graeme Ogden enough to sleep with him.

What she hadn't wanted to do was compare him to James or the other men whom she had known or been involved with, but he had passed her test with flying colors. Kayana knew he wanted her to sleep with him, yet he hadn't put any pressure on her to do so, while James had intimated on their second date that he'd found her to be the sexiest woman he'd ever met and fantasized making love with her. His ribald revelation had turned her off, and she told him that although he'd paid for dinner, she had no intention of being his dessert. James apologized profusely, and Kayana made him wait three months before sleeping with him.

*   *   *

Graeme was grateful Kayana had gone upstairs to leave her bag because it gave him time for his erection to go down. And, thankfully, the apron had concealed the bulge in his groin. He'd stopped wishing, hoping, and praying Kayana would stay overnight and in his bed, and that she would wake up beside him.

It was the second time he'd seen her wear a dress, and the transformation was shocking and hypnotic. Everything about her appearance was perfect: hair, face, figure, and legs, and he knew if she'd been taller, she could've easily become a high-fashion model. And there was no doubt that, when she entered a room on the arm of a man, men and women alike would turn and stare at her. He was no exception.

Graeme had put the flowers in the vase and filled it and lit the candles when Kayana returned. He pulled out a chair. "Please sit, babe." He seated her and then bent down to press a kiss to the column of her neck. "You look and smell incredible."

Kayana smiled up at him over her shoulder. "Thank you." She directed her gaze to the plate with ripe tomatoes, thinly sliced mozzarella cheese, fresh basil leaves, and black olives, topped with freshly ground black pepper and balsamic glaze. "You made this?"

"Yes, ma'am. I made everything except the glaze."

"I'm really impressed, Graeme. Thank you for taking the time to cook for me."

"It's something I enjoy and hope to do again after a few more lessons." Graeme went to the refrigerator and took the platter with the hens out to bring them to room temperature.

"What else is on the menu beside the caprese?"

"Grilled Cornish game hens. Also grilled parmesan and prosciutto-wrapped asparagus, and dessert is store-bought tiramisu with Irish coffee—an Ogden family favorite."

"I don't believe it! You've come up with all of this after two cooking lessons?"

Sitting opposite Kayana, Graeme winked at her. "What can I say? I have a brilliant teacher."

"That's nonsense, Graeme. You had to have had some prior experience cooking for yourself."

"I never said I couldn't cook. It's just that I would make the same things over and over. There's just so much steak I can eat in a week. I like red meat but prefer fish and poultry because there are so many ways they can be prepared. That's why I asked you to teach me how to roast a chicken. Now I feel confident trying new dishes."

Unfolding her napkin, Kayana placed it over her lap. "You're a natural. Maybe you missed your calling and should've become a chef."

He stared at her under lowered lids, silently admiring the black curls framing her round face with a barely there cover of makeup. "If I'd become a chef, then I doubt our paths would've ever crossed."

"There could've been a possibility if you were based in Atlanta, because I used to do a lot of entertaining."

Graeme chewed and swallowed a piece of creamy mozzarella that literally melted on his tongue. "Did you enjoy entertaining?"

A slight frown appeared between Kayana's eyes. "I hated it. Every weekend my home was like Union Station, with people coming and going. The exception was when my ex was on call. That's the only time when I didn't have to hype myself up and pretend to be a gracious hostess."

"Didn't he know how you felt about people taking over your home?"

"Of course, he did. It was only when I lost my temper and told him that I was going to act a fool in front of his friends, family, and colleagues or accidently on purpose burn the house down that he'd stop for a couple of weeks, but then it would start up again. During the winter, he'd entertain indoors, and during the warmer weather, it was on the patio with the in-ground pool and outdoor kitchen."

"It was obvious he had his own agenda."

Kayana pushed out her lips. "You've got that right."

"You never threatened to leave him?"

She lowered her eyes, staring at the contents on her plate. "I issued one threat, and that was before I married James. I told him if he ever cheated on me, I'd leave him so fast that he would forget what I looked like."

"And he did."

A sardonic smile twisted Kayana's mouth. "Yes. I don't know long he'd been sleeping with Alexis, but once I confronted him, he looked as if he was going to go into cardiac arrest. He believed I was naïve enough to never suspect that he was dicking around with the very woman who'd pretended to be a friend; in fact, she was always the first one to help me make certain my guests had everything they needed."

"That's really ballsy, Kay. What man invites his mistress to his house while he and his wife are hosting a gathering?"

"A man whose bank account has a lot less zeroes after I left him. Some women want to hold on to the big house with the pool in a gated neighborhood where folks have to use an intercom for you to let them in. But I wanted none of that, so James was forced to cough over the cash, or I was willing to drag out the divorce until the baby he'd made with the love of his life was old enough to attend college. And what he didn't want me to do was get really bitchy and talk about his screwing a coworker when there were rules at the hospital against supervisors fraternizing with subordinates."

Graeme leaned back in his chair. "What was she?"

"She was a first-year surgical resident."

"Damn. She didn't even wait to become a fully licensed doctor."

"Maybe it was what she'd done to get through medical school. But I'm willing to bet that she hadn't planned on getting pregnant, since it temporarily derailed her career."

Graeme listened intently while Kayana related the events that ruined one marriage and threatened to end another be-

fore it began. Her ex-husband had coerced his young para-
mour into taking a leave before the news of their affair threatened his position at the hospital.

"Should I assume he married her?" Graeme questioned.

Kayana nodded. "Yes. He arranged for Alexis to live with
a cousin in Raleigh–Durham until she gave birth to their son,
then he moved her back to Atlanta, and they were married in
a private ceremony with family and close friends."

"Did she ever return to the same hospital?"

"No. She applied to a smaller hospital in Macon, which is
about eighty miles from Atlanta. The latest news I heard
from a friend is that James hired a live-in nanny to take care
of the baby, while Alexis stays in an apartment in Macon and
only comes home when she has time off."

"What a mess!"

"That's what I said when my friend gave me an update.
But when I look back, I'm glad I don't have to put up with
that scene anymore. When I go upstairs after working in the
restaurant, my life is mine, and I can do whatever I want. I
don't have to concern myself with strangers invading my privacy and skinning and grinning at them when I don't want
to. Once I left that circus, I did not realize how much I was
willing to put up with and compromise on because I didn't
want a repeat of my parents' marriage, as they'd argued constantly. There was a running joke in the family that if Mom
and Daddy didn't argue, the sun wasn't going to rise the next
day. When Mom sat us down and told us she was divorcing
Daddy, we thought she was joking. One day, we came home
from school and discovered that all of his clothes were gone,
and that's when it finally sank in that we could live in a house
where we didn't have listen to our parents verbally attack
one another."

"Parents don't realize the impact they have on their children because most times they're concerned with what makes
the adults happy. My mother was like your ex-husband. She
loved entertaining, and whenever we spent time in Newbury-

port, she would invariably send out invitations to a luncheon or dinner party for some made-up social occasion. Dad and I would find someplace to go just to escape the lunacy."

"Did you ever host a function at the house after your parents passed away?"

"Never. Not even when I was married. Some of my colleagues would drop hints about using the house to host an end-of-the-year or retirement party, but after I turned them down a few times, they stopped asking."

"Do you close up the house whenever you come down here?"

"No. I have a full-time live-in housekeeper and caretaker, so there's never a need to close it. It's their home too, and I can't think of dispossessing them." Graeme dabbed his mouth with his napkin. "It's time I put the hens on the grill."

"The salad is delicious, and I can't wait for the entrée."

Graeme had to admit to himself that the caprese had exceeded his expectations. He mentally sent thanks to the clerk in the produce section who'd selected the perfectly ripe tomatoes and fresh basil leaves for the salad. Now, all he needed was for the hens to cook until they were crisp and golden on the outside and juicy on the inside.

If she hadn't seen it with her own eyes, Kayana would've thought Graeme had paid someone to grill the hens and asparagus. She watched him place the tender spears on strips of prosciutto, and then add shaved parmesan and wrap the thinly sliced, dry-cured ham and cheese around the asparagus before placing them on a heated grill. Minutes before, he'd grilled the hens to perfection; the herbed butter under skin had turned the birds golden and crisp on the outside, while infusing the meat with the flavors of fresh tarragon and rosemary. When she'd told Graeme that she wanted a boyfriend who could cook for her when she came home after a day of standing on her feet cooking for hours, she never would've imagined he would be able to put together a meal worthy of one served in a restaurant.

The food, the background music, the candlelight, and the man seated across from her, along with two glasses of rosé, created an atmosphere of total relaxation where anything and everything outside the house ceased to exist. It was only the two of them, cloistered in their own world, where she believed she knew what he was thinking and that he could also read her thoughts.

"Tonight has been nothing short of perfect." She'd spoken her thoughts aloud.

Graeme smiled. "That's because of you."

"It's just not me," Kayana countered. "You have a lot to do with it." A mysterious smile parted her lips when she said, "I think I'm going to keep you."

Although his mouth was smiling, Graeme's eyes were as dark as angry storm clouds. "Are you certain that's what you want to do?"

"Very certain."

Rising to stand, he came around the table and eased her to her feet, his arms circling her waist. "I hope you read the fine print, babe, because once you get involved with an Ogden man, there are no refunds or exchanges. It means you will have to keep me. Knowing this, do you want to back out now?"

Kayana realized Graeme was offering her a challenge and/or an out. That if she wasn't ready to commit, then this was her time to let him know. They had a little more than a month to be together, she thought, and if their relationship survived the season, she would have something to look forward to the following summer. And if not, then she would be left with the memory of a man who unknowingly made her aware that her love life did not begin and end with James, that she could have a mature relationship with other men.

"I am not a quitter," she said, in her best Richard Nixon imitation.

Lowering his head, Graeme took her mouth in a kiss that was more like a caress; she melted against the hardness of his body, glorying in the knowledge that she had not made a mistake becoming involved with one of the restaurant's customers. Not only was she playing in her own sandbox, but she had invited a man to share it with her.

"You don't know just how special you are to me," Graeme whispered against her parted lips.

Kayana closed her eyes as hot tears pricked the back of her lids at the same time her heart stopped and then started up again with his impassioned admission. She wanted to tell him how special and important he'd become to and for her.

Kayana did not want to love Graeme, because for her either she was all in or all out. She'd fallen in love with James and given him one hundred percent of herself to make their marriage work. She now had no illusions about marriage or children, because at age forty-six they weren't priorities for her. And she was no longer a twentysomething psychiatric social worker with stars in her eyes who'd caught the attention of one of Atlanta's leading trauma surgeons and felt as if she was on top of the world when she became his wife.

She knew it was impossible to turn her emotions on and off like a faucet, yet she would be offered a hiatus when Graeme left the island to return to his teaching position in Massachusetts. Their separation would give her time to take a step back and reassess their relationship until they reunited next summer.

"I'm not going anywhere," she whispered in his ear. "You'll always know where to find me." That was the last thing she said before he swept her up in his arms and headed for the staircase. Dessert and coffee forgotten, she knew and was ready for what was to come.

Words weren't necessary.

Graeme wanted to make love to her.

And she wanted to make love with him.

Chapter 17

Graeme felt as if he'd waited forever for someone like Kayana to come into his life. She embodied everything he'd sought in a woman, and then more. He hadn't known he was searching for something from the moment Patrick and Lauren Ogden revealed they weren't his biological parents: peace.

It no longer mattered who the woman was who'd slept with a man who'd deceived his wife when he got another woman pregnant. And whoever his biological mother was, he applauded her for not aborting the child created during their intimate expression of love but being willing to carry him to term and give him to a childless couple to love and raise as their own.

He'd sown his oats, dating more women than he'd slept with, while not actively looking for marriage until he met Jillian. Going into therapy following her death allowed him to understand why he'd married her: He thought of her as a bird who had fallen from the nest, abandoned by her mother, and it had become his responsibility to take care of her.

Entering the bedroom, he placed Kayana in the middle of

the bed and watched her intently staring up at him. The woman in his bed didn't need him to take care of her, and that meant they were equals. Although divorced, she wasn't emotionally broken, and it was her maturity, strength, and confidence he admired most. Grasping her ankle, Graeme removed her heels, placing them on the floor under the bedside table. He slipped out of his loafers, got into bed, and held her hand.

"I'm not going to do anything to you that you don't want me to do."

Shifting until she was facing Graeme, Kayana wanted to tell him to shut and make love to her. He wasn't teaching a class where he had to explain the steps in order to solve a math problem. "I'll definitely let you know what I don't like."

"I know you can't get pregnant, but I do have protection."

Kayana wanted to laugh. For a supposedly sexually experienced man, he sounded like a boy trying to convince a girl that she didn't have to concern herself with getting pregnant because he was willing to wear a condom. However, she had to admire him for practicing safe sex.

She pressed a kiss to his ear. "Thank you."

No further words were spoken as Graeme took his time undressing her and then himself. There was enough waning daylight coming through the glass on the doors leading to the veranda for Kayana to discern the silhouette of his body. There wasn't an extra ounce of fat on his tall, lean physique. She hadn't realized she had been holding her breath until he placed a condom under the pillow next to hers. More than two years of celibacy had prepared her for this moment with a man who'd managed to scale the fortress she'd constructed to keep men out. But Graeme Ogden, with his infinite patience, modesty, and reserved humility had worn down her resistance to not only become her friend, but one with benefits.

The side of the bed dipped when he got in and covered her body with his, supporting his weight on his elbows. She sucked in her breath when he suckled one breast and then the other. His mouth and tongue worshipped her body as waves of pleasure raced throughout Kayana's body and she was jolted with intermittent volts of electricity. The shocks, although strong, weren't enough for her to beg him to stop. At least not yet. Not until she gave him as much pleasure as he gave her.

Her fingers dug into his biceps, and she couldn't stop trembling uncontrollably as a rush of moisture flowed down her inner thighs and onto the sheets. Graeme reached down, stroking her clitoris as he continued feasting on her breasts. Kayana was losing control and didn't want to climax without him inside her.

"Please," she pleaded shamelessly, her body on fire.

Heat, followed by chills, then more heat singed her sensitive flesh. Graeme pulled her lower lip between his teeth. He kissed her again, this time on the hollow in her throat, his mouth charting a course down her body, lingering between her legs to taste her essence, then retracing his path as he explored every inch of her. Now she didn't want him to stop. He'd discovered erogenous zones on her body she hadn't known existed. Her heart pumped so hard she was certain it could be seen through her chest. She was offered a respite from his sensual assault when he reached under the pillow for the condom and slipped it over his erection.

Holding his hardened flesh in one hand, Graeme parted her legs with his knees and positioned his erection at the entrance to her sex. He pressed into her body, she watching as his penis finally slipped inside her. She was tight but managed to take all of him. They'd become the perfect fit.

Kayana gloried in the hard body atop hers, his erection sliding in and out of her wetness. A shiver of delight washed over her, as a moan slipped past her lips and she feared climaxing. She attempted to think about anything except the exquisite pleasure coursing throughout her body. However, she finally had to let go, and the first orgasm took over, holding her captive for mere seconds before another earth-shattering release shocked through her core, taking her beyond herself.

Graeme released his banked-up passions, ejaculating and sharing free fall with Kayana as her pulsating flesh closed around his, squeezing tighter and tighter until he was unable to hold back. He could not believe the selfless passion she'd offered him. He loved everything about her and unintentionally had come to depend on her emotionally. He went to bed thinking of her, woke looking for her.

"You are so incredibly beautiful," he whispered in her ear as her body calmed from her release. It took superhuman strength for him to move off her. Reaching for her hand, he cradled it gently, his thumb making tiny circles on her inner wrist. Making love with Kayana was more than he'd hoped for. "Are you all right, my love?"

Kayana sighed softly. "Yes."

"I didn't hurt you, did I?"

"No, sweetheart. You didn't hurt me. In fact, I can't remember when I've ever felt better."

He gave her fingers a gentle squeeze. "You know that I love you, Kay."

"You don't have to say it, Graeme."

He released her hand, his tightening into a fist. "Please, don't ever tell me what to say, Kayana. You can tune me out or not respond, but don't tell me what I don't have to say."

"You misunderstood me, Graeme, but if you're spoiling for a fight, then you're not going to get one from me. Not tonight. Not when I've had the time of my life with a man who went above and beyond to prepare an incredible dinner for me, then followed that up with making the most exquisite love I've ever had."

Graeme felt properly chastised. He had misinterpreted her comeback. "I'm sorry, babe. I didn't mean to snap at you. I—"

"Stop apologizing and kiss me," she said, interrupting him.

"Yes, ma'am." He complied, kissing her mouth, hair, ear, nose, and then her mouth again. In a moment of madness, he'd blurted out that he loved Kayana, and she probably believed it was because she'd allowed him to make love to her when he would've said the same even if she never let him touch her.

After all, he wasn't some sixteen-year-old randy boy who needed to jerk off several times a day. He was middle-aged man who was still virile enough to get and maintain an erection at this time in his life; it wasn't about sex but having a person with whom he wanted to share not only his current life but also his future.

He nuzzled her neck. "Let me know when you're ready for dessert."

Kayana giggled. "I've already had dessert. You were my dessert."

"Nah, babe. I'm the entrée, and you are dessert, because you taste a lot sweeter than I do."

"That hasn't been proven, Graeme, because I still have to taste you."

He went completely still. Making love with Kayana was the opposite of what he had had with Jillian because she wouldn't allow him to do more than kiss her mouth or touch her breasts. Everything below her bellybutton was forbidden, and she would only agree to the missionary position.

Graeme knew he had to stop comparing Kayana to Jillian. It wasn't fair to her. He kissed Kayana again. "I'll be back as soon as I throw away the condom."

He left the bed and walked into the bathroom to discard the condom. Staring at his reflection in the mirror over the vanity, he realized that although he looked the same, he wasn't the same, and he had to thank the woman in his bed for that.

Graeme returned to the bedroom to find Kayana asleep, her breasts rising and falling under the sheet she'd used to cover her nakedness. He got into the bed beside her, and it wasn't long before he also fell asleep.

Kayana's initial apprehension about spending nights with Graeme was belied because he did not disturb her whenever she retreated to the porch to read. She'd come over in the late afternoon; sometimes she brought dinner, or they'd cook together. He always insisted on cleaning the kitchen while she settled into a rocker with Barley stretched out beside her, to read.

They'd waited a day before making love again, where she'd assumed the dominant position; she sat atop Graeme's body, slowing and quickening the rhythm, stopping him from ejaculating by pressing her thumb under the shaft of his penis until he begged her to stop, but she didn't, until her orgasms overlapped one another and they climaxed together. As she lay there, attempting to catch her breath, Kayana knew that she had fallen in love with Graeme. She'd let her body tell him what she refused to verbalize and would remain her secret. And she was also looking forward to the end of the season when he would leave the island and she would have time to assess her feelings about him.

Kayana hadn't known what to expect when Graeme asked her to come and stay with him because she didn't want a repeat of what she'd had with James; she'd felt smothered by his presence and did his personal bidding whenever he invited hordes of people to their home. Looking back, she wondered how she had put up with it for so long, why it had taken his cheating for her to say no more.

The cellphone on the cushion vibrated, startling Barley, who stood up. Kayana set him on his feet before answering the call. "Hey, Mariah."

"Hey, yourself. It's been a while since we've chatted. How are things with you?"

Kayana smiled. "Wonderful," she admitted. She'd met a

wonderful man and had had wonderful sex, so all was right in her world.

"Good for you."

She heard something in Mariah's voice that indicated all wasn't right with her friend. She and Mariah called each other every couple of months, but Kayana hadn't heard from Mariah since early June, and she hadn't called her because of the therapist's heavy caseload.

"What's going on, Mariah?" A pregnant pause greeted her query.

"Haji and I decided to split."

It was Kayana's turn to become temporarily mute. Mariah had dated her CPA boyfriend for seven years. Haji had gone through a tumultuous divorce, and he finally was able to share custody of their children with his ex-wife; every other weekend, Mariah played stepmother to his son and two daughters.

"What happened?"

"One of his daughters called me a bitch because I wouldn't let her boyfriend hang out in her bedroom with the door closed."

Kayana's jaw dropped. "What!"

"I told Haji there was no way I was going to allow a thirteen-year-old to talk to me like that."

"Good for you. What did he say?"

"I don't know what the lying little heifer told him, but he had the audacity to say that Asia has a mother, so he would appreciate it if I didn't discipline his kids."

"No, he didn't!"

"Yes, he did. That's when I told him I was through. I know you'd complained to me about being the help whenever James invited folks to your home, while unsuspectingly I'd become a nanny to Haji's kids. He didn't have to pay someone to look after his children whenever he had to work his designated weekends during tax season, because yours truly was there."

"Didn't he realize you were trying to protect his daughter?"

"I suppose he didn't. There's one thing I know for certain, and that is that I will not counsel him or his daughter if she ends up pregnant."

Kayana had counseled clients in Mariah's practice facing the consequences surrounding a teenage pregnancy and its impact on the entire family. "Well, she does have a mother."

"You ain't lying," Mariah drawled. "I'm putting off seeing clients for the next two weeks. Would you mind if I drive up and spend some time with you?"

"Of course, I don't mind." How could she turn down her friend? When she had needed a shoulder to lean on, it had been Mariah who'd supported her once she'd decided to divorce James. "Just let me know when you're coming." Kayana knew she wouldn't be able to spend the night with Graeme once her friend arrived.

"I've already contacted my backup to alert him of any emergency. I still have to stop my mail and pack, so look for me either Saturday or Sunday."

Kayana smiled. "I want you to know that I'm part of a book club with two other women. We meet Sunday evenings, along with a light repast and beverages, to discuss a particular title."

"That sounds like fun."

"It is. So, if you come early enough, you're more than welcome to join us."

"By the way, are you cooking?"

"Yes."

"If that's the case, then I intend to be a spectator while eating and drinking until I burst."

Kayana laughed. Her friend was proud of her rounded body, which she referred to as fluffy. "Most times we manage to discuss a book in depth despite eating and drinking too much."

"I'm going to hang up now and put up several loads of

laundry before I begin packing. I promise to let you know when I'm coming. And thanks, Kay, for putting up with me."

"Bite your tongue, Mariah Hinton. How many times have you listened to me bitch and moan about my situation with James, and not once did you tell me to leave the narcissistic bastard."

"That's because I don't believe in advocating for the breakup of families unless there's verbal or physical abuse. Talk to you soon, Kay."

"Okay, Mariah."

Kayana hadn't experienced verbal or physical abuse, but what she'd put up with James bordered on emotional manipulation, as she'd decided not arguing with him would save her marriage. However, in the end it was the infidelity that ended it.

She knew she had to inform Graeme that her friend was coming up from Atlanta, and that she wouldn't be able to spend nights with him. She slipped a bookmark in the book and set it on the glass-topped table with tiny pots of succulents as the centerpiece. Walking out of the porch, she went into the family room, where he lay sprawled on the love seat, once again watching a baseball game.

He sat up with her approach, patting the seat beside him. "Sit down, babe."

"I wanted to tell you that a friend is coming up from Atlanta to stay with me for a while. I don't know how long she'll be here, so I'm going to ask for a rain check . . ."

"Don't sweat it, babe," Graeme said, cutting her off. "Have fun with your friend. We'll just have to make up for lost time once she leaves."

Resting her head on his shoulder, Kayana stared at the bundle of herbs resting on the grate in the unlit fireplace. She was practically living with Graeme, and each day she learned a little more about the man with whom she was falling in love. He was much more complex than she'd originally believed. There were moments when he appeared to be unusually quiet, and Kayana wondered if it had anything to do with her. That's when she went into therapist mode to wait until he felt comfortable and confident enough to open up to her. She'd promised herself she wouldn't coerce him to talk about something he preferred to keep hidden.

She sat up straight. "I think I'm going to turn in now."

"I'll be up in a little while. I want to get in a little more writing before I go to bed."

"How's the novel coming?"

He smiled. "It's coming."

"When do you anticipate completing it?"

"Hopefully before Labor Day."

Shifting on the love seat, Kayana met his eyes. "Will you let me read it once you finish it?"

Kayana was asking Graeme a question he wasn't able to answer. He didn't know if she was familiar with or had read any of the novels he'd published as Brendan Andersen. But under the conditions outlined in his contract, only listed designees were privy to his true identity: his agent, Alma Mc-Call; his editor, Peter Culhane; and his publisher, William Sopher. The small, privately owned book company sold nearly a half million copies of his first title in the first two months after its publication, and they were committed to safeguard his privacy with the dedication of Secret Service agents protecting the president. The two subsequent titles hit all of the best-seller lists shortly after their release dates.

"It's only the first draft," he lied smoothly. "I'll probably let you see it once it goes through several revisions." Graeme knew he would never tell Kayana that he was the reclusive, best-selling writer Brendan Andersen unless she was his wife. And if she stayed true to her declaration that she never wanted to marry again, that phase of his life would remain hidden from her.

"How many drafts do you anticipate?" she asked.

"As many as it takes before I feel comfortable enough to submit it to my publisher."

"If that's the case, I'll wait until it's published to read it. Then I can brag to everyone that I know a famous, best-selling author."

Graeme wanted to tell Kayana that she was already sleeping with a famous, best-selling author. "That may not be for many years."

"No matter," she quipped. "Even if we're no longer together, I can still say I knew you when." She pushed to her feet. "I'm going to take a shower and turn in. Some of us have to get up in the morning and go to work."

Graeme also stood up. "You're not going to make me feel guilty. I've spent the past twenty years staying up nights, grading exams and papers, then going in the next morning to face some students who didn't give a shit about math—except how to cheat in order to get a passing grade."

"It's almost impossible to stop kids from cheating."

A sly grin lifted the corner of Graeme's mouth. "I know, but I did devise a system that managed to curtail it. Whenever I administered a test, I made up two different exams and handed them out to different rows. Kids in rows one and three had the same test, while those in two and four shared the same one. If you decided to look on your neighbor's desk, you were assed-out because it was different."

"That's ingenious."

"No, it's not. I learned it from one of my high school teachers who couldn't figure out how kids were cheating. At first, he made up a different test for every student, but when that proved too taxing, he decided two tests were sufficient and distributed them to alternating rows."

"Did you ever cheat?"

"Oh, hell no! My father would've grounded me for life if I'd been caught cheating."

"Smart kid."

"No, Kay. Frightened kid. Dad wasn't one to blow smoke when he said something."

Rising on tiptoe, Kayana kissed his jaw. "Good night, honey."

"Good night, babe."

Graeme made it a practice to write during the hours Kayana was at the restaurant, stopping to eat and let Barley out, then going back to see how much he could accomplish before she returned later in the afternoon. He knew he would be able to put in a lot more hours while her friend was visiting. He would miss not having her sleep next to him, but knowing she'd return once her friend went back to Atlanta would heighten his anticipation.

Turning off the television, he let Barley out for his last romp, then dimmed the lights in the entryway. He whistled sharply for him, and within seconds, the puppy appeared and headed for his bed on the porch. Graeme set the alarm before he climbed the staircase to his study.

He booted up the computer and then inserted the thumb drive with his manuscript, rereading what he'd typed earlier that day. Graeme would've gone to bed with Kayana if it hadn't been so early. She made it a habit to get into bed by 10:00 in order to get at least six hours of sleep before getting up at 4:30 to begin work at 5:00. And when he varied his schedule and they went to bed together, they usually put off sleeping until after making passionate love to each other.

Making love with Kayana excited and frightened him at the same time. Each was so attuned to what brought the other maximum pleasure, and whenever she initiated the act, Graeme feared losing complete control. And once the act was over, he was left as helpless as a newborn, while praying she would never come to know the power she wielded over him.

Turning over his hourglass, he began typing. He'd completed two-thirds of the book and planned to write until the sand ran out. Graeme had learned from the episode when he'd compromised his health by writing around the clock for days, and he vowed not to repeat it. He'd just completed a chapter when his cellphone chimed a familiar ringtone.

He tapped the screen. It was his caretaker. "Yes, Rick."

"I'm sorry to bother you, Mr. Ogden, but I thought you needed to know that we just had a violent thunderstorm, and a tree fell onto the roof of the house. Several windowpanes on the bedroom over the dining room were knocked out, and I've tried putting a tarp over them to keep out the rain. I know you're going to have to call the insurance company—"

"It's all right, Rick. I'm coming up." He knew that, as the owner of the property, he would have to meet with the insurance adjuster to get an estimate of the cost to repair the roof and determine if there was any structural damage to the house.

"When should I expect you?"

"Tomorrow. I'm going to fly into Boston. I'll let you know when I'm expected to arrive, because I'd like you to pick me up."

"No problem, Mr. Ogden."

Graeme cursed under his breath. The year before, he'd replaced all of the windows in the house with energy-saving ones to reduce the expense of heating the large house with its twenty-foot ceilings. The house was listed on the national register of historic places, and he made certain to preserve it for its historical significance.

He scrolled through his directory to find a corporate jet to reserve a direct flight into Boston. He also had to call the groomer in the morning to board Barley until his return. Forty minutes later, he got into bed with Kayana. He was surprised to find that she was still awake.

"I have to go home tomorrow."

Turning over, she stared at him. "What's wrong?"

He told her about the phone call from the caretaker, and

that he'd reserved a direct flight to Boston with a private carrier. "I'm going to call the groomer tomorrow to board Barley until I come back."

Kayana sat up. "You can't, Graeme! The baby's going to be traumatized if he's caged up again."

"I can't take him with me, Kay. It would be different if I was driving."

"I'll take care of him. I'll house- and dog-sit while you're gone. Don't forget I have a set of keys."

"I can't ask you to do that."

"You're not asking. I'm volunteering."

"What about your friend?" Graeme asked.

"What about her?" Kayana countered. "She can stay at my place at night, while I sleep here. After work, I'll come over and check on Barley and make certain he's being a good boy. Meanwhile, Mariah can help out at the Café. She got a lot of experience waiting tables when she worked at a restaurant in high school and college. She will 'baby,' 'honey bunch,' and 'darling' a customer to death and wind up with a pocket full of tips at the end of her shift."

Graeme laughed, despite the seriousness of the scene that would greet him once he arrived in Newburyport. Many of the trees on the property were more than one hundred years old, and he realized he had to get someone to examine them for rot and/or to remove trees entirely or prune some of their branches.

"She sounds like a lot of fun."

"She's the best, Graeme. If everyone had a friend like Mariah, the world would be a lot happier."

He dropped a kiss on her hair. "You're very lucky, babe."

"I'm more than lucky," she whispered against his throat. "I'm blessed to have wonderful people in my life."

Graeme wanted to admit to Kayana that he was also blessed to have her in his life. "I'm not certain how long I'll be gone, but I'll text or call you with updates."

"Your house and your puppy are safe with me. What time and which airport are you leaving from?"

"Wilmington at twelve-thirty. I already called a car service to drop me off."

"Do you anticipate a lot of damage to the house?" she asked.

"The caretaker says it's only one bedroom, but I'll see once I get there. One of these days, I'd like you to come up and see the house. The best time is around the Christmas holidays because everything looks like a picture postcard."

"Maybe one of these days I'll come up to Massachusetts to see where the American Revolution began."

"You have to admit we were a bunch of badasses to challenge the mighty power that was the British Empire."

"They soon found out that a bunch of Yankee farmers with muskets, hoes, and pitchforks weren't going to roll over and submit to their tyranny."

Graeme pressed his mouth to her forehead. "I've kept you up long enough. Go to sleep, babe. I promise to get you up if you oversleep."

Kayana draped her bare smooth leg over his. "Good night again."

Graeme held Kayana until her breathing slowed, and she finally fell asleep. Reaching over, he turned off the bedside lamp on his side of the bed. Just when he was beginning to get used to sharing his bed with Kayana, he would have to leave her and Coates Island. She wasn't actually living with him because she hadn't moved all of her possessions into the house, yet it was the first step in his hoping to convince her that they could live together. He had given up on the likelihood they would marry, which meant he had to be content with whatever arrangement she would agree to.

Graeme closed his eyes and shook his head when he saw the aftermath from the storm. The top third of the massive tree lay across the length of the bedroom, and if anyone had been sleeping in the bed, they would not have survived. There were leaves, glass, and tree bark everywhere, and he knew nothing could be moved or cleaned up until after the adjuster arrived.

"What do you think, Mr. Ogden?"

He turned to find the caretaker standing in the hallway behind him. Richard O'Neill Jr. was only two years older than Graeme. The son of the former gardener and housekeeper, Richard Sr. and Dorcas, Rick had elected to stay on as the property's caretaker after his parents passed away. Graeme hadn't had much contact with Rick during the school year, but once his parents closed the townhouse in Boston to return to Newburyport for the summer, they were inseparable whenever the Ogdens weren't traveling abroad. When his mother chided him for spending too much time with the help's son, Graeme realized she wasn't as liberal-minded as she professed, but as he grew older, he'd come to understand that there was a distinct delineation when it came to social class. It was obvious Rick understood the differences because he'd gone from calling him Master Graeme to Mr. Ogden. And there was never a time when he'd slipped up and addressed him as Graeme.

"It's a wicked mess, Rick."

"I'd say it's more than a mess, Mr. Ogden. That tree is going to have to be cut into pieces before it can be carted away."

Graeme stared at the tall, slender man with bright blue eyes and strawberry-blond hair. Rick was in his early twenties when he fell in love with a local girl, but she broke his heart when she married an older man willing to give her what Rick wasn't able to.

"You're right about that. Once the adjuster finishes with his estimate, I'm going to call a company that will take care of everything."

"What about the furniture?"

"I doubt it can be replaced." All of the furnishings in the house had been appraised and authenticated for insurance purposes, but Graeme had no intention of hiring someone to go to auctions or estate sales to replace the antiques. Reproductions would have to suffice. "I believe I need a drink, but I hate drinking alone. What say you, Rick? Let's crack open my grandfather's aged scotch and see if it's as good as they make it out to be."

Rick's eyes shimmered like polished blue topaz. "Are you sure?"

"As sure as that big-ass tree that decided it was better inside the house than out."

"I'll go down to the wine cellar and dust off a bottle."

Graeme lingered in the bedroom, surveying the damage for another minute before turning on his heel and taking the back staircase to the first story. His grandfather had been a collector: antique cars, aged liquor, and imported wine, and he had a penchant for younger women. Although married, he'd had several mistresses who were young enough to be his daughter, while his blue-blood wife turned a blind eye to her husband's affairs; she loved the grand lifestyle even more than her husband.

Graeme folded his body down into a leather armchair in the library and watched as Rick poured a couple ounces of scotch into highball glasses. He'd lost track of the number of hours he'd spent in the room as a boy, sitting on a chair in the corner while his grandfather held business meetings. Laurence Jacoby Norris claimed he wanted to expose his six-year-old grandson to the way he conducted business. He wasn't allowed to say anything but was meant to just watch and listen. Once the meetings concluded, Graeme was tested on what he'd heard and was asked if he agreed or disagreed with his grandfather's decision to invest in or sell properties.

As he grew older, he understood what his grandfather was attempting to teach him. A country's economy wasn't only its lifeblood; it was the heart that pumped the blood.

He took the glass from Rick, held it up in a toast, and took a sip. "Boy, that is really smooth."

Rick nodded in agreement. "It's the best I've tasted. I bet the old man would be spinning in his grave if he knew the help was lounging in his inner sanctum, drinking his ninety-year-old single-malt scotch."

"Speaking of help, Rick. It's time you stop calling me Mr. Ogden."

Bright blue eyes met a pair of light gray ones. "What do you want me to call you?"

"Graeme. After all, this is my name."

Rick bit his lip. "Why now? What happened?"

Slumping lower in his chair, Graeme stared at row upon row of books lining the wall in a built-in bookcase. "Now that I'm retired and have nothing but time on my hands, I've done a lot of thinking about things. For example, I realize you're the closest thing I have to a brother."

"Don't forget a 'big' brother," Rick teased.

Graeme smiled. Rick was the one who had taught him how to drive, bought alcohol for them before Graeme was twenty-one, and introduced him to the cousin of his then girlfriend, who'd shown him a world of sexual pleasure he never could've imagined.

"You're right about that. We were brothers in crime."

Rick grimaced. "Not quite crime, but trouble," he said, and then gave Graeme a lingering stare. "I don't know what it is, but there's something different about you. Maybe it's because you're retired and more relaxed."

Graeme crossed his feet at the ankles. "That's because I'm at a different place in my life."

Pale eyebrows lifted questioningly. "Does it have anything to do with a woman?"

It was as if he and Rick had turned back the clock to when they were young boys and confided in each other about any and everything. "Yes."

"Are you in love with her—Graeme?"

"Yes, I am."

"Good for you. When are you bringing her home?"

Rick was asking Graeme a question he couldn't answer. Not now. When he'd mentioned home, he knew Rick was talking about the house in Newburyport. But for him the house on Coates Island was now home. It was where he felt more alive than he had in years. It was also where he felt most creative. But, more important, it was where he'd met and fallen in love with a woman who complemented him in every way.

"I don't know, Rick." He set his glass on a leaded crystal coaster. "Let's go out and get something to eat, because I'm beginning to feel the effects of Grandpa's liquid gold."

Rick stood up, placing his glass on a matching coaster. "I'm game. Give me a few minutes to change my clothes, and I'll meet you by the garage."

Chapter 18

"Do you put out a spread like this every Sunday?" Mariah asked Kayana as they carried dishes from the Café's kitchen to the patio.

She smiled at her friend, nodding. "Yes."

Mariah had arrived late Saturday afternoon, and after changing her clothes, she had immediately put on an apron and begun assisting the waitstaff taking dinner orders.

Kayana was shocked upon seeing her friend for the first time in six months. Although they talked on the phone every other month, Mariah had neglected to tell her that she'd gone on a diet, and the result was a loss of nearly forty pounds. She'd gone from a size twenty to a fourteen, and the transformation was complete when she'd stopped relaxing her salt-and-pepper, shoulder-length hair and adopted a close-cropped style. The result was stunning and head-turning. The weight loss had slimmed her face to reveal exquisite cheekbones in a gold-brown complexion with a faint sprinkling of freckles over her pert nose.

Mariah was married to her high school sweetheart when Kayana had met her in grad school, but the union ended once

Thomas Hinton revealed he was bisexual. Following her divorce, Mariah had dated a few men until she met Haji Davis. He became the love of her life, and she talked incessantly about wanting to marry again. But it was obvious her lover avoided the issue like the plague, and Kayana had suggested to her friend that she stop bringing up the subject, that no man wanted to be pressured into marriage.

Kayana had decided to prepare the quintessential southern Sunday dinner, with fried chicken, collard greens, macaroni and cheese, and buttery cornbread. Cherie had sent her a text saying she was bringing strawberry shortcake for dessert, while Leah had volunteered to bring the ingredients for a champagne punch.

"What are your book club friends like?" Mariah asked.

"You'll see when they get here."

A frown appeared between Mariah's clear brown eyes. "That's not telling me anything."

"I'm not saying anything because I don't want you to have any preconceived notions. The only other thing I'm going to say is that I look forward to discussing books with them."

She hadn't mentioned Graeme to Mariah; she didn't want her friend to accuse her of being a sell-out because she was dating a man who wasn't black. Mariah hadn't forgiven her mother for sleeping with a white man who'd abandoned her when she'd told him she was pregnant with his child, which had resulted in Mariah having unresolved issues about her father. And when she'd told Mariah she was house- and dog-sitting for a friend, Kayana let her draw her own conclusion as to the race of the man whose house she was looking after during his absence.

She and Graeme exchanged texts every night. He'd reminded her they would miss seeing *Les Misérables*, but promised to make it up to her when he returned. She'd told him not to worry because there was always next summer. He also gave her updates on repairs to the house; it would be at least another two weeks before he received confirmation from the insurance company because there was a backlog of claims due to the storm. Kayana reassured him that Barley was well and she was trying not to spoil him, but to no avail, though she hadn't gone against his wishes not to allow the puppy in the kitchen or the bedroom.

Kayana detected the sound of an approaching vehicle. "That must be Leah and Cherie. I'll be right back. I have to open the door for them." She left the patio and opened the door to find the driver of the jitney holding a large wicker picnic basket.

"It was a little heavy for Mrs. Kent, so I volunteered to carry it for her."

Kayana opened the door wider. "Please come in, Henry, and put it on one of the tables." The basket was filled with bottles of champagne and ginger ale and a half-gallon jar of a pinkish mixture.

Leah surreptitiously slipped the young man a bill. "Thank you so much."

"No problem, Mrs. Kent. You can call me when you're ready to leave."

With wide eyes, Leah shook her head. "That's okay, Henry. Miss Johnson will drive me back."

"I think someone has the hots for Mrs. Kent," Cherie crooned as she cradled a large white box tied with string and adorned with a sticker from the local bakery.

Leah rolled her eyes upward. "That kid is younger than my sons, and I can assure you that I'm no cougar."

"You can't be," Cherie said, "not with a husband who's old enough to be your father."

Leah cut her eyes at Cherie. "That's cold."

"Yeah, right," Cherie drawled. "You told me I could have any man I want when it's the same with you, *Mrs. Kent*. You attract young men, old men, and those in-between, so stop playing yourself."

Leah blushed under the deep tan that enhanced the color

of her bright blue eyes. "Well, all of that attention is coming to an end because I'm leaving in a couple of days. This will be my last book club discussion."

"Why?" Kayana and Cherie said in unison.

"I got a text from my boys that Alan's not feeling well, so they're cutting their trip short and coming back to the States."

Cherie set the box on the table with the basket and hugged Leah. "I'm sorry about teasing you about your husband."

Leah patted the younger woman's back. "It's okay, honey. Alan's going to be around for a long time. Adele is eighty-six and still raising hell, so he's got at least another twenty years to make my life a living hell before he kicks the bucket. Enough talk about my tormentors. I'm ready to get my eat and drink on and talk about books with my best friends."

Kayana put her arms around Cherie and Leah in a group hug. "We have to promise to do this again next summer."

"Yes."

"Of course."

Cherie and Leah had spoken at the same time.

"My good friend from Atlanta is staying with me for a few days, so she'll be joining us this afternoon."

Kayana led them to the patio and introduced them to Mariah, who'd rearranged the place settings to make room for the platter of crispy fried chicken. "Mariah, I'd like you to meet Leah Kent and Cherie Thompson. Ladies, this Mariah Hinton from the ATL. Mariah and I go way back to when we were in college together."

The three women exchanged pleasantries before sitting down at the table. Meanwhile, Kayana removed a chilled punch bowl from the fridge and emptied the jar that held a blended mixture of pineapple juice, triple sec, brandy, and black-raspberry liqueur into the bowl and then added chilled ginger ale and dry champagne. She ladled the punch into cold mason jars and took a sip after serving everyone.

"Wow! That's delicious, Leah. When you told me what you were going to use to make the punch, I never would've expected it to taste this good."

Mariah smiled at Leah. "It's sneaky as hell. First, you think you're drinking some fountain fruit drink—until it goes down and detonates in your chest."

"Word," Cherie drawled. "This punch is crazy good. But I'd better eat something, or I'll find myself on my hind parts."

The platter of Cajun honey chicken was passed around the table, followed by a bowl of collard greens with pieces of smoked brisket, the chef's legendary macaroni and cheese, and generous slices of buttery cornbread. Conversation was minimal as everyone ate and drank their fill.

Mariah, moaning, pressed a napkin to her mouth. "Damn you, Kay. If I keep eating like this, I'm going to gain back the forty pounds I lost."

Cherie patted her flat belly. "I'm ready for a nap right about now."

Leah sighed. "I'm with Cherie. Kayana, do you mind if, after we clear the table, we go upstairs and veg out until our food digests?"

Kayana shared a look with Mariah, who gave her a barely perceptible nod. Mariah was now staying in the apartment, and she'd learned years ago that her friend tended to be less than tidy, while she was obsessive about neatness.

Mariah pushed back her chair. "I'm going upstairs for a few minutes."

Kayana knew Mariah wanted to straighten up the apartment before the others went up. "Go on up. We'll be there directly." She picked up the platter with several pieces of chicken. "Leah, Cherie, do you want me to pack up the leftovers for you?"

"Please," Leah said. "Even though Cherie doesn't have access to a refrigerator, she can come over to my place to eat.

There's no way I'm going to be able to finish everything when I'm leaving in a couple of days."

Cherie pantomimed bowing to Leah. "Thank you, Auntie Leah." She sobered quickly. "I know I've said things to you that were out of line, and if you were offended, I'm sorry."

Leah waved a hand. "Honey, please. I've had a lot worse said to me, and I'm still here."

Cherie lowered her eyes. "I have a habit of saying hateful things to people who've never done anything to me, while I give the SOBs a pass. Maybe I should have a couple of sessions with Kayana."

Kayana slowly shook her head. "That's not going to happen. I can talk to you like a friend, but not as a client. The days when I had to counsel folks are over, and I don't want to resurrect them."

"You don't miss it?" Leah asked Kyana, as she stacked plates and flatware.

"Not now. When I first handed in my resignation, I spent several weeks second-guessing myself, while wondering if I was doing the right thing giving up everything I'd worked for. But then I realized I couldn't continue to work for the same hospital where my ex and his mistress were employed."

"Why?" Cherie asked. "Were you afraid you would confront them in public?"

"Not hardly, Cherie. There is no way I would embarrass myself like that. And if I did act a fool, that would just serve to inflate my ex's ego, and no man is worth that. Think of it. Males in the animal kingdom fight each other over a herd of females, while in the human species, women fight other women over a man. I've watched women go out to eat with men who spend the entire time on their phones, and when it comes time to pay the bill, he'll either get up to use the restroom, or she'll go into her handbag and push money across the table, so it appears he's paying for dinner. And the real ballsy ones just sit there while she signs the credit card receipt."

Leah went completely still. "Should I assume that it's a pet peeve for you when a woman assumes financial responsibility for a man?"

"Yes and no. If the man is able-bodied and just too lazy to work and support himself—then yes. But if he's been with you and holding his own and happens to fall on bad times, there's nothing wrong with helping him until he's back on his feet."

Cherie picked up serving pieces. "What happened to 'for better or worse'?"

Kayana gave the young woman a sidelong glance. "That's for folks who exchange marriage vows."

"What about people who live together?" Cherie had asked another question.

"That turns the relationship into a different dynamic. The two people are not legally bound to each other, and therefore it's not as complicated."

A beat passed before Leah asked, "What if they have children together?"

"Then they'll have to deal with child support and visitation."

"That's why it's easier to stay together."

Kayana wanted to ask Leah who was she kidding. She had convinced herself it was better to stay with a cheating husband than go through a divorce. "That brings us to *Ethan Frome*. We know Ethan is in love with his wife's cousin, wants to run away with her, but doesn't have the money he needs for them to start a life together."

Cherie followed Leah and Kayana into the restaurant's kitchen. "He never should've been lusting after his wife's cousin in the first place."

Leah lined up a number of takeout containers on the prep table. "It was apparent that Ethan's initial attraction to Mattie was innocent enough, but the longer she lived with him and his wife, the more he found himself tempted by her presence."

"And you think his wife didn't notice this when she decided to send her away?" Kayana questioned.

"Of course, she did," Cherie confirmed. "The woman may have been a hypochondriac, but she wasn't insane. It was obvious, although Wharton wasn't that descriptive, that Ethan's and Mattie's body language told Zenobia that something was going on between the two."

"Temptation is so dangerous," Leah whispered.

"That it is," Kayana intoned. "Temptation is a recurring theme throughout the Bible. Did not the snake tempt Adam and Eve in the Garden of Eden when he convinced them to eat the apple?"

Leah stared at Kayana. "They didn't have to eat it, because God had given them free will to choose to die or live forever."

Cherie rested a hip against the countertop. "A person can be warned that someone or something may not be good for them, but only when they have to deal with the consequences of their actions does it become a reality."

"True," Leah agreed, "but how many folks are strong enough to be able to resist temptation?"

"Apparently not that many, or our prisons wouldn't be filled to capacity with people who disobey the law," Kayana stated. "Ethan knew it was wrong to lust after his wife's cousin and then felt guilty when he attempted to get a cash advance from a customer for a load of lumber so he would have the money to run away with her. So he wasn't completely amoral."

Cherie sat on a stool as Leah and Kayana busied themselves storing food in containers and putting the containers away and stacking dishes in the commercial dishwasher. "If we're talking about morally, then he did sin in his thoughts."

"But did he act on them?" Leah questioned.

"Yes. Didn't he agree to the suicide pact Mattie suggested so they would always be together?"

"But look what it got them," Leah argued softly. "They

sled down a hill, hit a tree, and he's crippled and she's para-lyzed for life. So much for dying together."

"Are y'all talking about Ethan Frome?" Mariah asked, walking into the kitchen.

Leah smiled. "Yes."

Mariah sat on a stool next to Cherie. "I read that book in high school, and it wasn't until years later that I came to re-alize that karma is a bitch. Sow a bad seed, reap a bad seed. And vice versa with a good deed. Ethan knew it was wrong to hit on his wife's cousin, but if you were to ask him, he would say he couldn't help it, and that's what most men say when they're caught stepping out on their wives."

"Are you married, Mariah?" Leah asked.

"Not any longer. My ex-husband couldn't decide whether he liked men or women. I decided to make it easy for him when I told him to go and find himself."

Cherie's jaw dropped in shock. "You never suspected he was bisexual?"

"Nope."

"It didn't bother you that he also liked men?"

Mariah smiled. "No, Cherie. And that didn't make me feel any less a woman. I've counseled women who blame themselves for their husband or boyfriend's infidelity. What most don't realize is that it has nothing to do with them. They can be the perfect wife or mother, and their man will still cheat."

"But why do they cheat?" Cherie asked.

"Because they can," Kayana and Mariah said in unison, as they exchanged fist bumps.

Leah chewed her lower lip. "Do you think women make it easy for men to cheat?"

Mariah glared at the redhead. "I refuse to accept blame for someone else's bad behavior. I'm certain if we'd asked Ethan why he wanted to abandon his wife, he probably would've said he got tired of taking care of a sick woman. But then I'd tell him that's what you signed up for when you married her.

Did he forget he took a vow to be with her through sickness and health?"

"He did," Kayana quipped, "until his sap began to rise. Mattie was young, pretty, and full of life. And because she'd been living with the Fromes for a year, she was a constant reminder to Ethan that she was the complete opposite of his sickly, complaining wife."

"I really liked Zenobia," Mariah admitted, "because she is redeemed, even though she's not seeking retribution, when the roles are reversed and she has to care for her crippled husband and bedridden cousin."

"Didn't you say karma is a bitch?" Cherie said under her breath.

"Yes, she is. You don't have to wish for payback because when she comes with her sisters and aunties, she's going to even the score. It's like the Sandman who comes on stage at the Apollo Theater on Amateur Nights with a broom. Bam! You're done."

Kayana knew Mariah, with her outgoing personality, would get along well with her book club friends. They stayed in the kitchen talking and laughing like schoolgirls until she glanced up at the clock. It was time for her to return to Graeme's house and let Barley out. She dropped Leah off at her rental with a promise she'd come by the restaurant before leaving for Virginia and then left Cherie at the boardinghouse. They'd decided tonight would be their last book club meeting until the following summer.

Barley greeted her with excited barking when she opened the door. Kayana had become very attached to the tiny dog and constantly resisted the urge to let him sleep on the foot of her bed as she had done with her dog.

"Well, big boy, it's time for me to turn in for the night because I have to get up early to go to work," she crooned to the puppy staring up at her. "I promise when I come home tomorrow afternoon, I'm going to take you on a long walk around the neighborhood so you can get some exercise."

Kayana checked doors and windows, making certain every-thing was locked before activating the alarm. She stripped off her clothes and walked into the en suite bath to shower. It had been a long day, and the bed was calling her name. The first few nights she'd slept alone in the bed, it had taken her a while to fall asleep. But her days were full cooking and spending time with Mariah. Some afternoons, she retreated to her apartment to relax or take a nap to reenergize herself.

It was only at night that she missed Graeme: their cooking together, sharing meals, and making love. He hadn't given her a date for when he would return, but Kayana had begun counting down the days, because they had less than three weeks before the mass exodus of vacationers, when Coates Island would settle into the slow, laid-back normalcy long-time locals craved.

Graeme felt as if he had been holding his breath during the three weeks he'd spent in Newburyport. Within minutes of the jet touching down in North Carolina, he'd slipped onto the rear seat of the limo and knew he had come home. Legally, he wasn't permitted to sell the house in Massachu-setts; it was to remain in the family for perpetuity, and if he didn't assign an heir, then it would go into receivership to the Commonwealth.

The adjuster arrived, noted the damage for his records, and without waiting for receipt of the check, Graeme con-tacted a company to remove the massive tree and cut it into firewood. Cleaning up the bedroom was a herculean task, as the cleaning crew had to locate hundreds, if not thousands, of shards of glass. The furniture was removed and sent to a factory, where it turned out that many of the pieces could be restored to their original condition. After the windows were replaced and the roof repaired, Graeme felt comfortable re-turning to Coates Island. Rick had promised to keep him abreast of each stage of the repairs.

Reuniting and spending time with Rick made Graeme

aware of why they'd had a tight bond as young kids. Rick felt comfortable enough to be forthcoming about his on again, off again relationship with a parochial schoolteacher. The fact that he only had a high school diploma made him feel insecure in his relationship with a college graduate. And when Graeme suggested he take online courses, Rick said he would think about it.

While Rick was thinking about furthering his education, Graeme could not stop thinking about Kayana. He knew he had to tell her about his plan not to return to New England at the end of the summer season, yet he wanted to wait for the right time.

He opened the door to the house and saw Barley staring up at him. "What's the matter, buddy? You don't remember me? Have I been gone that long?" Barley walked slowly toward him before jumping up against his leg. Graeme scooped up the wiggling puppy and held him against his chest. "It looks as if Kay took good care of you."

Graeme put Barley down and mounted the staircase. He wanted to shower and change before Kayana arrived. He purposely had not told her when he was returning because he wanted to surprise her.

Kayana opened the door and froze. She hadn't expected to find Graeme standing in the entryway grinning at her. Her smile matched his. "Welcome home."

Graeme extended his arms, and she walked into his embrace. "It's good to be home." He rested his chin on the top of her head. "Did you enjoy having your friend stay with you?"

"Mariah and I had a ball. She left to go back to Hot Lanta last week."

Lowering his head, Graeme brushed his mouth over hers, and the scent of mint from his mouthwash wafted to her nostrils. "I've missed you so much," he whispered over and over.

Kayana reached up, her arms circling his neck. "Show me how much you missed me."

She did not remember Graeme kissing her or sweeping her up in his arms and carrying her upstairs to the bedroom. Her hands were as busy as his when they undressed each other. There was no prolonged foreplay when he parted her legs with his knee, both groaning in pleasure once he was inside her. Not having the layer of latex between them and the ferocity of his penetration sent her libido into overdrive.

Grunts, groans, gasps, moans, arching, and thrusting punctuated their lovemaking. They strained to get even closer, and together Kayana and Graeme found a tempo where their bodies were in perfect harmony. Waves of desire and ecstasy held them captive until the dam broke and Kayana surrendered to the passion that left her shuddering in a shared released with the man she had been falling in love with.

Graeme lay heavily on Kayana as he waited for his heart to resume its normal rhythm. He hadn't meant to make love with her without a condom, but it was too late because he had come inside her.

"I'm sorry, babe."

"What are you sorry about?"

"I didn't use a condom."

Kayana exhaled an audible breath. "Are you carrying an STD?"

"No."

"Then not to worry, my love. We don't have to worry about making babies, and because I'm not carrying an STD, then we're good." She pressed a kiss to his throat. "Maybe you should go away more often if only to experience this type of reunion."

Graeme rolled off her body and stared up at the ceiling. "Is that what you want me to do? Go away?"

Rolling over her side, Kayana nuzzled his nose with her ear. "No. I want you to stay."

"For how long?"

"I don't know, Graeme. How long can you stay?"

"I can stay as long as you want."

Kayana rose slightly on her elbow. "What about school?"

"What about it?"

"Why are you answering my question with a question, Graeme?"

"Because I want you to know that I don't have to go back to Newburyport to teach."

She sat up straight, staring down at the man who made her feel things she didn't want to feel. Had he fallen and injured his head? Was he on drugs? Or had he taken leave of his senses? "Say that again."

"I said I don't have to go back to Newburyport to teach because I retired."

Kayana's mouth opened, but nothing came out. "When did you do this?" she asked, finally finding her voice.

"Last school term. I handed in my resignation in May."

She closed her eyes and counted slowly to ten. "All this time you let me believe you were leaving here at the end of the summer. You must have been laughing your head off at my gullibility. Or should I say my naïveté."

"You're wrong, Kay."

"Yes, Graeme, I'm wrong. I am so wrong for trusting you when you didn't trust me enough to tell me that you plan to live here. Do you remember what I said to you about trust? It means more to me than love. You're the second man I've let myself fall in love with, and I can't trust either of you." She swung her legs over the side of the bed. "I've got to go."

Graeme panicked. He would've felt better if Kayana had raised her voice or thrown things; he was thrown by the soft tone he called her therapist's voice. "Please don't leave."

She shook her head as she gathered up the discarded garments strewn on the bed and floor. "I have to leave now before I say something I'll regret later."

"Please, Kayana." He was begging and didn't care if she knew it. He would grovel if he had to if that would keep her from walking out of his life.

"No, Graeme. I can't. I need time to process this . . . this shit you just dumped on me. Why couldn't you have told me this before we slept together?"

He ran a hand over his face. "I don't know."

"Neither do I. You claimed your mother kept secrets you didn't find out about until after she'd died. Do you realize you're no different than she was? Better yet, don't answer that, because I'm certain you're probably hiding other things from me."

"There is something else, but I can't tell you."

"You can't or you won't? Which is it?"

"I can't."

"And why not?"

"Because you're not my wife."

Kayana slipped into her underwear. "And I'll never become your wife, so your secret is safe."

He watched as she finished dressing, wanting to tell her he was Brendan Andersen, but his tongue seemed to be stuck to the roof of his mouth, rendering him mute. "There's one more thing I have to tell you."

"Keep it to yourself,' she spat out.

"I love you, Kayana. I fell in love with you the first time I walked into the Café last summer, and it wasn't until I'd discovered you were single and not seeing anyone that I decided to buy this place."

Kayana turned to look at him. "Was I also the reason you resigned your teaching position?"

"No. After Jillian died, it was as if nothing was the same. The house had become a tomb where people go to die. I got tired of my colleagues asking me if I was all right or feeling the need to invite me somewhere. All the things I'd enjoyed up to that time were no longer important, and I knew I had to change things."

She gave him a forced smile. "Then you found me."

"Yes, I found you."

"Look, Graeme, you're going to have to give me time to sort this out in my head."

"Does this mean you still love me?"

"I don't know about you, but I'm not able to turn my feelings on and off like a faucet. And the answer to that question is yes, I still love you, but if you fuck up again, then forget you ever knew me."

Graeme felt as if he'd won a battle, but it wasn't clear about the war. And Kayana had declared war on him because he hadn't been forthcoming about his future, and he knew he owed that to her before he asked her to come live with him.

It wasn't as if she hadn't warned him about trust; yet he didn't trust her enough to let her know he'd planned to make the island his chief residence. He left the bed, picked up his briefs, and stepped into them. He would give her time to calm down and not put any pressure on her to reconcile. Now that she knew he would live on Coates Island, she wouldn't be able to avoid him.

Chapter 19

Kayana tried to ignore the incessant tapping on her apartment door, but she knew that if she didn't answer, the person would not go away. "Who is it?"

"Derrick. Will you please come and open the door?"

Groaning, she managed to pull herself off the love seat and walk to the door. The summer season was over, life had returned to normal, and now she and Derrick were responsible for a buffet brunch from 10:00 a.m. to 2:00 p.m., Monday through Saturday, which left her with more time on her hands than she knew what to do with. Last year, she couldn't wait for the vacationers to leave so she could do all the things she'd been denied when living in Atlanta. But this year was different; she did not want to believe how much she had come to depend on spending her free time with Graeme.

She missed him so much, yet she still wasn't ready to forgive him for his deception. She was aware that he came into the Café several times a week for brunch, and the one time they saw each other, he'd smiled and acknowledged her with a slight nod of the head before walking out.

Kayana unlocked the door, and Derrick brushed past her and sat on a chair in the living room. "Well, hello to you too."

Crossing his arms over his chest, her brother glared at her. "Cut the bullshit, Kayana."

"What!"

"You heard what I said. Now, sit down so we can talk."

Her temper flared. "Have you forgotten that this is my place, brother? And I give the orders, not you?"

Derrick ran a large hand over his cropped gray hair. "Please sit down, sister love."

"Oh, now you're being fake."

"No, Kay, you're the fake one. I don't know what went down between you and Graeme Ogden, but I need to know before I kick the man's ass for hurting my sister."

Kayana panicked. Derrick and Graeme shared equal height, but Derrick had managed to stay in top physical condition despite not going into the NFL. He'd set up a gym in his house and worked out practically every day. And if he did hit Graeme, there was no doubt he would seriously injure him.

"No! You don't understand."

"What I do understand, Kay, is you going around with a long face while acting like you lost your best friend. You weren't this down in the mouth when you divorced that blowhard masquerading as a doctor."

"How did you know I was seeing Graeme?"

"How could I not know? This island is two miles long and three miles wide, and there's nothing that goes on here that folks don't know about. A few people mentioned to me that they saw your BMW parked at Graeme's house, so it's obvious you were spending nights there." He held up a hand. "And I also know you stayed over to watch his house and his dog when he flew back to Massachusetts for several weeks."

"Well, damn!"

Derrick smiled. "Yes, damn. Now tell me what's wrong that you don't want to see him."

Kayana sat down on a chair facing Derrick's and told him everything. It was as if they'd turned back the clock to the days when she'd come crying to him about some boy she liked who didn't seem remotely interested in her. She could always count on her brother to make her feel better when he told her she was too good for the boy; if he couldn't recognize a diamond, then he wasn't worth her time.

"You overreacted, Kay. The man not telling you something doesn't mean he lied to you. To be honest, he isn't obligated to tell you anything, because, after all, you're not his wife. And even husbands and wives have secrets from each other."

"Oh, don't I know that."

"I'm not talking about cheating, Kay. You claim Graeme has something else to tell you, but he can't because you're not married."

"Yes."

"Do you want to marry him?"

Derrick was asking her a question she'd asked herself again and again the past two months, and each time she found herself in a quandary. Not only did she love Graeme, but she had fallen hopelessly in love with him. And she did not want to believe that she'd waited until she was forty-six to find a man so attuned to her wants and needs that she sometimes believed she'd conjured him up.

"I think I do."

"You think or you know?"

"I know, Derrick."

"Well, Miss Kayana Cassandra Johnson, what are you going to do about it?"

Kayana buried her face in her hands. "I suppose I'm going to let Mr. Graeme Norris Ogden know he can tell me his secret because I'm willing to become his wife."

Derrick slapped his thigh. "That's my girl. You're off this week, so why don't you spend some time with the man I wouldn't mind calling my brother-in-law?" He stood up. "I meant to tell you that the week I'm off, I'm driving down to Florida to check up on my baby girl. I'm not going to tell her I'm coming because if I find her hugged up with some little shit, I'm going to snap his neck and make her come back home for her last year."

Deandra had elected to spend her senior year in Florida while applying to schools in the state as a permanent resident. "You will not do that to my niece, or she'll never forgive you."

"I gave her the rules, and I expect her to follow them, or she'll suffer the consequences."

Kayana knew her brother was overprotective when it came to his daughter, but there was no need to go Neanderthal because she liked a boy. Deandra's life had been planned for her, while Kayana still had to get hers together. She would take Derrick's advice and talk to Graeme. But there was one thing she would not do: grovel.

Graeme stood in the doorway, waiting for her, as she closed the door to her vehicle. She could see by his smile that he was happy to see her. Barley scampered over to her, sniffing her toes, as she bent down to pick him up. He was heavier than when she'd last seen him.

"Hey, baby boy. I miss you too," she crooned when he attempted to lick her chin.

Graeme cradled the back of her head and pressed a kiss to her forehead. "His daddy also missed you."

Kayana inhaled the familiar scent of his cologne. "Graeme. We have to talk."

"No, we don't, babe. We talked enough the last time you were here. You know that I love you, and you said that you love me. Now, what are we going to do about it?"

"What people in love normally do."

His eyebrows lifted. "And that is?"

"They get married and live happily ever after."

He angled his head. "That sounds about right. When and where do you want to marry?"

"Christmas in Newburyport."

"Hot damn! The woman's a mind reader. Do you think it's possible to have your family come up? There's plenty of bedrooms, and if they come during the winter break, they can stay the entire week. After they leave, we can honeymoon in Dubai for a couple of weeks."

"You really have everything planned out, don't you?"

"Why not? Did I not plan to buy property on Coates Island when I saw a woman who'd become my muse?"

"I'm the muse for your novel?"

"Yes. Now that we're going to be married, I want you to know I'm not an aspiring writer but a best-selling author of several books. I use the name Brendan Andersen, but the only people who know my identity are my agent, editor, and publisher. And now you."

With wide eyes, Kayana placed her fingers over her mouth. "For real?"

"Absolutely for real."

She didn't want to believe he was Brendan Andersen, the mysterious, reclusive writer who refused to be photographed and declined to be interviewed and whose books were snatched up the first day they were released.

Kayana pantomimed locking her lips and throwing away the key. "Your secret will never pass these lips."

Graeme took her hand, threading their fingers together. "Come with me to the study. I want to show you my next book."

"Am I in it?"

"Yes, you are."

Kayana did not want to believe her decision to come back to Coates Island and help her brother run the Seaside Café would result in her falling in love with a man whom she could not wait to marry despite her protestations she never wanted to marry again. And she was also looking forward to next summer to reunite with her book club buddies when she would inform them she was no longer Kayana Johnson but Kayana Ogden.

We hope you enjoyed THE SEASIDE CAFÉ,
the first book of
The Book Club series
by
Rochelle Alers.
The next book in the series, THE BEACH HOUSE,
is due out in
December 2020

If you missed the first book of Rochelle Alers's last series,
THE INHERITANCE,
just turn the page and take a sneak peek at an excerpt from
this best-selling book!
Available at your favorite bookstore or e-retailer.

Chapter 1

Smiling, the doorman touched the shiny brim of his cap with a white-gloved hand. "Have a good day, Ms. Lowell."

Hannah DuPont-Lowell returned his smile with a warm one of her own. "Thank you, Max."

Her smile still in place, she inhaled a lungful of warm air. It was mid-May, a glorious morning, and her favorite time of the year. The daytime temperature was predicted to reach seventy-eight degrees; the weather in New York City had gone from a damp and chilly spring to summer overnight, forcing her to modify her wardrobe.

Today she'd selected a navy-blue linen gabardine pantsuit with an emerald-green silk blouse and navy kitten heels. Hannah favored wearing lower heels because they were not only comfortable but practical. Since moving to New York, Hannah found herself walking everywhere: the three blocks from her apartment building to the office, and whenever she didn't eat lunch in the bank's cafeteria it was the half mile to her favorite French-inspired café; on weekends it was either strolling to Battery Park or to the South Street Seaport.

Hannah didn't meet the eyes of the stoic guard standing outside the historic four-story structure in the Stone Street Historic District that housed the private international investment bank where she'd worked for the past five years. No matter how many times she greeted him with a smile he never returned it. She wondered if he even knew how to smile. She knew his job was to monitor everyone coming into and leaving the building, but a nod of acknowledgment would have been nice. And it wasn't the first time she reminded herself she wasn't in the South, where most people greeted strangers with a nod and "mornin'," or "good evenin'."

Whenever she returned to New Orleans for vacation or family holidays, she unconsciously settled into her childhood home training. She'd been taught never to sass older folks, nor use profanity in their presence, and to speak when spoken to. In another two years she would celebrate her sixtieth birthday, and old habits were still hard to ignore.

Hannah swiped her ID before punching the button for the elevator to the second floor where the bank's legal offices occupied the entire space. The doors opened, and she came face-to-face with the attorney who ran Wakefield Hamilton Investment's legal department like a drill sergeant. Lateness—his pet peeve—extended from not coming in on time to not completing a project by a pre-determined date.

"You're wanted in the small conference room. Now!" he snapped when she hesitated.

Hannah resisted the urge to snap to attention and salute him as she stepped back into the elevator. The doors closed, shutting out his cold ice-blue eyes and the thin lips that were a mere slash in his corpulent face. The car descended to the first floor, and a minute later she entered the conference room. She recognized the occupants seated at a round oaken table: CEO, CFO, and a member of the bank's security staff. The three men rose to their feet.

CEO Braden Grant gave her a steady stare. "Please sit down, Ms. Lowell."

She sat, the others following suit. Hannah didn't know why, but she felt like she'd been summoned to the principal's office because of an infraction. A shiver raced over her body and it had nothing to do with the frigid air flowing from overhead vents. She rarely, if ever, met with the bank's senior officers.

Braden continued to stare at her. "Ms. Lowell, I'm sorry, but we're terminating your employment, effective immediately."

The CFO pushed an envelope across the table. "We've direct deposited three years' severance and the last quarter's profit sharing into your bank account, and we'll also cover the cost of your health insurance coverage for one full year. Earlier this week the board of directors held an emergency shareholders' meeting, and the stockholders voted to merge with another institution. The result is the entire New York operation will move to Trenton, New Jersey, this coming weekend."

She inhaled deeply in an attempt to slow down the runaway beating of her heart. Talk about being blindsided. Five years ago she'd resigned her position with a prominent law firm in midtown Manhattan to work for the bank, and it had been her plan to stay long enough to retire at sixty-seven.

"Am I the only one being terminated?" she asked, after an uncomfortable silence.

"No. Unfortunately, we've had to lay off half our employees," the chief financial officer replied in an emotionless monotone, "including upper management *and* support staff."

Hannah saw his mouth moving but she wasn't listening to what he was saying because she'd suddenly tuned him out. She knew that someday she would go back to her roots, because she'd always yearned for a slower pace in which to live out the rest of her life. It was apparent that day had come much sooner than she'd planned.

Braden cleared his throat. "Is there anything else you'd

like to ask or say, Ms. Lowell, before security escorts you to your office so you can retrieve your personal belongings?"

Her lips twisted into a cynical smile as she tucked a platinum strand of hair behind her left ear. He really didn't want to hear what she really longed to say. She stood, the others rising with her. "No. Thank you for everything. You've been most generous," Hannah drawled facetiously, when she wanted to curse them soundly for disrupting her life without prior notice.

She viewed the merger with skepticism, because there had been no discussion or rumors of a merger among any of the employees. She complimented herself for not losing her composure. If her mother had been alive there was no doubt she would've been very proud that her daughter had retained her ladylike poise, and poise was everything to Clarissa DuPont. Picking up the envelope, Hannah dropped it into her handbag and left the conference room.

The first thing she saw as she entered what would no longer be her office was the banker's box on the desk. It took less than ten minutes to remove laminated degrees from the wall, family photos, personal books and magazines off a credenza and store them in the box. She surrendered her ID badge, and the guard carried the box until they arrived at the entrance to the building.

It was apparent the CFO hadn't lied about the number of terminations, as evidenced by more than a dozen employees huddled together on the sidewalk. Their shock was visible. Those who were crying were comforted by their coworkers. She approached a woman who'd worked in human resources.

"Did you know about this?" she asked Jasmine Washington.

Jasmine shook her head, raven-black wavy hair swaying with the gesture. "Hell no!" she spat out. "And as the assistant director of personnel you'd think someone would've given me a heads-up."

Hannah glanced away when she saw tears filling Jasmine's eyes. She knew Jasmine had recently gone through a contentious divorce, even going so far as to drop her married name, and now being unemployed was akin to dousing a bonfire with an accelerant.

Recently certified public accountant Nydia Santiago shifted her box. "I don't know about the rest of you, but I could use a real stiff drink right about now."

Tonya Martin, the bank's former assistant chef, glared at Nydia. "It's nine flipping thirty in the morning, and none of the local watering holes are open at this time."

"I know where we can get a drink," Hannah volunteered. "Y'all come to my place," she added quickly when they gave her incredulous looks. "I live three blocks from here and y'all are welcome to hang out and, as you young folks say, get your drink on."

Tonya shifted an oversize hobo bag from one shoulder to the other. "Count me in."

Nydia looked at the others. "I'm game if the rest of you are."

Hannah met Jasmine's eyes. "Are you coming?"

"I guess so."

"You don't have to sound so enthusiastic, Jasmine," Nydia chided.

Hannah led the short distance to her apartment building. As the eldest of the quartet, she suspected she was in a better position financially than the other women, who were nowhere close to retirement age. And she didn't know what possessed her to invite them to her apartment, because she rarely socialized with her coworkers outside the office. She occasionally joined them at a restaurant for someone's birthday or retirement dinner, but none of them had ever come to her home.

The doorman gave Hannah a puzzled look, aware she'd left less than an hour ago. He opened the door to the air-cooled vestibule, nodding to each of the women. She wasn't about to tell him she was jobless, because New York City doormen were notorious gossips—at least with one another.

Tonya glanced around the opulent lobby with a massive chandelier and mahogany tables cradling large painted vases overflowing with a profusion of fresh flowers. "How long have you lived here?" she asked Hannah.

Hannah smiled at the chef, who had a flawless henna-brown complexion and dimpled cheeks. Lightly graying curly twists were pinned into a neat bun on the nape of her neck. "Almost eight years."

"And how long has it been since you left the South?" Tonya had asked another question. "Your down South was showing when you said 'y'all.' "

"I really never left," she admitted. "I go back to New Orleans at least twice a year."

"Do you prefer Louisiana to New York?" Nydia questioned.

Hannah waited until they were in the elevator, punching the button for the twenty-sixth floor, and then said, "It's a toss-up. Both cities are wonderful places to live," she answered truthfully.

She'd spent years living on the West Coast when her naval officer husband was stationed in San Diego, but after his second—and fatal—heart attack, her life changed dramatically, allowing her to live her life by her leave. Hannah gave each woman a cursory glance. She felt a commonality with them despite their differences in age, race, and ethnicity. And despite being educated professionals, they were now four unemployed career women.

The doors opened and they exited the car, their footsteps muffled in the deep pile of the carpet that ran the length of a hallway decorated with framed prints of various New York City landmarks. Hannah stopped at her apartment door, swiped her cardkey, waited for the green light, and then pushed opened the door to what had become her sanctuary. The dwelling was high enough above the streets that she didn't hear any of the city's noise and she could unwind at the end of a long, and an occasionally hectic, workday.

"Please come in and set down your boxes next to the table." A bleached pine table in the entryway held a collection of paperweights in various materials ranging from sterling to fragile cut-glass crystal. Hannah watched Nydia as she made her way across the open floor plan with a dining room, living room, and floor-to-ceiling windows.

"This is what I'm talking about," Nydia whispered, peering down at the cars and pedestrians on the streets below. "My boyfriend and I are looking for a place to live together, but nothing we've seen comes close to this." She turned, giving Hannah a long, penetrating stare. "How much do these apartments sell for?"

"Every apartment in this building is a rental."

Nydia grimaced. "And I can imagine the rents would be more than paying a mortgage."

She didn't have a comeback for Nydia, because Hannah never had to concern herself with mortgage payments. She'd inherited a house in New Orleans' Garden District that had been in her family for two centuries. She kicked off her shoes, leaving them under the table.

"Y'all make yourself comfortable. There's a bar under the credenza in the dining room, and I also have chilled champagne in the fridge if anyone wants a mimosa or Bellini."

Jasmine dropped her handbag on one of the straight-backed chairs flanking the table. "A Bellini sounds wonderful."

A smile parted Hannah's lips. "And I don't know about the rest of you, but I've never been able to drink on an empty stomach, so if you can wait for me to change into something a little more comfortable, I'll whip up something for us to eat."

Tonya nodded. "I'm with you. If you don't mind, I'm willing to cook."

Pressing her palms together, Hannah whispered a silent

prayer of thanks. Even though she was a more than adequate cook, it had been a while since she'd prepared a meal for someone other than herself. "Check in the fridge and use whatever you want." She'd planned to empty the refrigerator of perishables in the coming week anyway before she left to attend her high school's fortieth reunion.

Recipes

Deviled Egg Pasta Salad

4 cups cooked elbow macaroni
½ cup mayonnaise
¼ cup sour cream
1 tablespoon mustard
1 tablespoon white vinegar
1 teaspoon salt
¼ teaspoon pepper
8 hard-cooked eggs, chopped
¼ teaspoon paprika
¼ cup diced dill pickles

Place cooked pasta in a large bowl.

Add mayonnaise, sour cream, mustard, vinegar, salt, and pepper. Mix until well combined.

Gently stir in the hard-cooked eggs.

Refrigerate 1–2 hours or until chilled. Just before serving, top with paprika and pickles.

Makes 8 servings.

The Best Potato Salad

8 medium to large potatoes
10 hard-boiled eggs, chopped
2 cups chopped yellow onion
1 cup diced dill pickles
1 cup mayonnaise
¾ cup yellow mustard
¾ cup dill pickle juice
Salt and pepper to taste
Paprika (optional)

Boil the potatoes whole in the skin until fork tender, about 20–30 minutes.

Run water over the potatoes to cool.

Peel and chop the potatoes.

In a large bowl, combine the potatoes, eggs, onion, dill pickles, mayonnaise, and mustard.

Pour in the dill pickle juice and stir to combine.

Season to taste with salt and pepper.

Sprinkle with paprika, if desired.

Refrigerate until serving.

Sheet Pan Shrimp Fajitas

1 (1-ounce) package fajita seasoning
1 tablespoon olive oil
1½ pounds raw shrimp, peeled and deveined
1 red bell pepper, sliced into strips
1 yellow bell pepper, sliced into strips
1 red onion, sliced into strips
1 jalapeño pepper, sliced into rings

Preheat oven to 450° F (230° C).

Mix fajita seasoning and olive oil together in a large bowl. Add shrimp; toss to coat.

Lay out seasoned shrimp in a single layer on a baking sheet. Add red bell pepper, yellow bell pepper, red onion, and jalapeño pepper; mix with shrimp and spread out evenly.

Roast in the preheated oven until shrimp are opaque, 8–10 minutes. Transfer shrimp to a serving plate.

Broil pepper mixture until lightly blackened, 2–3 minutes. Transfer to the serving plate with shrimp.

Nashville Hot Fried Chicken

1 (3-pound) chicken, quartered
1 tablespoon kosher salt
2½ teaspoons freshly ground pepper, divided
1 cup milk
2 large eggs
1 tablespoon Louisiana-style hot sauce
2 cups all-purpose flour
2¾ teaspoons sea salt, divided
12 cups vegetable oil
½ cup lard, melted and heated (optional)
1–3 tablespoons ground red pepper
1 tablespoon light brown sugar
½ teaspoon each garlic powder and paprika

Wash chicken and pat dry. Combine kosher salt and 1½ teaspoons of pepper in a large bowl. Add chicken pieces and toss to coat. Cover and chill 8–24 hours.

Whisk together milk, eggs, and hot sauce in a large bowl; set aside.

Combine flour and 2 teaspoons of sea salt in a separate large bowl. Dip l chicken quarter into the flour mixture, then the egg mixture, and again in the flour mixture. Shake off the excess after each step. Repeat procedure with remaining chicken.

Heat oil in a 6- to 8-quart Dutch oven to 350° F. Set a wire rack on top of a rimmed baking sheet.

Fry chicken, in batches, 15–17 minutes for breast quarters and 18–20 minutes for leg quarters, or until crisp and dark golden brown and a thermometer inserted into the thickest part of the chicken registers 165° F; turn the chicken during the last 5 minutes of frying for even browning, if necessary. (The temperature will drop after chicken pieces are added to the oil. Adjust the temperature during frying, as necessary, to maintain a steady temperature of 325°.)

Remove the chicken from the hot oil, and drain on the prepared rack. Carefully ladle ½ cup frying oil into a medium-size, heatproof bowl. Whisk in red pepper, light brown sugar, garlic powder, paprika, and the remaining pepper and sea salt. Baste the hot chicken with the spiced oil. Serve immediately.

Makes 4 servings.

Best Caesar Dressing

1½ cups olive oil
1 tablespoon red wine vinegar
¼ cup lemon juice
1 tablespoon Worcestershire sauce
2 tablespoons anchovy paste
½ teaspoon mustard powder
4 cloves garlic, crushed
3 tablespoons sour cream
½ cup grated Parmesan cheese

In a food processor or blender, combine the olive oil, vinegar, lemon juice, Worcestershire sauce, anchovy paste, mustard powder, garlic, sour cream, and Parmesan cheese. Process until smooth.

Pour into glass container, seal, and refrigerate until ready to use.

Cornish Game Hens

10 tablespoons butter, softened
1 tablespoon chopped fresh tarragon or rosemary
4 Cornish game hens, weighing 1½–2 pounds each
Salt
Freshly ground black pepper

Blend the butter and herbs together, cover, and leave to marinate overnight in the refrigerator.

Prepare the hens by cutting along both sides of the backbone. Discard the bone. Lay each half skin side up and gently press down with your hand to flatten. Thread 2 or 3 soaked wooden skewers to hold the hens flat. Season with salt and pepper to taste, cover, and leave to marinate at room temperature for 1 hour.

After marinating, loosen the skin around the breast and thighs, and slip in tablespoons of the chilled butter and herb mixture.

Grill over medium-hot charcoal for 20–30 minutes until crisp and golden brown on the outside and juicy on the inside.

Creole Chicken and Buttermilk Waffles

½ cup buttermilk
3 tablespoons hot sauce, such as Tabasco, plus more for
  serving
1 chicken (about 3 pounds), cut into 10 pieces
1⅔ cups all-purpose flour
⅓ cup sorghum flour
½ teaspoon salt

¼ teaspoon freshly ground black pepper
2 teaspoons Creole seasoning
Vegetable shortening for frying
Buttermilk waffles (recipe follows)
Softened unsalted butter, for serving
Sorghum syrup, for serving

Combine the buttermilk and the hot sauce in a large, zip-top bag.

Add the chicken, seal the bag, and refrigerate for 3–5 hours.

In a large bowl, whisk together the all-purpose flour, sorghum flour, salt, pepper, and Creole seasoning

In a large heavy skillet, heat the shortening over medium heat to 375° F. It should be 1 inch deep when melted. Set a wire rack over a rimmed baking sheet.

Working with half of the chicken at a time, remove the pieces from the buttermilk mixture, dredge in the flour mixture, and carefully place in the hot oil. Fry for 14–15 minutes, or until the chicken is brown and the juices run clear. Maintain a frying temperature of 330° F. Drain the chicken on the wire rack. Repeat with the remaining pieces.

Serve the chicken over the warm, buttered waffles. Sprinkle with hot sauce and a generous pour of sorghum syrup.

Buttermilk Waffles

2 cups all-purpose flour
3 tablespoons sugar
1 teaspoon baking powder
½ teaspoon salt
¼ teaspoon baking soda
2 eggs
¾ cup buttermilk
¾ cup milk
⅓ cup unsalted butter, melted

In a large bowl, whisk together the flour, sugar, baking powder, salt, and baking soda, and in another bowl, the eggs, buttermilk, and milk. Add the liquid ingredients to the flour mixture, and whisk until blended. Stir in the melted butter.

Preheat and oil a Belgian-style waffle iron. Cook the batter in batches, until golden brown. Cooking times will vary depending on the waffle maker.

Makes 12 waffles.

Connect with

Us

Visit us online at
KensingtonBooks.com
to read more from your favorite authors, see books
by series, view reading group guides, and more.

for sneak peeks, chances to win books and prize packs,
and to share your thoughts with other readers.

facebook.com/kensingtonpublishing
twitter.com/kensingtonbooks

Tell us what you think!

To share your thoughts, submit a review,
or sign up for our eNewsletters, please visit:
KensingtonBooks.com/TellUs.